Hugh Reginald Haweis

Sir Morell Mackenzie

Physician and Operator

Hugh Reginald Haweis

Sir Morell Mackenzie
Physician and Operator

ISBN/EAN: 9783337306724

Printed in Europe, USA, Canada, Australia, Japan

Cover: Foto ©Raphael Reischuk / pixelio.de

More available books at **www.hansebooks.com**

SIR MORELL MACKENZIE

PHYSICIAN AND OPERATOR

A Memoir

COMPILED AND EDITED FROM PRIVATE PAPERS AND

PERSONAL REMINISCENCES

BY

THE REV H R HAWEIS MA

AUTHOR OF "MUSIC AND MORALS" "MY MUSICAL LIFE" ETC

LONDON

W. H. ALLEN & CO. LIMITED

13 WATERLOO PLACE

1893

CONTENTS.

PAGE

PROLOGUE 1

I. FAMILY TREE.

St. Neots 13

II. SURROUNDINGS.

A Literary Circle 19
Letter from T. B. Macaulay 21
Aged Fourteen 23

III. BOYHOOD.

Early Kindness 29
Lessons and Games 31
Boyhood at Wanstead 33
Death of his Father 35
Growth of Character 37

IV. A VOCATION.

Voluntary Medical Study 43
Medical Career entered upon 45
London Hospital College 47
The Laryngoscope 49
Physician to the London Hospital 51
The Brass-plate Period 53

A 2

V. THE THROAT HOSPITAL.

	PAGE
Free Dispensary for Diseases of the Throat . . .	59
Doctor and Dispenser in one	61
The Throat Hospital	63
Attack on the Throat Hospital	65
Withdrawal of the Hospital Sunday Grant . . .	67
Attempted Alienation of Subscribers	69
Mackenzie's Resignation	71
Arming for the Fight	73
The Report is not read	75
How the Requisition was signed	77
The Committee of Inquiry	79
An Unforeseen Episode	81
Senior Physician at Golden Square	83
Samaritan Branch	85

VI. PRIVATE PRACTICE.

" He did cure me "	91
A Patient's Home Treatment	93
Sympathy with his Patient	95
Testimonials of Gratitude	97
" A Good and True Friend "	99
Self-reliance and Perseverance	101
The Emperor's Confidence	103
Celebrated Confrères	105

VII. LEISURE HOURS.

Incident at the Theatre	111
Life at Wargrave	113
An Exhilarating Tonic	115
His Daily Routine	117
Capacity for bearing Pain	119
" One of my successes "	121

VIII. THE EMPEROR.

PAGE

The Verdict of Posterity 127
Intelligible Facts 129
German Surgeons in Council 131
First Operation 133
Intimacy with the Royal Patient 135
Virchow's Analysis 137
Return to Potsdam 139
Operation in London 141
Danger Ahead 143
Mismanagement 145
Announcement of Cancer 147
Mackenzie given Sole Charge 149
Five Months' Progress 151
Frederick's Journey to Berlin 153
The German Public 155
Visit to the Empress Augusta 157
Life at Charlottenberg 159
The Empress' Consideration 161
The Emperor's Malady increases 163
The Bergmann Incident 165
"Von Bergmann's roughness" 167
Bergmann's unsatisfactory Explanations . . . 169
Leyden and Senator 171
The King of Sweden's Visit 173
The Emperor's Death 175
Mackenzie's Report 177
The Autopsy 179
German Comment 181

IX. THE GERMAN DOCTORS.

Right, First and Last 187
German Charges 189
Answer to Bergmann 191

PAGE

First Popular Charge 193
Second Popular Charge. 195
Suffering alleviated 197
Life prolonged 199
No Operation without Positive Evidence . . . 201

X. THE BOOK.

A Stigma on his Book 207
"My Lips were sealed" 209
The Emperor Frederick's Opinion 211
Leading a Forlorn Hope 213
German Criticism 215

XI. THE RESPITE.

Mackenzie leaves Charlottenberg 221
Rest at Venice 223
The neglected Practice 225
The Queen's Letter 227
Ovation at Edinburgh 229
Welcome in Scotland 231
At the Philosophical Institution 233
University Training 235
Voyage to Teneriffe 237
The Canary Islands 239
Natives of Teneriffe 241
Ready for fresh Work 243
Volunteer Interest 245
A Lecturette 247
Literary Activity 249
Inventive Ardour 251
All-round Ability 253
The Essay on Smoking 255
The Smoking Question 257
Two Evils of Tobacco 259

XII. THE LAST VOYAGE.

PAGE

On the *Chimborazo* 265
Fellow-passengers 267
" The Omnibus " Yacht 271

XIII. LAST GLIMPSES.

Back in Harley Street 277
A Presentation 279
The Toast of the Evening 281
Lord Randolph Churchill's Speech 283
Mr. Henry Irving's Speech 285
A Gift not a Testimonial 287

XIV. THE END.

Influenza in the 16th Century 293
Superficial Improvement 295
A Rally 297
" A Happy New Year" 299
The last Days 301
" It is no use " 303
The Memorial Service 305

EPILOGUE 309
Appendix A 313
    „ B 317
    „ C 325
    „ D 335
    „ E 341
    „ F 349
    „ G 355
    „ H 361
    „ I 367
    „ J 373

SIR MORELL MACKENZIE.

PROLOGUE.

THE last scenes in the life of Sir Morell
Mackenzie are naturally those which rise first
in the recollection of all who are familiar
with his name. There was something in that
sustained and skilful vigil beside the dying
Emperor which attracted world-wide attention
and almost world-wide sympathy. The English
physician had set himself to prolong to the
utmost, if not to save, one of the most valuable
lives in the civilized world, and in the process
he also became personally devoted to his august
patient, Frederick the Noble. It was a post of
peril, anxiety, and severe trial, but it was also
a labour of love.

As a number of alternatives promising personal safety or release passed before him, he

turned away from each, like Elaine from every
offer of sordid compromise, saying :

"Of all this will I nothing."

There was in Mackenzie the stuff out of which
heroes are made ; the singleness of aim, the
concentration of purpose, the settled enthusiasm,
the forgetfulness of self, the unconscious and
unquestioning surrender of lower aims, and last,
but not least, a quiet, unostentatious and tireless
enthusiasm of humanity seldom seen and not
always understood ; these were the qualities
which made themselves felt at San Remo and
Berlin, and which attracted latterly so much
public attention to Mackenzie's personality.

Sir Morell came back from Berlin a broken
man a month after the death of the Emperor.
Soon afterwards I lunched with him in Harley
Street. I was shocked at his appearance. His
speech was slower, he was reticent and indis-
posed to refer to the Emperor or the terrible
time through which he had passed, just as great
soldiers can seldom be got to describe sieges and
battle-fields, or as Stanley declared there were
scenes in his African travels of which he could
not trust himself to speak until years had
dimmed the terror of their details.

Mackenzie's face seemed suddenly and com-

pletely to have lost, for a time at least, its restless vivacity. It looked stiff and elongated and
thin and haggard. He moved stiffly and more
deliberately. His alertness seemed gone, and
although a timely respite abroad, an ovation in
Scotland, and a cruise in the Mediterranean,
restored something of the old exuberant energy,
and in the autumn of 1891 there seemed more
than a flicker of his old self, yet between 1888
and 1892 he fell a prey to various diseases ; he
was never, in fact, the same after that last
terrible vigil of 1888 at Berlin.

Nor did he find on his return to England the
reception most calculated to soothe nerves tried
almost beyond human powers of endurance.

Instead of applause and admiration, he was
met by the bitterest general criticism and the
severest official censure.

In spite of the largest fee ever received by a
medical man—12,000*l.*—he found that he had
suffered professionally.

In his absence many of the specialists whom
he had formed and aided had not been slow to
absorb a number of his patients, and he returned
to a diminished *clientèle*. This I have reason to
know caused him some anxiety.

Soon afterwards he consulted me about
lecturing in America—he had been offered high

terms. I had had some experience there myself and strongly advised him to go. However, that fell through.

He was much pulled down in 1890 with a first attack of influenza, and on his partial recovery I was extremely anxious he should leave England and accompany me to Tangier. He would and would not. He seemed so keen upon picking up the lost threads of his practice. Patients who had been listening to other charmers discovered that, after all, there was but one Mackenzie, and they were flocking back to him. He was also in great request at Marlborough House, and in high favour generally with our Royal personages, and therefore, of course, with the cream of the aristocracy. The tide had again turned, and Mackenzie was on the top of the wave.

Ill and worn, he could not tear himself from London. The London fogs of winter 1891 were setting in, and in November Mackenzie was again down with influenza. Soon afterwards I got ill myself. In December, not realizing how seriously affected he was, I wrote and told him my symptoms. He sent word back immediately, " My dear fellow, I would come and see you myself instantly, but I can't leave my bed, and if I did I could not get out of the house. Get out of London yourself as quickly as possible."

It was the last message I ever got from my poor friend. Would he had taken his own advice.

I left for the Riviera, *en route* to Tangier. In February at Tangier I was unspeakably shocked, if not surprised, to open the *Pall Mall Gazette* of February 3rd, 1892, and read,—

" DEATH OF SIR MORELL MACKENZIE."

So closed a friendship of thirty years' standing. On my return to England his family and executors approached me with a request that I would undertake some account of his life. I felt that my love and admiration for the man constituted my only qualifications, or, as some people will perhaps say, my greatest disqualifications.

Those who saw most of Mackenzie saw little of him. I had been on his Hospital Committee as well as Chairman of the Throat Hospital Samaritan Society for many years; but this brought me only into occasional contact with him. He was in the habit of consulting me whenever there was any difficulty. I was, on and off, a frequent guest at his house, godfathered his eldest daughter and christened most of the other children. The family had been seatholders at St. James', Westmoreland Street,

Marylebone, for more than twenty years. Certainly I could not decline to arrange for publication any records the family chose to put into my hands; but those records were meagre to a degree. Mackenzie wrote few letters—very few indeed have come into my hands—though some correspondents have assured me that they possess interesting ones, which, for reasons best known to themselves, they refuse to allow me to see, intending, I believe, to publish them separately.

A few relatives have drawn up a few memoranda; many correspondents have favoured me with accounts of Mackenzie's extraordinary skill and boundless generosity; some doctors have contributed a few less flattering letters which, on the whole, it will hardly be necessary to publish ; here and there, from family report or intercourse with his friends, I have been able to recover glimpses of his professional life of toil and his spare moments of recreation ; I can fill out some details from personal knowledge or recollection, and I can appeal to his own writings, his book "Frederick the Noble" and several charming essays and addresses, the " proofs " of which are before me.

Such is my moderate equipment. (Appendix A.)

I have thought it right to submit the

proof-sheets to a representative member of the family, and I have felt bound, both as regards what is said and what has been left unsaid, *as far as possible* to respect their wishes. I have, in fact, been an arranger of material placed at my disposal by the friends and family of Sir Morell. I have not thought it necessary to listen to or record mere gossip, sometimes very unfriendly, concerning much of which it may be said,—

> "Surely, after all,
> The noblest answer unto such
> Is kindly silence when they brawl."

This Memoir, like Sir Morell's own book, " Frederick the Noble," is addressed to the general public, whom he served, and not to the profession, whose opinions and prejudices he so often—in my opinion needlessly—defied.

I expect to make no medical conversions, but I wish to leave some picture of a very remarkable man, who certainly contrived to excite the extremes of hatred and love, leaving to his biographer the difficult task of striking a balance and doing some justice to his memory. Those who loved him will know how to value this tribute ; and those who loved him not are not obliged to read the book.

I.

FAMILY TREE.

I.

FAMILY TREE.

The great question of whether the "Mackanzes" "Makainzes" or "McKenzes"[1] (spelling in old times was notoriously a matter of taste) were descended from the ancient kings of Desmond in Ireland, or from some other inconceivably remote and probably ragged potentates, is a question which I feel myself quite unable to " wrastle " with.

I may also here add that the bloody struggles between the Makainzes who stuck to the Earl of Seaforth as head of the clan, the Makcanzes who stood by the Earl of Cromarty, and the Mc-Kenzes who acknowledged the Baron of Kintail, need not engross the reader's attention. The favourite family motto which embalms the memory of a certain amount of " peculation " in a very literal sense, smacking of the good old times and the old established plan, that he should

---

[1] *Vide* " Parochiales Scotia," vol. ii., p. 393.

take who has the power, and he should keep
who can, is still often quoted by the Mackenzie
family. It runs thus, and certainly betrays some
lively doings of a sort, happily now no longer
reputable. " *As long as there are cows in Kintail
there will be Mackenzies to lift them.*"

Out of the thirty-five families with their
cows, whose varying fortunes are recorded in
the History of the McKenzie clan, the McKENZIES
OF SCATWELL alone need here be mentioned.
They came from one Roderick McKenzie of
Coigeach, and evidently acknowledged the
BARON OF KINTAIL as head of their clan, since
Sir Roderick acted as tutor of Kintail, and was
also cousin to his pupil's father, the first lord.

In 1619, Sir Roderick's second son, Kenneth
McKenzie, settled at Scatwell. His heir,
another Kenneth McKenzie, was made a
Baronet of Nova Scotia in 1703. Sir Morell
Mackenzie, the subject of this memoir, is
directly descended from Alexander, the *second*
son of this Nova Scotia Baronet, Sir Roderick
McKenzie, through Alexander's son, John Mac-
kenzie, born 1751, whose son was another John
Mackenzie, born 1783, who was the father of
STEPHEN MACKENZIE, born 1803, who married
MISS HARVEY, and became the father of the late
distinguished physician, MORELL MACKENZIE.

Exactly when the Mackenzies migrated from
Scotland and took up their abode in England
I have not been able to ascertain, but it is
certain that the second John Mackenzie, Sir
Morell's grandfather, after many years' service as a lighterman and wharfinger—having
presumably feathered his nest—threw up business and settled at St. Neots in Huntingdon-
shire. What his personal claims to attention
may have been does not appear, but a certain
family halo gathered round the head of the
retired lighterman now in the enjoyment of
otium cum dignitate, when it became known
in St. Neots that his wife had been a Miss
Symonds, daughter of a medical practitioner in
Worcestershire. This lady boasted that she was
co-descendant together with the Symons or
Symeons of Pyrton, the heiress of which branch
married the great John Hampden. The Mackenzies seem to have always been extremely
proud of this patriotic connection, which certainly proves that the clannish instinct undoubtedly strong in the Scotch, has not in the least in-
terfered with their hearty sympathy with British
interests and traditions. When we remember how
bitter the feeling still was between Hampden's
English contemporaries and the Scotch, we
cannot but be thankful that so complete an

amalgamation of sentiments has since taken place.

Two of Morell Mackenzie's uncles made for themselves names. John Morell, a well-known Nonconformist minister, was drowned at sea after a distinguished career at Glasgow University, where he was the friend and contemporary of Professor Swinton and Archbishop Tait. The other uncle was Charles, better known as Henry Compton, the well-known comedian and exponent of Shakespeare's clowns.

When I have further mentioned that the present (Morell) Mackenzies claim kinship with Mr. James Addington Symonds, the critic, through John Mackenzie's wife, a Miss Symonds, as mentioned above, and with Sir Rowland Hill of Penny Postage fame, and Mr. James Davenport Hill, Q.C., through a marriage between Mr. John Mackenzie's sister and Mr. James Hill, grandfather of the celebrated Secretary to the Post-office, I think I shall have done all that the most exacting reader can fairly require in the way of genealogy, besides setting at rest the ingenious speculations of certain imaginative German journalists who declared that he was not a Scotchman at all, but a Polish Jew, and that his real name was not " Morell Mackenzie," but " Moritz Marcovics."

II.

SURROUNDINGS.

II.

THE father and mother of Morell Mackenzie were no ordinary medical man and his wife. Stephen Mackenzie (*père*) was a man of great taste, various learning and much literary enthusiasm. His wife Margaret (*née* Harvey) was a woman of great liveliness and ability, a ready and entertaining talker—even as I recollect her in later life—a first-rate manager, a devout soul withal ; over-zealous at times that others should do their duty and profess correct opinions on all religious and social questions upon which she might happen to feel strongly herself ; a woman not to be talked over or talked down, with a tendency to have a finger in every pie ; whose advice was often given unasked, and was not always acceptable, but generally worth listening to, even when it could not be taken. I remember well this Margaret Mackenzie, who died in 1877, a

c

fresh-coloured, well-preserved old lady, with great powers of narrative and talk, not to say rattle, and always incisive and pointed, with a certain vivacity and *empressement*, which attracted strangers, but occasionally wearied familiars. There was no doubt a certain want of repose about her, born of a life of bustle and anxiety, but she was a faithful and devoted mother and idolized Morell, who in turn worshipped her with a tenderness and practical liberality which knew no bounds up to the day of her death.

As Morell's father and mother were exceptional so also was the atmosphere and *entourage* into which he was born.

The little village of Leytonstone, only six miles from London, and then quite "countryfied," was in the forties the favourite resort of hardworked City men. They built villas and came out to breathe the fresh air, as Coleridge and Charles Lamb resorted to Hampstead, or as later on people flocked for the same purpose to Norwood and Sydenham before those exquisite woodlands became merely tributary towns to London. The names of that coterie of literary and scientific men whom Stephen Mackenzie delighted to gather round him, for social intercourse and literary recreation, from Saturday to Monday, out of the ferment of the great neighbouring

Babylon, have unhappily not been preserved.
The children were all very young when their
father died. But it is certain from the first that
they were accustomed to see men of refinement
and culture and t› hear good literary talk. It
was indeed a grand period, 1837-51.[1] The star
of Byron had not long set, and Shelley's voice still
seemed to haunt the air. The rippling verses
and the guitar of Moore still tickled the ears of
the polite cognoscenti, Wordsworth had followed
Southey as laureate, the influence of the lake school
was still paramount—Walter Scott had not yet
been pushed aside for Bulwer. People had begun to whisper strange praises of a young poet
called Alfred Tennyson, Carlyle was fighting for

		Born		Died
[1] Moore		1779.	...	1852.
Southey . . .		1774.	...	1843.
Wordsworth . . .		1770.		1850.
Scott		1771.	...	1833.
Lord Lytton (Bulwer) .		1805.	...	1873.
Tennyson . . .		1810.	...	1892.
Carlyle		1795.	...	1881.
Ruskin		1819.	...	...
Dickens . . .		1812.	...	1870.
Thackeray . . .		1811.	...	1863.
Lockhart . . .		1794.	...	1854
Shelley . . .		1792.	...	1822.
Byron		1788.	...	1824.
Macaulay . . .		1800.	...	1859.

C 2

a Public, Ruskin was beginning to get abused by
the architects, Dickens was lounging about the
sands at Broadstairs, Thackeray was hardly
known ; and last but not least the *Edinburgh
Review* under the guidance of Lockhart, Walter
Scott's son-in-law, was driving a coach and four
through the old methods of criticism by substitut-
ing for dissection and analysis creative synthesis
and picturesque construction. Of this method, a
rising young writer, whose articles periodically
fluttered the literary dovecotes of Leytonstone
and a good many others besides, was the acknowledged master. His name was Thomas Babington
Macaulay.

Stephen Mackenzie, in the midst of his
literary symposium, which as has been said
lasted from Saturday to Monday, eagerly discussed these remarkable articles. Their novel
style made them comparatively easy to single
out ; but at last, when the list had assumed the
proportion of a bulky volume, the desire of the
Mackenzie coterie was so great to have them
certified, that the zealous doctor wrote to
Macaulay himself, telling him of the enthusiastic
and admiring circle of readers at Leytonstone,
urging him to employ his great powers on writing
a history of England, and finally requesting him
to note any errors in the list of articles ascribed

to him and to supply any omissions. All this may not seem strictly relevant to the life of Sir Morell Mackenzie, but if the characters and pursuits of great men's parents—as has been generally held—are calculated to throw some light upon the tendencies which influenced their early days, and therefore their whole subsequent careers, antecedents so remarkable as those which I have digressed to relate, should not be thought entirely out of place here. The sequel to Stephen Mackenzie's letter to Macaulay is far too interesting to be omitted.

There was, indeed, a flutter of excitement and delight when the following reply to the doctor's diffident and apologetic letter, arrived from the great but urbane writer :—

Albany, London,
January 22*nd*, 1843.

SIR,—Your apology was quite unnecessary. It is most gratifying to me to learn that I have given any pleasure to an intelligent reader who is a stranger to me, and whose judgment must be unbiassed by personal considerations.

Most of the papers which you mention are mine. You are wrong, however, about three "Uneducated Poets," "Alison" and "De Witt." The bulk of what I have written for the *Edinburgh Review* will be republished. But some selection it has been necessary to make. The collection will make three large and not loosely printed octavo volumes. If two more volumes had been added, filled with juvenile declamation, or with controversy on questions which had only a transitory interest, the patience even of readers so indulgent as yourself, would have been worn out.

I have long entertained the design of writing the History of England from the time of the Revolution. The execution of this design will probably be the chief employment of my life. But some years must elapse before any part of the work is fit for publication.

I have the honour to be,
Sir,
Your faithful servant,
T. B. MACAULAY.

It may interest admirers and students of Macaulay to know that amongst the articles which Stephen Mackenzie had bound up with the others in a volume now before me, were the three on Mill's Utilitarianism, Barère and Mirabeau, none of which did Macaulay include in the edition that was published of his Essays during his lifetime, but which have found a place in Sir George Otto Trevelyan's edition of his uncle's " Miscellaneous Writings."

Such, then, was the literary atmosphere, and such the wide and cultured interests which Morell Mackenzie, the eldest born son of Stephen Mackenzie, had the advantage of enjoying up to the age of fourteen (1851).

III.

BOYHOOD.

III.

"*MORELL*" MACKENZIE was named after his uncle, who received his name from a respected minister of St. Neots, where his father had once resided. The Rev. gentleman's fame chiefly survives through his brother Daniel, author of "*Morell's* Grammar," and his far more illustrious namesake SIR MORELL MACKENZIE.

A large head with some tendency to water on the brain—a certain mental sluggishness, accompanied by an emotional sensibility beyond his years, occasioned his parents much anxiety. Indeed, his head seemed too heavy for his body, and had a tendency to roll about awkwardly, so that for some years he was even forced to wear a protective pad. The little picture of him at the age of seven, still in existence, probably toned down these personal peculiarities which as he grew up entirely disappeared. He is there represented, as his sister Agnes describes him, " with long curls of bright auburn hair. He generally wore a velvet suit (of the period) with a broad linen collar trimmed round with a frill."

He seems to have been a good deal let alone educationally, as he had " several severe illnesses," according to his eldest sister Bessie, now the wife of Archdeacon Aglen, and could not be " taught much." Nevertheless, in spite of tardy mental development, so often favourable to originality, the dominant notes of his character were early and spontaneously struck. These certainly were a total absence of self-consciousness combined with that kindness of heart and simplicity of purpose, which never rested in mere sentiment but passed at once into action. " Do noble things, not dream them all day long."

" I remember," writes his sister " (and it is one of my earliest recollections of him), looking out of the nursery window at Leytonstone, and seeing my little brother Morell, who must then have been between seven and eight, carrying a faggot of sticks. There was an old woman in our village, Mrs. Parker by name ; she is vividly impressed upon my mind by the red cloak she wore, as every one, high and low, wore red cloaks or jerseys about that time, but the winter distribution of red cloaks in our village was chiefly made by Mrs. Cotton, mother of the Lord Justice Cotton. One very severe winter Morell had been hearing about the hardships of the poor, what a comfort a cup of hot tea was to them, and especially how much the aged poor suffered from cold. The long ears of little pitchers were never filled to better purpose. He began saving up his money to buy tea and sugar for old Mrs. Parker, and asked to be allowed to gather up sticks for firewood out of the garden. Every morning early he rose to perform this pious work of supererogation, and might be seen in all weathers—though far from strong himself—trudging along to Mrs. Parker's cottage with his bundle of wood.

" The old lady was at one time ill in bed, and Morell used to hurry out to light her fire for her, and run back in time for breakfast. When Mrs. Parker could get out, she was wont to come up to our house, and be made welcome in the kitchen. She seldom returned without a bundle of sundry comforts, which my little brother used to carry back for her. One day, for a frolic, he pretended to act the thief, and snatching the bundle from the old dame, was making off with it, when a passing carter mistaking his action raised his whip to chastise the young ruffian ; but the tables were soon turned, when the old woman, flourishing her stick in a terrible state of excitement, screamed out, " Hoo ! hoo ! how dare you touch my young master ! "

Little could Morell's sister or old Dame Parker have guessed how much of the invalid boy's life would afterwards be spent in gathering sticks for the use of others, and in providing solace gratuitously for the suffering and the needy ! This could not indeed be written before-hand, but the remembrance of it throws a halo round the life of one who has been sometimes accused of loving high fees to excess (as if no doctor had ever been known to care for such things). But those, and their name is legion, who were benefited by his generous and gratuitous services, know that he cared for suffering humanity far more than for money.

> His memory long will live alone
>   In all *their* hearts like mournful light ;
> That broods above the fallen sun,
>   And dwells in Heaven half the night.

Like all boys whose early education has for any reason been neglected, Morell was very backward when he began to attend school at Walthamstow

House under Dr. Glennie Greig. He was even thought slow and wanting in application, but this period of mental stagnation could not have lasted very long. His improving health now enabled him to enter more fully into the delights of the country, and fishing, climbing trees, collecting birds' eggs, and riding were indulged in with the happiest physical and mental results. From the first he had been a favourite with his schoolfellows, and his masters soon began to change their opinion of his intellectual powers. The drawing master especially noted the delicacy of his *hand* and the correctness of his *eye*, qualities which, in later life, not only enabled him to reach the acme of technical skill in operating, but also rendered him capable of making original drawings and diagrams for professional purposes, often in coloured chalks, of which he was particularly fond. Dr. Greig now discovered that young Morell had a turn for Latin verse, and a schoolfellow describes how, " looking back over the long years, he seemed to hear the Doctor lilting the lines—for he seemed unable to scan unless he lilted—with Morell, proud and confident in their correctness, standing by." The same school friend describes him about the year 1850 as " a chubby, round, powerful, strong ruffian, who played excellently well fives and cricket,"

thus showing how completely, in a few years,
the boy had outgrown the valetudinarian tendencies of his early days. This was, no doubt,
largely due to the judicious, if somewhat doc-
trinaire, views of his father on health, diet,
and general *régime*.

Stephen Mackenzie was a great advocate
for out-door sports and exercises of all kinds.
In the summer the children were all made to
bathe in the little river Roden, which flowed
through Wanstead, and they early became accomplished swimmers. In winter they were
encouraged to skate, which they were nothing
loth to do, on the famous Eagle Pond in Snares-
brook, and the commodious Bason in Wanstead
Park. The bathing was only permitted at certain hours, and the boys were then put under
the supervision of an old gardener who had been
many years in the family. There seems to have
been, thus early, a spice of carelessness and
defiant self-reliance in Morell Mackenzie, for on
one occasion, he, and at his instigation, his
brother thought they would like to try a little
bathing unprotected, and in the forbidden hours
of the afternoon. They unfortunately chose a
spot close to the Red Bridge, on the road from
Wanstead to Ilford; but, as Thackeray says, " a
hi was fixt upon 'em which these raskles little

saw, which it was"—the eye of the local consta-
ble and guardian of the Peace and Propriety of
Wanstead. Down from the bridge, silently
but swiftly, stole this inexorable vindicator of
outraged law, and before the wretched little
naked urchins could fly to the banks from the
sweets of stolen waters, their clothes had been
secured, and a humiliating surrender at discre-
tion had to be made. At first the policeman
seemed inexorable, and it looked very much as
if the young scapegraces, Morell and Alfred,
would have to be personally conducted by the
arm of the law through the village in a state of
nature to durance vile. Fortunately, on dis-
closing their identity, it was remembered that
their father was the medical officer to the police
force, whereupon the boys were released and
allowed to return home " clothed," if not exactly
in " a right mind."

The home exercitations were sometimes of a
less exciting character. The reading aloud,
especially on Sunday afternoons, by the mother
was much relished, but an attempt to force
sweet music on the boys was decidedly unpalat-
eable. Morell seems not even to have been of
Dr. Johnson's opinion, that " music was, perhaps,
of all noises, the least disagreeable." To sit
still, as their father obliged them to do, whilst a

seriously musical friend seriously played serious
pieces of classical music, was to Morell, at least,
an almost unendurable infliction. He was never
what could be called musical, though he appreciated, in his own way, fine singers like Nilsson,
whom I have often heard in his drawing-
room, as well as many other great vocal stars,
such as Patti *par excellence*. Most of them,
sooner or later, came under his professional care,
and being variously indebted to him, were always
ready, and even eager, to show their gratitude
by singing for him at all times and seasons.

But I must not anticipate. It was in 1851, the
year of the great Exhibition, when Morell was just
fourteen, that an event happened which certainly
had an extraordinary effect upon his character,
indeed upon his whole mental and moral development. One day the boy was suddenly called
out of school and told to go home immediately.
He found his father lying dead in the house.
Both he and his groom had been thrown out of
the old-fashioned doctor's gig; the man escaped,
but Stephen Mackenzie fell with his head
against the curb stone and never recovered
consciousness.

There are times in life when growth, both
physical and mental, after seeming to be at a
standstill, advances suddenly by leaps and

bounds, and in a moment we place our foot
upon a higher platform, and survey, for the
first time, a new and wider prospect. At the
touch of his first great grief—which fell like
a bolt from the blue upon the sensitive and
affectionate heart of the boy—Morell seemed to
become suddenly aged and sobered, with that
sense of family responsibility which never afterwards left him.

The family consisted of four brothers and four
sisters, exclusive of one brother (Harry) who
died very young. The sisters were Bessie,
Fanny, Agnes, and Emily, and the brothers,
Alfred, Stephen, and Herbert. They were all
extremely affectionate and united, and, it need
hardly be said, watched the career of the eldest
brother with great interest. It is a somewhat
remarkable fact that, with the exception of the
young brother mentioned above, there was no
death in this generation for nearly forty years,
and that of the eldest and most eminent among
them last year (1892) broke the spell of family
life.

His widowed mother, with her eight young
children, and a ninth in prospect, turned instinctively to him as to a trusted friend and
almost adviser, young as he was in years.
From that moment he became his mother's chief

stay and support, and in later years rejoiced to be able to give her out of his professional income a handsome allowance until she died,— before the great *cause célèbre* in Germany, but not before he had reached as a physician the zenith of his fame, fortune and popularity.

"Soon after his father's death," writes an old friend, "I well remember Morell coming for the first time to our old home in Westminster. He was a fine, tall, dark boy, dressed in deep mourning, and, though older than myself, was introduced to us by a mutual friend as a boy who had just sustained a terrible bereavement, and might possibly turn out a suitable companion for me, although I was then two or three years younger than himself. He was still at Dr. Greig's school, and I had not yet entered at Westminster. We saw a good deal of him, and my father and mother took a great fancy to him, and encouraged our boyish alliance, which grew into the settled friendship of manhood, but of which it may be said that death cut it short before the shadows of life were lengthening, or the twilight had commenced." His friend (T. W. Wheeler, Q.C.) then goes on to say that underlying a certain strenuous earnestness of purpose, there was ever that immense elas-

ticity of mind, that joyous and serene temperament, and that capacity for interesting himself
in everything and everybody which accompanied
him through all the vicissitudes, disappointments
and crises of his remarkable life, and enabled
him to keep a level head even when on giddy
heights that would have dazzled or wrecked a
lesser man. Mr. Wheeler, however, adds what
has been corroborated in substance by more
than one old friend : " I cannot say that his
boyhood indicated his brilliant successes in life.
It was the boyhood of a gentle, kindly and
reflective lad, but the purpose of his life grew
with his growth, and strengthened with his
strength. He was a man of whom it may be
said that " his faculties were climbing after
knowledge, infinite and ever-moving as the
restless spheres, willing him to wear himself and
never rest until he reached the ripest fruit of
all."

IV.

A VOCATION.

IV.

FAMILIARITY with his father's surgery and dis-
pensing-room had by no means bred contempt in
Morell. There was at first, however, no thought
of his adopting his father's profession, and he
was far too young to succeed him in practice.
When all the debts were paid the family means
were found to be straitened, and the *res
angusta domi* to be a question of *urgence*, as
they say in France. Morell was good in Latin
and strong in French and drawing. Still it did
not at once appear how he was to commence the
pecuniary battle of life so as to become self-
supporting and a prop to the family besides.

Friends had been very kind. Mrs. Mackenzie
being a woman of education and enterprise, set
up a school and managed to bring up and launch
most of her children, until Morell came nobly
to the rescue later on. He was about sixteen,

when a niche was found for him in the Union
Assurance Company by Mr. Nicholas Charring-
ton, an old friend of the family. The family
then lived at Woodford, and as the nearest point
touched by the railway was Stratford, he trudged
daily three miles on foot, morning and evening,
to and fro from his office. The steady figure
tramping along, always book in hand and
apparently absorbed in reading, soon attracted
the attention of a gentleman who drove into
town on business every morning. He stopped
one day, and offered to give the lad a lift, and
from that time Morell found in his chance bene-
factor a constant and life-long friend.

Like many young fellows who are pitch-
forked *faute de mieux* into the nearest office,
his heart was not there, though it may be
questioned whether at that age two years
rubbing down in an office of any kind, with
regular hours and regular routine work, is not
about the best preparation for any kind of systematic work which may be afterwards taken up.

There is evidence enough to show that all the
time the young man's head was running not so
much on life and fire assurance as upon life-
saving and disease-healing. He propounded
to his friends theories of inoculation for scarlet
fever. He showed himself already a proficient

in the treatment of stomachic difficulties. On one occasion, when a young friend having poured out and drank off a glass of raw brandy, supposing it to be light wine, was in danger of choking, Morell seized him and, hurrying him out of the room, administered a tremendous thumping on the back, which had the desired effect.

It soon appeared that, in addition to an omnivorous appetite for general reading, Morell was a special and interested student of medical books. Certainly a doctor he intended to be— but how?

Whilst still at the Union Assurance office, he entered his name for a series of evening classes at King's College, which he attended most regularly. In order to profit to the utmost, it was necessary to "read up," and in order to read up it was *de rigueur* to get up. His mother and sister entering his room to wish him good night, cn one occasion found him tying himself up in a most ingenious manner, his right thumb being connected with his left toe, so that the least movement would wake him. This was to enable him to rise at five every morning, so as to secure a couple of hours of medical reading before he started for his office. After this his sister Agnes undertook to call him every morning at five, and always made a point of being down herself at 7.30 o'clock to give him his break-fast, which, she adds, with what may be called a touch of local colour, " was extremely simple, but which he always liked to finish off with a piece of buttered toast."

It is this lady, who married my old college friend, George Foster Cooke, to whom I was indebted soon after leaving Trinity College, Cambridge, for my first introduction to Morell Mackenzie, then a rising but almost unknown physician, but already most reputably estab-lished in Weymouth Street.

His sister Agnes was before his marriage with Miss Bouch his constant and most helpful companion, and in some sort his gentle guide, philosopher, and friend. I can remember even now, though 'tis well nigh thirty years ago (*eheu fugaces!*), the exultant look of pride in her pretty face when she told me that Morell had presided over a large dinner party of eminent doctors, in his new Weymouth Street House, and how eager they were to learn his opinion, and how frankly they deferred to it, and " he," she added, with all a sister's affectionate pride, " the youngest of them all, and isn't it nice ! "

Thus early and irresistibly did the future trusted physician and friend of imperial

crowned heads assert himself, and thus spontaneously and ungrudgingly, before bitter
rivalries had obfuscated their professional minds,
did his medical brethren admit his supremacy
in his special department.

But the early brass plate in George Street,
Hanover Square, was not reached without a
struggle. Step by step, obstacle after obstacle
had to be surmounted—fees for instruction,
books, the necessary certificates, time for study,
and the inevitable " what shall we eat and what
shall we drink question," without solving which
obviously no doctoring could begin—and where
was it all to come from ?

Doctoring and Union Life Assurance could not
go on together. At this crisis Miss Harvey,
Morell's aunt, who kept a ladies' school at
Notting Hill, stepped into the breach. Morell
Mackenzie has never been without friends who
believed in him, because, perhaps, he has always
believed in himself ; but to take him out of an
office, where he was earning a living, when he was
penniless, and put him into training for a profession already overstocked to repletion, was either
an act of folly or an act of faith, which deserved
on the face of it severe criticism or unbounded
praise. It is difficult to say whether, had there
been no Miss Harvey there would have been no

Dr. Mackenzie. It is quite possible but for her timely help Morell's energies might have been forced into a different channel. " What would you have done," asked a friend, "if you had not become a doctor?" " I don't exactly know," answered Mackenzie. "I think I should have written. I would have made myself known some-how." I think I may say that he always felt a sort of confidence in being able not so much to win as to *command* success, and certainly in no one's case has the proverb, *"Fortune helps those who help themselves,"* been more startlingly verified.

Fortune certainly smiled on Mackenzie in the person of his kind and prescient aunt, Miss Harvey. She advanced him the wherewithal to withdraw from the assurance office, and her *protégé* was not slow to justify her liberality, and in later years to repay—and more than repay —her kindness.

Morell had always been a prize winner. He now enrolled himself at the London Hospital College, was soon noted by his teachers and examiners, who testified their high appreciation of his abilities and general proficiency by awarding him the gold medal for medicine and surgery, which, at that time, was the only acknowledgment given to students. Mackenzie, too, " was ever a fighter," as Browning has it, and he took a keen interest in what the students considered a gross perversion of their privileges, viz. the drawing of teeth by the chief Dispenser. I do not quite gather whether Mackenzie penned the famous *Lancet* letter, which declared that the " committee, altogether disregarding the interests of the students, and the *claims of humanity* (there is one for the chief Dispenser !), have transferred one branch of our studies to an officer of the institution, who will now have to perform the onerous but somewhat anomalous duties of butler, dispenser, and dental surgeon."

This certainly reminds us of the trenchant and sarcastic style of one who wrote some thirty years later, in his famous attack upon the College of Surgeons : " By the Act of 1540 the union between the surgeons and the elegant fraternity of specialists for the hair was finally consummated. Although at that period sur-geons ranked in social scale with ' common ' bakers, brewers, and scriveners, from a study of the Act it appears that a union between the surgeons and the shavers was rather a mechanical mixture than a chemical combination. The difference between the crafts is clearly recognized in the Act itself, and no member seems to have been allowed to practise, what

for convenience may be called both branches of
the profession." (P. 135,"Mackenzie's Essays.")

A little later we find young Morell Mackenzie
to the fore again at a meeting in St. Martin's
Hall, when the late Rt. Hon. Acton Ayrton,
M.P., took the chair, to expose and ventilate
the grievances of naval medical officers.

In due course he became a member of the
College of Surgeons, who found him later on
an extremely candid friend and caustic critic.

After taking their diploma, as also that of the
Apothecaries' Company, and carrying off the
Jacksonian prize, he qualified generally for work
in the hospitals in the usual way, and became in
turn resident accoucheur, house-surgeon, and
resident medical officer. To fill up his time he
also took the post of resident surgeon to the
Tower Hamlets Dispensary, in the Commercial
Road. Meanwhile he had matriculated, and
taken the degree of M.B. at the London
University.

But his good genius, in the shape of his
maternal aunt, who had helped him so far, had
no idea of doing anything by halves, and from
what she had heard she gathered that a course
of study at the medical schools of Paris, Prague,
and Vienna would be of the utmost advantage
to the young medallist.

The funds were again forthcoming, and Morell now prepared to go abroad and study for himself the practice and procedure of the foreign schools. He made few professional friends in Paris, but he became intimate with M. Vautrain, a distinguished advocate, afterwards President both of the Municipal Council and the Council-General of the Seine.

It was in Germany, 1859, that the note of his future destiny was struck. He there met Professor Czermack, and was introduced to the laryngoscope, an instrument invented by Manuel Garcia, the great singing master, which Czermack was then bringing into clinical use.

When he returned to England, he had accumulated a vast store of experience and learning. He had already, as stated above, graduated as Bachelor of Medicine at the London University in 1861, and he took the degree of Doctor of Medicine in the following year, 1862. He also filled the vacant office of assistant physician at his old hospital—the London Hospital. To qualify himself the better for this post, the young doctor had judiciously provided himself with the regulation testimonials from the acknowledged princes of the medical art, couched in more than the

E

regulation terms of eulogistic eloquence. He was perhaps wise to exhaust on the threshold of his career the medical horn of plenty from which then, and then for almost the last time, flowed such unstinted professional recognition and praise. Later on, when his magnificent success had more than justified the prescience of Sir William Jenner and Mr. Hutchinson, both of whom went out of their way to prophesy his brilliant future, Morell Mackenzie might have found it difficult to obtain a word of commendation from many of the leaders of his profession. He certainly never sought it, and did not require it. Here are some of his early testimonials.

"I have formed," writes Sir Andrew Clark, M.D., in his most flowing style, "after long acquaintance, a very high opinion of the abilities and professional acquirements of Dr. Morell Mackenzie. Formerly," the great doctor went on to say, "one of the most distinguished pupils and resident medical officers of the London Hospital, author of the College of Surgeons' prize essay on Diseases of the Throat, devoting himself to professional advancement with rare activity and perseverance, and already well known by his connection with the Hospital for Diseases of the Throat, his book on laryngo-

scopy and his numerous contributions to the pages
of medical journals and the proceedings of medical
societies, I am satisfied that no one can have
greater professional claims to the appoint-
ment of assistant physician to the London
Hospital. Dr. Morell Mackenzie once acted as
my clinical assistant in the wards of the London
Hospital, and it is only bare justice to say that
I never knew assistance more ably, zealously,
and punctually rendered."

Mr. Jonathan Hutchinson, himself an ex-
president of the Royal College of Surgeons, adds
his tribute. " I entertain," he writes, " the
highest opinion of the abilities and professional
attainments of Dr. Morell Mackenzie. He has
already enriched the literature of medicine with
some very valuable contributions, and has earned
for himself a wide reputation. After an unusually extensive course of study both abroad
and at home, he has now for some years been
engaged with remarkable success in the practice
of his profession. He is at once remarkable
for originality of mental endowment, and for
energetic zeal in the pursuit of knowledge.
Should the governors of the London Hospital
elect him to the vacant office, they will secure
the services of an excellent physician and of

one who *in the future* (sic) *will sustain and enhance the reputation of that medical staff.*" (The italics are mine.)

Sir William Fergusson is more concise, but hardly less emphatic. "I have long entertained," writes the great surgeon, " a very high opinion of the abilities and attainments of Dr. Morell Mackenzie, and have much confidence in stating my conviction that he is eminently qualified to fill the office of physician to the London Hospital, or any similar institution."

Sir William Jenner's encomium is no less valuable and significant. " Dr. Morell Mackenzie," wrote the Queen's physician, " is well known to me by his writings, by personal intercourse, and by having been examined by me in medicine, when he graduated at the London University. The opinion I have formed of Dr. Mackenzie's ability, energy, and knowledge of his profession is very high, and *I anticipate for him a distinguished career* (sic).

Litera scripta manet, and at a time when the German papers were denouncing Mackenzie as a charlatan and impostor, and the Royal College of Surgeons and Physicians, upon whom he had shed so much lustre, were cutting him off from their fellowship on account of his having published a few facts which jarred on professional ears,—the above printed and signed matter must have afforded Sir Morell Mackenzie very pleasant and seasonable fireside reading.

With these testimonials, which stand for ever as sentinels and guardians of his fame on the very threshold of his career, I may fitly usher in the brass-plate period, which began at No. 64, George Street, Hanover Square, in the year 1862.

V.

THE THROAT HOSPITAL.

V.

Soon after Mackenzie returned from his con-
tinental studies, he began to chafe at the
slowness of hospital routine as a road to independent practice. He had taken a house in
George Street, Hanover Square, in view of his
approaching marriage with Miss Bouch (now
his widow, Lady Mackenzie). His sister Agnes
(who, all through his life, in conjunction with
Bessie, his eldest, and Fanny and Emily, his
younger sisters, have been his faithful and
trusted friends and companions) now came to
stay with him. Agnes helped him to get the
house in order for the young wife, and many long
conversations were there between them, as to
how to make both ends meet under new conditions of life and coming marriage responsibilities. His brother Alfred was also at this time
his constant adviser.

"Ag (Agnes)," said Morell one day, "if I am ever to make anything of the throat" (that was his dream ever since he had seen Czermak's laryngoscopic work at Pesth) "I must see more patients. Put on your things and come out with me, and I will tell you what I shall do."

It was characteristic of him that he should say "*make anything of the throat*," instead of "*increase my practice*," or "*get an income*;" it betrayed unconsciously the order of ideas in his own mind, first his art and specialité, and all other considerations afterwards.

Forth went brother and sister striking into Regent Street, then all around in the less expensive purlieus of Oxford Street, and Leicester Square and Soho. At last they fixed on two rooms at No. 5, King Street, Regent Street.

It was Friday, but not to Morell an unlucky day, surely a Good Friday, hereafter to be associated with infinite relief of distress— alleviation of suffering poverty, and salvation of life !

It was found, however, that the two rooms could not be hired alone, and that it was necessary to take the whole house. This did not deter the young doctor, and the house was but a short time on his hands, for a sub-tenant was soon secured, and ultimately the two rooms cost but a very trifling sum. From the first moment of decision there was no pause or delay. Carpenters, painters, and glaziers were called in, and in an incredibly short time a bold printed placard was got out—rather lengthy, it must be owned,—"Metropolitan Free Dispensary for Diseases of the Throat and Loss of Voice;" whilst up in the window in large letters was painted "Attendance, etc." Empty benches (not long to remain empty) filled two rooms and looked very business-like, and the little dispensary seemed to the eager specialist (already!) quite prophetic and encouraging.

From the first printed announcement of the hospital, drawn up in the little consulting-room in George Street, Hanover Square, and which is now before me, I append in a foot-note the statement which was put forth as the *raison d'être* of the new institution, and which may be taken as the founders' " own words." [1]

[1] Formerly, when diseases of the throat were merely treated on general principles, it was easy to attend to such affections at the ordinary hospitals and dispensaries, but the progress of science, and more especially the recent invention of the laryngoscope, have added so considerably to our knowledge of throat affections, that a special dispensary for their treatment is felt to be an urgent want in the metropolis.

Though it is still a point of contention as to who was the actual inventor of the laryngoscope, there can be no doubt as to

From the very first patients began to flock. There had never been before any special *throat* dispensary, and the existence of this modest harbour of refuge, soon to be crowded with all

its utility. By its means the larynx and a considerable portion of the windpipe can be inspected, and suitable remedies applied to the diseased parts ; indeed, there is no doubt that its more general use will effect a great change in the manner of treating the deep-seated affections of the throat. Till now, as it was impossible to see the condition of the larynx, it was equally impossible to treat it satisfactorily when diseased, but now "the eye directs the hand," and a new era in the treatment of throat affections has commenced. Artificial illumination and reflected light being, however, essentials in the employment of the laryngoscope, the instrument cannot well be used at the general hospitals, where the diseases are of so varied a character that it is impossible to employ the same elaborate apparatus which is practicable when the affections are all of the same description.

The introduction of the stethoscope led to the more accurate investigation of pulmonary affections, and statistics testify to the immense amount of relief which the hospitals for diseases of the chest have afforded to the poor of London. The numerous eye infirmaries, likewise, where the ophthalmoscope is in daily use, have done much to alleviate misery. Nevertheless, up to a certain period, both consumption and eye diseases were treated in the general hospitals, and it was only when a more delicate method demanded a more organized system that special institutions became necessary. The time has now arrived for the establishment of a dispensary for the treatment of throat affections. By the institution of such a charity the projectors hope to secure to the poor the advantages already enjoyed by the rich.

kinds of storm-tossed and weather-beaten
sufferers, the victims of a climate specially
favourable to the incubation, growth and progress of diseases of the throat, soon revealed
the fact that a want had not only been discovered, but efficiently met.

At first Mackenzie seems to have worked
single-handed, and he used to relate with much
gusto in later days how after examining or
operating on the patients in one room, he was
in the habit of popping behind a door, and then,
in such a way that his face could not be seen,
personating the dispenser, who, after making up
the prescription in a separate department,
handed it to the patient through a window ; was
there indeed any occasion throughout his life
to which he did not prove himself equal ?

So was " inaugurated " the famous Hospital for
Diseases of the Throat, whose pharmacopœia has
become a medical classic, and whose doors have
been entered by some 100,000 sufferers, many
of whom have found recovery and all relief.
But the importance of this special institution,
which is the creation of Morell Mackenzie's
brain and the child of his heart, has not only
been recognized by every class of society, from
imperial and royal personages down to the

lowliest and poorest dregs of the London streets, but its wards, consulting and operating rooms have been annually the object of special visits, made by foreign medical men of the highest distinction, and hosts of medical practitioners and students, many of whom have thought it worth while to travel long distances, and even to cross the Atlantic, in order to visit the Throat Hospital, and "*see*" Morell Mackenzie.

At the close of the second year, the committee (for though there was a full-fledged committee at first, there was now also a staff of physicians and all other things generally necessary), including Lord Stratheden and Campbell, who became its first President, and remained a firm friend up to his death, were able to announce that no less than 5915 patients had received medical treatment at the Free Throat Dispensary, Golden Square.

In 1869 the battle of Special Hospitals had still to be fought. The simple fact of their prosperity had hardly been grasped by a conservative section of the medical press, or only admitted as an insoluble mystery—one more astonishing tribute to the infinite gullibility of the public.

The two simple propositions which are at

once the cause and the justification of Special Hospitals only got themselves formulated very gradually under high outside pressure. It has taken, in fact, about twenty years for the medical papers to admit : *First* that a disease once diagnosed, those doctors who had given most attention to that disease were the most likely to cure it—and *secondly* that the pig-headed public who did not always read the medical papers always went in largest numbers to the places and the doctors which cured them quickest. This, for instance, is how the *Lancet* of the period spoke of the Royal Ophthalmic Hospital, now universally admitted to be one of the grandest and most important medical institutions in the land :—

" The business was so well managed that this infirmary shop was opened for the reception of *gulls* (*sic*) &c.—and *three years afterwards* the proceedings of the ophthalmic *warehouse* were laid before the public ! "

The Throat Hospital, directly it was quite evident that its success was admitted, met with a like genial criticism. But the patients who took the physic did not, as a rule, read the criticism, and so no great harm was done.

By the tenth year the hospital had opened an important ward with twenty beds, and with a staff of medical men, including the honoured names of Sir William Jenner, Dr. Archibald Billing, and Sir William Fergusson, whilst His Royal Highness the Duke of Cambridge, figured as Patron, with the Earl of Clarendon as President. The funds were reinforced by a Bazaar which realized 1000*l*., and an anonymous donor gave another 1000*l*.

In 1875 the hospital opened allied branches at Notting Hill and Walworth.

In 1873 the Prince of Wales had become Patron and continued joint Patron with the Duke of Cambridge till 1878, when both these Royal personages retired—and thereby hangs a tale. Lord Calthorpe then became President— a post which he has nobly occupied ever since— piloting the establishment through a few stiff storms, due largely to discord and misrepresentation within acting upon professional feeling without.

In 1884 the Patron's place, which had remained vacant since 1878, was filled, and continues to be filled, by His Grace the Archbishop of Canterbury, down to the present time (1893).

1878 is memorable as the turning point which decided whether or no it would be possible at once to deal an effective blow at specialism and to effectually damage the professional career of

Morell Mackenzie by an attack upon the Throat Hospital.

In 1878 the attack was made and was conducted, up to a certain point, with great skill and some success. It was of a curiously complex and exciting kind. Some minor officials connected with the hospital had constituted themselves into a sort of Cave of Adullam—which not unnaturally ended in their resignation. These became the new wire-pullers. It required no special insight to suggest that those within the citadel could open, if they pleased, the gates to the enemy, or at least that persons intimately acquainted with the details of the hospital, could act as very effective enemies and critics if they deserted to the enemy and were prepared to throw all scruples to the wind. Rumours were now heard of "*Internal mismanagement*"—the only internal mismanagement I became aware of was that of retaining the complainants so long in office—"*hole-and-corner business managed by Dr. Morell Mackenzie and his family*"—this was plausible at least, for Dr. Morell Mackenzie had founded the place—rallied all his friends and relations round him—collected funds, and no doubt the committee consisted, at first, largely of his personal friends and relations; but it could

F

hardly be pretended that they, myself, or Lord Calthorpe, for instance, got anything out of it, and few could fail to see that to secure a man like Mackenzie to act as medical superintendent was a singular advantage to any hospital. The only profit he could derive was a prestige entirely dependent upon the success and popularity of the hospital.

The ears of people eminent in the faculty were, however, at that time sensitively alive to any rumours, damaging at once to a special hospital and a man of genius whose methods were not always in strict accord with professional etiquette, whilst his manners were not always affable towards his medical critics, and his income was large.

To cut a long story short without raking up the details of an extinct controversy, his Royal Highness the Prince of Wales, was approached by those who at that time had won, not undeservedly, his Royal Highness's confidence. And from the statements laid before him he was led very naturally to infer that the Golden Square Hospital was not deserving of his Royal support. He accordingly, in company with the Duke of Cambridge, withdrew, and the illustrious names no longer figured as Patrons in the annual reports. The

same influences were at work on the London
Hospital Sunday Fund Committee at the Mansion House, and another blow was aimed at
the hospital and its perilously successful medical
superintendent by the withdrawal of the Hospital Sunday Grant from the Hospital for
Diseases of the Throat. Thus far the attack
had succeeded beyond the hopes of its promoters. They had appealed boldly to professional *esprit de corps*, and the response had been
hearty. I remember this stormy epoch was
well marked by two rather dramatic episodes.

Mackenzie had often pointed out to me certain
defects in the basis of administration adopted by
the Mansion House Committee, upon which I
was then sitting with Cardinal Manning, Sir
Spencer Wells, and several others. Into the
details of this business it is needless now to
enter. I quite agreed with Mackenzie, and did
not scruple to say so in committee, and the basis
of distribution was, I believe, subsequently
modified ; but I ceased to sit on the Committee
after the attack upon the Throat Hospital, as I
was then on the Committee of management and
Chairman to the Hospital's Samaritan Society.[1]
But in 1878 there was a densely crowded

[1] See Appendix B.

Annual Meeting at the Mansion House, and
Dr. Mackenzie in the teeth of considerable
opposition led a fierce attack on the principle,
which guided at that time the distribution of
the Funds, showing how the numerical test was
misleading, and how some Institutions got too
much and others too little or nothing at all, and
so forth. The speech was pluckily delivered
with extraordinary volubility, and I must admit
considerable animus. The effect produced
was not good ; the argument was a good deal
peppered and sugared with hisses and applause.

In such a perturbed and mixed atmosphere of
course the real points under discussion could not
be grasped much less weighed, and the majority
assembled being, as usual, quite innocent and
ignorant of the question in debate, naturally
trusted to the infallible wisdom of the Mansion
House Committee and the Lord Mayor ! I
doubted altogether the wisdom of Mackenzie's
policy in exposing himself to an open defeat at
such a crisis. I felt, in short, that his charge
was very plucky, " bien beau, mais ce n'était
pas la guerre ! " and I prudently held my tongue,
reserving myself for another occasion which
presently came.

The general impression was that Mackenzie,
being very angry at the slight put upon the

Hospital (merely a thin disguise for the blow aimed at himself) had hit out right and left, but was quite in the wrong.

The Mansion House Committee withdrew its grant. The conspirators had scored again. They had shown their power and had succeeded in wounding Mackenzie, which, indeed, was one of their principal objects. The thing had been cleverly managed, too. It all seemed to come about so naturally—prejudice, spite, professional jealousy, all had been pressed without apparent effort into cause of an insignificant faction of malcontent officials, who had determined to celebrate their secession, expulsion, resignation, or whatever it was, by acting the gadfly, intent on driving the noble war-horse mad.

They did not, however, quite know the limit of their own power or the mettle of the noble war-horse with whom they had to deal. Emboldened to rashness by their success, they now proposed to turn against the very fabric of the Hospital, and inflict upon it an incurable wound by poisoning the wells; that is to say, alienating the subscribers by privately-circulated statements so highly flavoured that even the papers, always on the *qui vive* for a scandal, refused to touch them. But the game was too good to be thrown up.

The Prince of Wales and the Duke of Cambridge had resigned. The Mansion House had withdrawn its grant. The next thing to do was to get the public to stop the supplies. The document which the papers refused to print was the report of a so-called Committee of Inquiry, from which the Hospital Committee representatives retired when they learned that an open and avowed enemy of special hospitals, and a well-known and professed opponent of Dr. Morell Mackenzie, was to take a leading part at the special request of His Royal Highness the Prince of Wales, who acted throughout with perfect impartiality on the only statements, unreliable as they eventually turned out to be, which had been laid before him.

Although the Hospital Committee of Management were refused an opportunity of seeing, let alone answering, the charges of the Committee of Inquiry, a few of the charges of course leaked out, and amongst them rumours of the old stale complaint that the Hospital was exploited by Dr. Morell Mackenzie and his relations—exactly *how* did not appear. When this came to the ears of Mackenzie, he promptly resigned his post as Medical Superintendent (and his brother Alfred his place on the committee).

The instant Mackenzie resigned everyone connected with the Hospital (myself amongst the number), or who knew and understood anything about its interests, felt that the establishment had sustained a severe loss. I talked the matter over with Mackenzie, and urged him to reconsider his decision. I was Chairman of the Samaritan branch, and still on the Committee of Management. I pointed out that his resignation would be hailed as another victory by the conspirators, and might give colour to their statements, and play into their hands by inflicting a blow upon the Hospital.

But nothing would move him. He was galled to the quick; but he was, as the event proved, more far-seeing than I was. He had a robuster faith in the vigour and stability of the Institution which he had created.

The Hospital funds throughout 1879-1880 rose in spite of the crisis of 1878, the culminating scene of which I am about to relate.

The malcontents ejected from office had been busy playing, through letters and circulars, upon the credulity of a section of the Hospital subscribers, who knew as much or as little as most hospital subscribers about the inner working of the hospital which they support. But when these

anxious "inquirers" had not been able to get
the newspapers to print their damaging report,
a bright idea struck them. The problem was, how
to obtain damaging publicity for their charges
without incurring a libel action ? And this was
the solution : Twenty-one subscribers had the
power to call a special meeting to consider any
question affecting the interests or welfare of the
Hospital. What could be simpler or more
straightforward, than to get twenty-one subscribers to convene such a meeting? No sooner
said than done. Such a meeting would *receive*
the obnoxious report, a copy of which had
been refused to the Committee of Management,
the newspapers would simply report it *as news*
of Hospital proceedings, and it would thus be
"privileged," the desired currency would be
given to the libel, and no liability incurred.

The meeting was accordingly called. The
Beethoven Rooms were selected ; Lord Calthorpe
was in the chair ; the clique packed the place as
well as they could, but *we*, the committee had
no fear. The date fixed was 2nd March, 1878.

I think it was one Monday when I got one of
those little notes which Mackenzie was in the
habit of sending me from time to time when
he was bothered about anything and wanted

ARMING FOR THE FIGHT.

to consult me. " I should like to see you, if you could spare a few minutes ; very important ; won't keep you waiting if you would call in about twelve to-morrow morning."

I went up to 19, Harley Street. It was a fine morning. I got drafted almost at once into his inner sanctuary, but he was not there, and there I waited.

About half-past twelve he came in, laid down a pair of forceps, and said, "I want to consult you very particularly, and ask you to do something for the Hospital. The enemy are going to play their trump card on Saturday. You have received a circular. Very well ! I want you to attend and to speak. You don't mind a row ? They'll try and pack the place, and interrupt you, but we are going to beat them."

" Why don't you fight it yourself ? Fight half as well as you did at the Mansion House, and you will do ever so much better than I can, because you know everything and can answer every objection."

But Mackenzie was decided.

" No," he said ; " I want to be out of it, although I may have to speak." (He did speak, and his speech, together with the charges, which we had at last obtained, will be found under Appendix C.). " I have resigned my post; I no longer superintend. I wish to stand aside, and let others fight it out; but I will give you all the material, if you will only state the case. *Your* connection with the Hospital cannot be misconstrued; it must be absolutely *disinterested.* You can get nothing by it; the whole body of subscribers can see that at a glance. You will then in this affair carry immense weight, and we have a splendid card."

" What is that?" said I.

" They want to get the Report of Inquiry *read* ; they want to throw the mud, like the little street boy at the footman's calves. I'm the footman, and they think we can't help ourselves."

" Well ?"

" Well," says Mackenzie, " the chairman will call upon you to move a resolution that their report be *not read*, that the meeting refuse to ' receive ' it; in your speech you can unmask the conspiracy, and the papers will print *that* instead of their libel ! "

The newspaper verbatim report will now best record this summary defeat of what I may call the last serious attack which has been aimed against the Hospital for Diseases of the Throat.

March 2nd, 1878, Beethoven Rooms, the Right Honourable

Lord Calthorpe, President, in the chair, then rose and called upon the Rev. H. R. Haweis to move the first resolution.

I need hardly say that the upturned faces of the meeting exhibited considerable anger and disgust as I read the resolution, which ran as follows :—

"That considering the circumstances which led to the formation of the committee of inquiry, and the manner in which the investigation was conducted (as detailed by the committee of management at the annual meeting of subscribers, held February 9th, 1878), and considering further that no copy of the report of the so-called committee of inquiry was ever forwarded to the committee of management, the elected executive of the subscribers, this meeting declines to receive such report."

At the close I paused to let them blow off steam, which they did not fail to do, and I waited patiently until the uproar of mingled hisses and counter cheers had subsided. This was the resolution that so disappointed the conspirators, but which, of course, a large body of well-informed subscribers present came prepared to support. The shorthand writer thus recorded my speech, which I have ventured to insert here as a compendious summary of the *casus belli*. It also gives what is Mackenzie's general reply to the cavillers.

When silence had been restored—

The Rev. H. R. Haweis continuing said that, in moving the

resolution which stood in his name, he claimed their indulgence, not as the honorary chaplain, though he had held that
office for ten years, nor as an independent subscriber, but as
the representative of the Committee of Management. He felt
that his position was a somewhat peculiar one, because the
meeting having been convened upon a requisition, the object of
which was that a certain alleged report should be read to the
subscribers, he was going to strike the first note of disappointment by proposing that this report, which probably many
persons were anxious to hear, should not be read. Now,
in bringing forward this resolution, it might be said by some
that he was endeavouring to burke the charges which had
been made against the committee of management; but these
charges would be fully stated and answered by the speakers
who would follow him, and he should therefore confine himself
to stating the reasons why the committee of management
objected to have this report read. Two circulars had
been issued, and he would now call attention to the first
of them, namely, that containing the requisition of the
twenty-one subscribers. To begin with, it was inaccurate
in its statements that certain officials there specified had
" resigned." The late chairman and the vice-chairman had
not resigned as chairman and vice-chairman ; but after
the annual meeting held last year those gentlemen were
not re-elected to their respective offices, because they showed
an intention of carrying matters with a high hand, and of
introducing something very like martial law into the management of the Hospital ; and that being so—and there being no
probability of their working any longer harmoniously with
the committee—they were not re-elected. They then withdrew with two friends on the committee. The late secretary
and the late matron had resigned ; and with regard to the late
surgeon, the friend of the secretary, he thought fit to send in
his resignation also, but in a form which showed it was not his
intention that it should be immediately accepted; however,
to his surprise, his resignation was immediately and unani-

mously accepted by the committee. He (Mr. Haweis) ventured to say that, if the surgeon's resignation had not been accepted, the committee and the public would not have heard a syllable about these charges against the committee. (Cheers.) In ordinary cases the regular course of business at a meeting of this kind would probably be to hear the report read and to take the opinion of that meeting upon it ; but, in the present case, it would be necessary to examine into the circumstances under which the requisition was signed, and to see how far those who had signed it were qualified to form an opinion upon the subject. Now it was an undoubted fact, as appeared from what took place at the annual meeting last month, that in more than one instance the requisition had been signed by subscribers who had little or no knowledge of what it was about.

Sir Charles Legard, one of the subscribers who had signed the requisition, asked for the name of any subscriber who had signed it in ignorance of its contents.

The chairman rose and said that Sir Charles Legard had himself informed him that he had signed the requisition at the request of the then Chairman of the Committee, and because he saw several influential names among the requisitionists.

Mr. Haweis then continued his speech by saying that this showed the way in which the requisition had been got up. Without making any reflection whatever upon the *bona fides* of the noblemen and gentlemen who had signed the requisition, everyone knew how easily a petition of any description could be got up and signed, if necessary, by almost any number of respectable persons, and it very often turned out on inquiry— and he had known several instances of it himself—that a person signed his name simply because he had been asked to do so by some friend, and without taking the trouble to look into the matter for himself. In ordinary cases that might not be of much moment ; but when you came to a petition or requisition of this sort, conveying serious charges against the executive of a large and influential charity like this, it became a matter of great importance to ascertain what amount of authority such a document represented. (Cheers.) But many people would, no doubt, ask, "What is this report? What is the nature of it? Why cannot it be read?" In answer to that he would say the committee had never themselves seen the report, though they had accidentally heard something of it. It was as well that the meeting should know that this report had been in the hands of the promoters of the requisition for eight months; that those persons had not, on account of its libellous character, dared to publish it themselves, and that, notwithstanding the most persistent efforts on their part, they could not induce a single newspaper or periodical to publish it in its entirety, though some extracts from it had, he believed, appeared in one or two medical papers. Now the object of these persons in calling this meeting was evidently to get this report brought before the public by having it published in the form of a newspaper report of proceedings at a public meeting, and thus to escape the legal liability which they would be under if they published the report themselves. In short, a calumny being unable to run of itself, the committee were asked to provide it with legs. (Laughter, and "Hear, hear.") The committee would have no objection to its going forth to the world, if the answers and explanations could go with it, but it was notorious that out of numerous persons who might read a libel only a few might happen to see the explanations subsequently published. Now he wished to disenchant the meeting with any desire to hear this report. As a body of subscribers it would not become them to be the means of publishing a report obtained under the circumstances he was about to relate, even supposing it were steeped in flattery. (Laughter.) The circumstances connected with this so-called inquiry, which was a private, and not an official inquiry, and which resulted in this report, will be presently related; but it was sufficient now to say that his Royal Highness the Prince of Wales had been worked upon to withdraw from the hospital, and, in order to satisfy his Royal Highness, the Committee

had consented to the holding of an inquiry. They had, however, been obliged to protest against the constitution of the
so-called committee of inquiry which could only result in one
verdict. He should remind the meeting that these charges
had been made before the annual meeting last year, and that
the chairman, who was one of the gentlemen who had made
these charges, under the private instructions of the conspirators,
discharged matron, surgeon, etc., was present at that meeting;
had heard votes of confidence passed and pleasant speeches made
on all sides, and yet never ventured to rise in his place and say,
" We are going too far : I have certain charges to bring against
this committee." (Hear, hear.) Why did not the late chairman take that opportunity of bringing forward those charges, if
there was any real ground for them ? (Hear, hear.) Then
came the annual meeting of 1878 which took place the other
day ; there again the charges were not brought forward. In
the different attempts that had been made to throw discredit on
the medical administration of the hospital, there seemed to
have been a certain amount of connivance on the part of the
hall-porter and the late matron, who, apparently, thought she
knew more of medical subjects and of surgical operations than
Dr. Mackenzie and the rest of the medical staff. (Laughter.)
Well, it was proposed that a committee of inquiry should be
held. The committee of management, of course, could not
consent to their late chairman being on the inquiry, but what
they said was this : you select three gentlemen and we will
select three from amongst the subscribers. That, though unconstitutional, was at all events fair ; and it was thought that
the whole matter might have been discussed in a friendly
spirit. The committee, accordingly, selected their three
representatives, and these were approved of by the chairman's friends ; but a day or two before the day fixed for
the inquiry those friends objected to the members appointed
by the committee of management, and a letter was suddenly
produced from his Royal Highness the Prince of Wales
in which the representatives of the committee were altogether

ignored, and Sir William Gull was appointed as a member
of, or assessor, to the committee of inquiry, the result being
that the committee of management were not represented
at all. Now Sir William Gull was well known to be a
great opponent of special hospitals ; but he was also a famous
physician, and, therefore, the committee felt that under the
circumstances he was scarcely fitted to assume the office of
judge, and, to do Sir William Gull justice, he did his best to
get out of the inquiry, especially as there was some little
personal feeling between himself and Dr. Mackenzie ; he wrote
no less than six letters asking to be excused, but at the urgent
request of his Royal Highness Sir William at last consented to
sit upon the inquiry, and on to the inquiry he went evidently
determined to do his work in accordance with his stated views
and natural feelings. The inquiry then took place ; but it
was of a most absurd character, and there was not the smallest
pretence of impartiality. (Hear, hear.) The committee of
management, therefore, were compelled to withdraw. Ultimately all sorts of reports were circulated as to the extraordinary revelations which were to be made respecting the
hospital. Some of these charges had been solemnly communicated to himself ; and he was perfectly astonished at
them. They were of the most paltry character. For instance,
one was that Dr. Mackenzie had acquired an undue ascendancy
over the committee. Supposing it were true that Dr. Mackenzie
did possess great influence with the committee ; was that to
be wondered at, when it was entirely due to his energy, ability,
and experience that the hospital owed its origin, and had
arrived at its present distinguished position ? Another charge
was that a patient had died some hours after Dr. Mackenzie
had given him up ; but was that a surprising circumstance ?
It might have been a reflection on Dr. Mackenzie if the patient
had recovered. He had once heard that a patient whom
Mr. Abernethy attended got well after he had given him
up, and, when Mr. Abernethy met him in the street, he declined to recognize him. But after all, that was not the only

ground for declining to receive the report. His objection was that the report was utterly informal and unconstitutional. Further, although the report had been sent to the Hospital Sunday Fund with the hope of injuring the hospital, it was not forwarded to the committee of management with the view of its leading to any administrative reform. He would also point out that the report might have been brought forward at the annual meeting held only three weeks ago; this would have been a fair and legitimate proceeding, but would not have suited the purpose of those who are now trying to publish it. Their object was to injure the institution, and to gain publicity for a libel they dared not publish in any other way. I am making no charge against the honourable gentlemen who have been made the catspaw of the wire-pullers. The committee of management could not be made—they ought not to be asked—to receive a report elicited by an anonymous person, a report wholly informal, and drawn up directly in contravention of the printed rules of the hospital. (Cheers.)

A considerable amount of by-play followed, gentlemen rising in the room asking the noble chairman questions, others blurting out wild words and charges, which they refused to formulate as amendments or counter resolutions. One of which, as it was gravely insisted upon, perhaps deserves a passing notice on account of the extremely comic and unforeseen episode to which it led up.

There had been, it was said, a poor patient at the Throat Hospital who after having been unskilfully (!) operated upon at our hands, had at last been turned out to die, a case

G

in which, if a little common prudence had been used, let alone skill or kindness, a life might have been spared and great suffering and bitter injustice and cruelty avoided! The meeting seemed deeply affected, many eyes glared at the late medical superintendent, who was present, but opened not his mouth, yet was there an inscrutable and sphinx-like twinkle upon his otherwise well-controlled face. At this point there were loud demands for the name of this victim of cruel mismanagement, and the name was actually given. The fact is the Committee happened ' *to know that patient*,' and had somehow got wind that her sad case and premature death would be brought up at the meeting by those who never dreamed that any-one would hunt up and verify one obscure case, one out of many thousands ; but they were mis-taken. The Committee had kept their eye on that victim of hospital mismanagement (case of Fanny Brooks, see appendix C.), and at consider-able trouble and some expense had got her up from the country, and when her name was called, the " dead " answered from the bottom of the room and testified to the great skill and kindness with which she had been treated, as also to her complete restoration and present good health. The roars of laughter and applause which

greeted this last exposure of the exposers fairly
knocked the bottom out of their little tub, the
meeting resulted in their entire discomfiture, and
from that day to this, I have never heard of
any charge of mismanagement or neglect being
brought against the Throat Hospital.

After this period the story of the Throat
Hospital ceased to be in the same absorbing
manner connected with the personal career of
Dr. Morell Mackenzie.   He still retained the
position of Senior Physician, but he had many
able coadjutors, and took very little part in the
administration of the place.   His enormous
practice seldom allowed him time to spare
except for the most critical operations and the
most urgent consultations at Golden Square.
Although the place had been started as a free
dispensary, yet Mackenzie early advocated the
wholesome principle of patients contributing
what they coul l afford to the Institution which
helped them, and it was with open gratification
that we were often able to announce in our
annual reports that out of an expenditure of
from £3000 to £4000 the patients had contributed
over £2000.   This most salutary practice of
making people pay according to their means,
for benefits received has been extensively

adopted in many other hospitals, although some older and more conservative institutions still affect to look upon it as a contrivance beneath their dignity.

Whether we regard the leaps and bounds by which the Throat Hospital has advanced in public favour, with varying fluctuations, by the numerical measure of patients or the £ s. d. test, the result must strike even a careless reader as remarkable. (See Appendix D.)

At the close of the first decade, 1873, the Committee announced that in *ten* years it had relieved 949 *in-patients* and 37,859 *out*.

In 1891 *alone* its in-patients amounted to 526, and its out-patients 7260, whilst its attendances amounted to 37,319.

In 1873 its receipts amounted to £5966, but in 1891, with a varying expenditure per annum of from five to seven thousand pounds, it had an investment account of £17,579, and this after having built a splendid hospital which has cost in all about £10,000.

It is now agitating for a Mackenzie Memorial Branch, which is to consist of a wing named after the founder of the Hospital.

Of the Samaritan Branch, which I conducted and was largely instrumental in raising funds for, much need not be said. I found Mackenzie always most anxious to impress upon us the great importance of assisting medical treatment with nourishments and sometimes pecuniary aid calculated to abate anxieties which fretted our patients and retarded their cure, our motto being,

> " 'Tis not enough to help the feeble up,
> But to support him after."

It was often represented to Sir Morell in later days when he became a trusted medical adviser of the Prince of Wales and our Royal Family, that the Royalties might again figure as patrons of the Hospital for Diseases of the Throat. The late Emperor Frederick visited its wards admiringly, and so did our *quondam* Princess Royal, as Empress, and we all know it was at the special suggestion of Her Majesty that our great throat specialist was sent for to Berlin.

Her Majesty also supplied the material (and wrote a preface) for a " Life of the Emperor," which was written by Mr. Rennell Rodd, and published for the advantage of the Hospital, and produced a sum of £300.

But Mackenzie often said to me nothing would induce him to request the replacement of any patron's name that had once been withdrawn. He even valued the absence of the Royal names

under the circumstances; he said it was like a
standing record of an attack *that had failed con-
spicuously.*

It is now time for us to take a glance at Sir
Morell Mackenzie's private practice.

VI.

PRIVATE PRACTICE.

VI.

THE interviewer, who sometimes, under the disguise of a patient, entered Mackenzie's consulting-room, found a man sitting at a table full of an orderly disorder—heaps of letters, telegrams, filed prescriptions, and memoranda, paper weights, curios, testimonials, knicknacks; on the walls presentation portraits of Royal persons, framed letters from the late Emperor of Germany and our own Queen; but Mackenzie himself he found a man of few words, and he could be on occasion more brief than brief.

To a globe trotter, who forced his way in to "see Mackenzie," as a "thing to do" before leaving Europe, the distinguished specialist merely said, "My fee's two guineas!" and showed him the door. To the *bonâ-fide* press reporter he was more courteous; and there was one class to whom he never turned a deaf ear— for whom he always had advice, physic, and often money—it was the poor and needy, of whom more presently.

Mackenzie's average day was fourteen hours of steady professional toil. He rose early, was out of the house by nine to visit certain urgent cases, which he usually contrived to get lodged in Devonshire Street or Beaumont Street. He was back by ten, by which time his various consulting-rooms were crowded. Then he plunged into the thick of the day's work. He passed from one room to another, and carried on several cases simultaneously, often with astonishing speed. Whilst one patient was removing his wrapper, Mackenzie passed through a door and gave a gargle to a second. Whilst this one cleared his throat, he would pass into another room and puff a powder down a third's throat, by which time the first would be ready for him, and, whipping his instruments out of his carbolized silk case, he would deftly remove his tonsils.

His diagnosis with the laryngoscope was astonishingly rapid. The mirror was instantly fixed, the light instantly caught, the throat illumined and scanned down to the breast-bone, and the inspection was over in a moment. .. The patient was often dismissed with a prescription or advice before he had well surveyed his physician. Unlike some doctors, Mackenzie seldom needed explanations from his patients. At a glance he seemed intuitively to grasp the case. They say he made mistakes— I suppose all doctors do sometimes—but he seldom failed to inspire confidence and hope, and in the vast majority of instances he wrought great alleviation or a lasting cure.

"He only puffed a powder down my throat and charged me two guineas!" complained one patient, "and whenever I went the same thing happened."

"But you got well?"

"Yes, I certainly got well; he did cure me."

"Then you ought to be thankful, and consider your guineas well spent. A less skilful man might have cut your throat, or bungled over you for months."

Mackenzie's methods were sometimes denounced as risky, and it was said a good many of his patients died. Indeed, he often spoke to me on this very subject. "Of course," he said, "the mortality at our hospital is very great; patients try the other hospitals first, and many come to ours only when their case is hopeless. I have still greater difficulties in my private practice. People come up from the country,

probably after a certain amount of mismanagement. What am I to do? If I could keep
them up in town I might cure them even then.
I know the best treatment it is useless to suggest,
because their own doctor, who sends them up to
me, will not or cannot carry it out. I then
think of the next best, or some treatment that
may possibly be carried out when the patient
returns; if it fails, of course I get the blame.
Then wretched people come up to me, who have
very little chance—they are too far gone or
have been shockingly neglected or misunderstood. Sometimes I cure them; if I do not,
they say, ' You see, your specialist is no better
than the others after all.' "

I have a letter containing a curious anecdote,
illustrating at once the jealousy which the doctors had of Mackenzie, together with their real
confidence in his power. My correspondent says
he had an obstinate throat, and he asked his
doctor whether he should see Mackenzie. The
doctor said, " No, I wouldn't go to that quack;
no, don't see Mackenzie." So my correspondent
did not, and got worse and worse. One day, to
his surprise, his doctor (who had probably for-
gotten his former advice) said, " Oh, if you are
so very bad, and don't get any better, why of
course you must go to Mackenzie ! "

A word more now about Mackenzie's high
fees. It is easy to misrepresent this matter.
Two guineas for a puff of powder seems a good
deal; but I have a letter from Mr. Ulick Burke,
now Town Clerk of Dublin, who apparently
required this very treatment, and after the first
operation for which Mackenzie took his fee, he
turned to Mrs. Burke and said, " Don't you think
you could do for your husband what you have
seen me do if I show you how? It is quite
needless for him to come here and pay a fee
each time." Mrs. Burke at once made the experiment with success, and the patient was
saved all further expense.

On the other hand, I was visiting one of
Mackenzie's patients in Beaumont Street, when
enter the great specialist. He goes up to the
sick man.

" Taken your medicine? "

" Yes."

" Very well, good-bye ! " and into his hand is
dropped a fee of two guineas, and out goes
Mackenzie.

I could not help saying to him, " That's rather
sharp practice, isn't it? " as we went downstairs together.

" Not at all," says Mackenzie. " I told that
man a fortnight ago, that he would die in three

weeks, that nothing could save him, that I could do nothing more for him, that the only alleviation he could get would be from the medicine I had prescribed. 'Very well,' said he, 'then I want you all the same to visit me every day till I die.' 'Very well,' I said, 'you know my fee is two guineas.' 'I know,' said the gentleman, 'and I am quite willing to pay it.' Now," added Mackenzie, "some people might get hold of that story, and give it an ugly twist and say that *I* insisted on visiting a dying man every day, and taking his two guineas, when I knew I could do him no good."

There was no end to the extortion said to have been practised by Mackenzie. I have a heap of abusive letters, but singularly enough they *are all from medical men*. It is curious that out of the piles from *patients*, not *one* accuses Mackenzie of extortion, or even complains of his fees; yet I invited, through the newspapers, correspondence from all quarters.

It was said that an eminent solicitor paid him £100 for a simple operation. In the case alluded to Mackenzie refused his fee.

It was said that a poor student, who on his first visit had been fleeced, was told to call three times a week, but on the second visit, being unable to pay his fee, was told he need not call again. This, I need hardly say, is not true.

I am not in a position to say whether Mackenzie ever mistook consumption of the lungs for throat disease, or failed to detect chest complaints and treated imaginary symptoms, or even created them, so imperilling human life, until some really good doctor round the corner rescued the patient, only just in time, from the consciously fraudulent specialist. Into such nice points it would ill become me to enter.

It is more pleasant to cull from the mass of letters sent me, sent me by all sorts and conditions of men and women, a few specimens of which I will place before my readers and allow such to speak for themselves.

I knew that Mackenzie was kind and generous, that he had a feeling heart, that sometimes when he had to perform a delicate operation, his anxiety for and sympathy with his patient, well-nigh overcame him at the close, though his deep feeling had never been known to allow his hand to falter. I knew in a general way he was good to the very poor, and I had myself brought before him cases of poor governesses, servants, reduced clergy, and worn-out schoolmasters, whom he had invariably treated for nothing, not unfrequently providing them with wine from his own cellar, and food from his kitchen, but until his death let loose the cloud of living witnesses, I had no idea of the extent and frequency of his generosity.

Here is a case which came under my own notice whilst I was Chairman of the Samaritan Society. I am indebted to Miss Stuart, one of my lady Almoners, for the exact details. She writes as follows.—

"When I was administering the funds of the Samaritan Society of Golden Square Hospital, we had a patient, Sarah C., who had fatally injured her throat and chest, in attempting suicide, by drinking carbolic acid. She lingered on, receiving a little assistance weekly from the Society, for fifteen months. At first Sir Morell Mackenzie had seen her once or twice, but afterwards, when her case was pronounced hopeless, she was moved to her own home in Walworth; just before she died she became possessed with the idea that she could not die easily without seeing him again, he had always spoken so kindly to her, and she gave me no peace till I promised to go and tell him. I hardly liked to trouble him with such a useless request, but the woman was dying, and insistent. 'Is it any good my coming?' he asked. 'None to her health,' I had to answer, 'but it will ease her mind.' 'All right, I'll come,' and he went all the way down to South-East London, sat by her, talked to her for half-an-hour, and called her, 'my dear,' which comforted her beyond expression. She died the next day; there were two sovereigns which he had left with her, under her pillow, 'for her funeral,' a great help to her struggling relations, but the time and sympathy which he had given her were beyond the price of gold."

A poor Board School teacher writes :—

EXTRACT.

" Whenever I sought his advice there was a kindly greeting ; he was always the same solicitous, courteous gentleman. I was treated as though I paid huge fees, and in no wise as an object of charity. Should I be kept waiting, there was invariably an apology. To prevent my calling upon Sir Morell to no purpose, it was made known to me when he expected to be from town. On leaving him he expressed best wishes for my welfare and offered his medical aid should my throat again prove troublesome.

" I deeply regret the loss of one to whom I owe my health, and who was so self-forgetful and such a great power for good."

Mr. Plumpton Wilson, an Elstree schoolmaster, writes :—

" I suddenly lost my voice almost entirely, and began to fear that I should have to forfeit my place at Elstree and try a new career. As a last resource, I paid a visit to Harley Street, where Sir Morell Mackenzie was kindness and encouragement itself, and after six visits my voice had completely recovered under his treatment. On my asking what fee was due to him, he replied that he could not think of taking a fee of any kind from an Elstree master, and added that he should always feel grateful to Elstree for what it had done for Kenneth (his son, who had been at school there)."

Miss V— writes from Lausanne :—

" I am unable to contribute materially towards your work, yet I cannot refrain from adding my testimony, to hundreds of other sufferers, to Sir Morell's great kindness of heart and *utter unselfishness.* Sir Morell attended me *gratuitously* for two years, indeed until his last illness, seeing me every day, and I

H

grieve to say I was never in a position to make him any return whatever. Sir Morell always treated me with the utmost kindness and courtesy. On one occasion I remember his apologizing for having kept me waiting whilst he saw the Prince of Wales. When I came up from the country to see him last November, I was told that he was very ill in bed, but he actually got up to see me rather than that I should have a lost journey. I believe he was recovering from influenza, and he was almost too weak to stand. Although I sometimes waited for hours to see Sir Morell for a few minutes, yet I felt fully recompensed for waiting; he was always so kind and thoroughly sympathetic that even seeing him seemed to do one good. I used to say it was better than a tonic. I am certain that no man was ever more misunderstood. People have often said to me, 'Oh, Mackenzie won't see you without a fee; he's too *grasping!*' How *utterly untrue!* In Sir Morell his patients have lost a friend, and a most skilful physician, who can never be replaced. I shall look forward with the greatest eagerness to reading your ' Memoir,' and I am quite sure that every friend of Sir Morell's will be deeply grateful to you for the work you have undertaken."

Another writes how Mackenzie, hearing of a sick person desirous to see him, but unable to pay, drove six miles into the country, and then another six miles out of his way to tell the country doctor what he had done and what he would advise.

When at San Remo, his scanty leisure was often used up in walking to see patients who could afford to give him no fee, at the same time he declined heavy fees offered him during his stay abroad whilst in attendance on the Emperor.

It is well known that he would never accept a fee from any actor or singer. I have received the following letter from Mr. Henry Irving :—

"I have been trying to recall some story which would picture to the readers of a Memoir the man I knew, his infinite kindness and patience, the breadth of his sympathies, and the simplicity of his character.

"I cannot call to mind anything that will serve the purpose in the way of an anecdote, but I should like to testify not only to the debt which I personally owe to his memory, but also to the affectionate remembrance in which he is held by many members of my profession, who had special need of his ministering skill, and who still have reason to speak of him with gratitude."

The Earl of Londesborough writes to Harry Mackenzie :—

"I unfortunately have no letters of your father's, and I could only say I found him a good and true friend, always pleased to come and see me when ill, although suffering himself and at great personal inconvenience. I can speak personally of his extreme liberality and kindness; in one case, I knew a clergyman whom he saw daily for six weeks without a fee.

"There is no one who will be so missed by those who knew him, he was always so kind and considerate in giving his opinions."

Mr. Edmund Yates writes :—

"For fifteen years I lived in closest intimacy with Sir Morell Mackenzie, and I may therefore claim some insight into and knowledge of his character. And I say, in full deliberation, that in a long and much-varied experience, I have never known a more thoroughly kind-hearted or a more unselfish man, using his unequalled skill in well-doing liberally and without stint,

H 2

and commending himself to vast numbers of his fellow-creatures by sympathy which found its issue in practical result, and benevolence which took the form of immediate victory over disease.

" I have never known a man more misunderstood, more mis-represented, or more sedulously lied about. For years there have been going about in society men, many I grieve to say of his own calling, who have disseminated stories of his rapacity and greed, his wild haste to make money, his exaggeration of small complaints into large ones as an excuse for raising his fees, and of his general charlatanism : but even these men were perforce silent as regards his professional skill, for the results of that were before the world. The real fact about the other matter is, that while the wealthy had to pay Mackenzie heavily for the services which he. rendered, services often of absolutely vital importance, and which, it should be remembered, no one else could render, no member even of that large-hearted, generous profession did more gratuitous work, or did it more readily. Such service on his part was constantly volunteered : read in the Bancrofts' book, where his keen eye detects on the stage a grievously ailing man, a ' super,' whom he has brought to him, and whom he tends at his poor home for a year, till his death. ' Send him to me ' was his cry whenever a ' sad case ' was mentioned to him, and the inner hall at Harley Street was never without its complement of waiting poor. The amount of work which he got through was extraordinary, as besides his immense practice he generally had an article in one of the current monthly reviews, was always well up in literary and scientific subjects, and all this while under the influence of such wearing and depressing disease that his ordinary night's sleep was broken at half-hourly intervals by the necessity for inhaling a stramonium cigarette to relieve acute asthma.

" In his special branch of his profession, Morell Mackenzie was unassailable. I have seen him in close conflict with fell disease, where the conquest was achieved by greatest skill and

most indomitable, unswerving, dogged perseverance ; success
and triumph over apparent odds following on the determined
effort of will.   He had the enormous advantage of thorough
self-reliance, acting with unhesitating despatch, and com-
municating, magnetically as it were, to the patient his own
inspiring courage.   No man was more intrigued against, no
man more frequently attacked obliquely by envious rivals;
but he won.   For years they succeeded in keeping him out of
Marlborough House ; but he was there in daily attendance for
weeks last summer, and was the recipient of much grateful
acknowledgment on the part of the Prince of Wales."

Of course these testimonies might be multiplied
indefinitely.   He was full of real charity.   After
his death this was the aspect of his life and work
which seemed most to impress the newspapers.
They published pictures of him interviewing the
poor ; Sir Morell sitting on the bedsteads of sick
children and coaxing them with toys, alternated
with Sir Morell Mackenzie walking out with the
Emperor, driving with the Empress, or chatting
with Bismarck.   He was always the same earnest, kindly, devoted, genial spirit, equally at
home in the hovels of the poor, the hospital
wards, or in kings' palaces.

In his intercourse with his patients there
was something extremely reassuring, and invariably sympathetic.   They always felt no
stone would be left unturned, and that everything short of the impossible would be accomplished.

There was something singularly persuasive—
almost magnetic — about his authority.   One
patient describes with admiration how after a
skilful operation he had felt inclined to cough,
when Mackenzie turned round and looked at
him, sternly saying "Don't cough !" and every
desire to cough or choke instantly left him.

Another singular anecdote reaches me, of a
death which happened most unexpectedly in his
consulting-room—one of those cases which Sir
James Paget used to call "a calamity of surgery."   The brother of the unfortunate man
arrived furious, and determined to give Mackenzie
a piece of his mind.   Such, however, proved the
fascination of Mackenzie's manner that the in-
furiated relative "slowed down" by degrees,
and in a short time found himself conversing
quite calmly about the fatal case.   The triumph
was reached when, before departing, the aveng-
ing brother found himself in the operating chair,
and, after allowing Mackenzie to examine his
throat, paid him his fee without a murmur.

Perhaps no man felt this curious ascendancy
more strongly than the Emperor Frederick.   He
would habitually turn to Mackenzie and say,
"If you advise this I will obey," "If you
think it necessary I will submit," "I am quite
satisfied."

It was this absolute, almost unquestioning, confidence of the Emperor in his English adviser which was the bitterest pill which the German doctors had to swallow, and the bitter attacks and underhand conspiracies against him at Berlin date from the time when this strong preference was unmistakably shown.

Although Mackenzie was an avowed specialist yet many people had the most unbounded confidence in him as a general medical adviser. He would at once tell you if he did not think he could treat your case, and send you impartially to the most suitable doctor—friend or foe, for I must admit that Mackenzie was often unstinted in his praise of men who spoke very indifferently of him. But personally I can only say that in an acquaintanceship of nearly thirty years, I have found in numerous cases, including my own wife and other members of my family, that Mackenzie's insight has usually led to the adoption of remedies which have sometimes been quite startling in their speedy efficacy. In one special case of obstinate hay fever, after trying different things patiently for a month, he hit upon something which has proved an absolute specific, and for over twenty years, his prescription has never failed absolutely to

stop the first symptoms. But if I indulge in
this vein I shall be in danger of trespassing
upon technical matters of which I have no
special knowledge ; I must, therefore, reluctantly curtail this section on the much criticized private practice of this unconventional and
strikingly successful specialist.

A very general impression prevails—and it is
one sedulously fomented by a section of the
medical faculty—that Sir Morell Mackenzie was,
to use the language of a prominent doctor, " a
free-lance and semi-outlaw in his profession—a
sort of Ishmael whose hand was against every
man, and every man's hand against him." That
he walked through some medical conventions
which he deemed injurious, that he was not
only a physician but a skilful surgeon (to combine the two seems a great medical offence in
itself by the way), that when attacked he was
in the habit of hitting back rather smartly,
that he wrote and spoke freely, and did not
think it necessary to decline any newspaper,
magazine, or pamphlet, or book form of utter-
ance calculated to render generally intelligible
what he had to say to a generally intelligent
public—these are no doubt qualities possessed
by the few but obnoxious to the many.

A professional income of from twelve to fifteen thousand a year was, however, the chief source of his distinguished unpopularity. But on the other hand, in France and in America, and before he became an awkward rival, in Germany too, the name of Mackenzie was held in something like exalted reverence, as undoubtedly the greatest throat specialist alive—whose book was the standard one on throat disease, and whose genius by o'erstepping those limits of routine prescribed by use and wont, which are the fatal watch-dogs of vested interest and mediocrity— had opened up a new sphere in surgery and popularized and developed a new instrument in diagnosis which has saved thousands of lives and relieved millions of sufferers.

In his own country written medical testimonies of admiration and esteem of the highest weight are conveniently ignored by some whose apparent object it is to cheapen their too successful and too celebrated confrère; yet he numbered amongst his friends men like Sir Spencer Wells, Sir Andrew Clark, Sir William Dalby, Sir Henry Thompson, Mr. Christopher Heath, Dr. Robert Barnes, Dr. Langdon Down, Dr. McCall Anderson, Mr. Walter Rivington, Mr. Anderson Critchett, Mr. Walton Coulson,

etc., etc. In France, Fauvel and Péan, etc. ;
in Germany, Krause, Billroth, Senator, and
many others ; whilst in America he was looked
up to by the Profession as an oracle on Throat
Diseases from whom there could be no appeal.
(See Appendix I.)

VII.

LEISURE HOURS.

VII.

A CASUAL observer might suppose that a man, who, for many hours a day walked from room to room operating, prescribing, and diagnosing, and varied the strain only by driving to other houses or hospitals and treating more patients, must have almost lost the habit of play. Not at all ; Mackenzie was as good at play—I had almost said the Play—as in the laboratory or consulting-room. He was a steady first-nighter. If the delicate throats of actors and singers caused the operatic and dramatic stars to gravitate towards 19, Harley Street, Harley Street returned the compliment. And a first night of any importance was seldom unmarked by the presence of the busy doctor. He was a great admirer of the histrionic profession, members of which he invariably treated free of charge, and many a pretty story is told of the notice he took of the lowliest. Observing sometimes from his stall or box some "super" or novice evidently suffering from throat or chest, he would present himself between the acts, behind the scenes, ready with advice and sometimes handy with the promptest remedies. His skill on emergency was certainly incomparable, and it was no unusual thing for a singer or speaker to turn up *hors de combat* and say to Mackenzie, "I must have my voice back for two hours to-night," and Mackenzie would say, "So you shall, but then go home and go to bed, and don't stir till I come."

Mr. and Mrs. Bancroft, in their Autobiography, relate the following anecdote :—

"During a run of *Caste*, one night we received a message from the stalls that "Dr. (now Sir) Morell Mackenzie would like to speak to us." He had been for years a friend —indeed, it would be impossible to over-estimate the services he has rendered us, sternly refusing at all times to accept any fee or reward, whenever sent for, and however tried his time ; even to the extent of paying three visits in a day. This goodness is well known among singers and actors, and we hope he will forgive us for speaking of it to a wider circle. Dr. Mackenzie was brought round to the green-room and startled us by saying quietly, "You have a dying man upon your stage, who is only fit to be in bed." Inquiries told us that a poor fellow who only appeared as a servant for one minute in the second act of *Caste*, had been for some weeks ill, but was for so short a time in the theatre, and kept his troubles so much to himself, that we knew nothing of them. Dr. Mackenzie for a long while drove almost daily to a humble lodging in a remote part of London, where by no chance could he be likely to have other patients, to keep this one alive. He was patched up for a time through unceasing kindness; but his state was beyond the power of doctors to do more than let him enter another year, when his troubles ceased for ever."

From early childhood his own children delighted in private theatricals, and on such occasions, their father was always foremost as prompter, stage manager and general adviser.

After a laborious day, a short retirement, a nap, a stramonium cigarette for asthma, seemed to restore him.

When he corrected his proofs, wrote his letters and postcards, always of the briefest, was a mystery. A perfect system, fixed hours,

and delegated details, add to which, servants
who understood his ways, especially the hall
oracle, Mr. Bowden, who for many years "controlled" the patients, and protected the doctor
from countless loafers, pilgrims and strangers;
all this fails to account for the immense range
of his work, both quantity and quality.

But Mackenzie was never more genial than
at his own dinner table. He would eat and
drink most sparingly, whilst providing all the
most *recherché* and indigestible delicacies for his
guests.

His income being large, his expenditure was
somewhat lavish, and wife and children were
refused nothing that money could buy.

One might suppose that his tender affection
for his children would lead him to spoil them;
but that was only one side of his nature. He
was in many ways a strict and even exacting
disciplinarian, but it was his example, his spirit
that moulded and controlled them more than
his words. A truer glimpse into this side of his
family relations than any I could give, will be
derived from a perusal of his eldest daughter's
notes which I print without alteration at the
end of this chapter. Lady Mackenzie's well-
known afternoons once a week, at which all
the rising musical and dramatic stars were

wont to put in a quite informal appearance,
singing, playing or not, as fancy or occasion
served, were, of course, seldom graced by the
presence of the busy doctor, but the late re-
ceptions and suppers lasting into the small
hours, were of the most brilliant character, and
it was not uncommon to find Irving, Toole,
Ellen Terry, the Bancrofts, Nillson, Nachez,
and such like dazzling combinations, all together between twelve and two in Mackenzie's
electrically - lighted and splendidly-appointed
saloon in Harley Street.

But it was at Wargrave, on the banks of the
Thames, a locality he was never tired of denouncing to his patients, as bad for complaints,
such as he himself habitually suffered from
—Wargrave, loveliest of waterside townlets,
studded with old-fashioned picturesque streets
and houses—it was here that Mackenzie really
enjoyed his leisure hours. Need I say that to
him leisure could never mean idleness? He
planned and built his house, he laid out his
garden. He set a gondola on the river, taught
his daughters, Ethel, Olga, and Hilda, rowing
and swimming, and they soon became admired
experts in both accomplishments. Here in the
cool of the day in summer, with chosen companions, overtaxed professional men, artists,

I

authors and distinguished foreign visitors, Mackenzie took his truest leisure.

When alone with his family he was equally
happy, and equally busy, planting trees,
arranging flower-beds, pruning roses, devising
new rustic seats and leafy alcoves, or taking a
ride with his girls, Ethel, Hilda, or Olga. In
earlier days, lawn tennis was his delight, and
to the end chess was an unfailing source of
interest. His method of playing is thus characterized by a gentleman who played with him
frequently on board the *Chimborazo* during a
cruise in the Mediterranean. "I am sure,"
writes his friend, "that he must have often
played a dozen games a day. I remember
myself playing three with him in three quarters
of an hour. But he played the game as a game
—with him it was neither science nor skittles,
but a playful mixture. In chess, too, his good
nature showed itself repeatedly. He was never
put out when he lost, and I have known him
play most patiently with bores who took half an
hour to think over a move and then did the
wrong thing."

The same companion says of him : " He was
an accomplished sight-seer. He did *not*, like
some of our ladies, attempt too much, or like
some of our men attempt too little for real

enjoyment . . . it is no small praise to say that if we had decided by ballot who was the most agreeable man in the company, Mackenzie would have been easily first . . . Sir Morell seemed to have combined with the genial morality of the *homo sum* the keen observation of the naturalist. He took a positive pleasure in making the acquaintance of every one, and entered with zeal into their interests. He was equally at home with the little girl of seven and the old man of seventy, the man of business, the lawyer, the author, the actor or the artist. He enjoyed talking and talked well."

Few who noticed the extremely short sentences, brief and rapid words bestowed upon them in the consulting-room, suspected the eloquent and sustained power of description, the humorous exposition, the sharp incisive epigram, the shrewd appreciation of character, the genial, almost boyish overflow of spirits, the bursts of natural impulse which made a ramble with him amongst the hills or a walk in the summer woodland as good as the most exhilarating of tonics.

But I now willingly hand my pen to his eldest daughter Ethel, who has been good enough to write a few charming paragraphs, some notes of his professional and family daily life, expressive of her affectionate appreciation of her father, chiefly as he lived and moved amongst his children.

ETHEL'S NOTES.

" He always woke early, for he did not know what it was to have a good night, and was obliged to sleep in a sitting position, and generally would begin reading before seven. An early breakfast, after which came the reading of his correspondence and dictating replies. Then in summer time he would take a short walk, either to see a few special cases or, if no one needed an early call, in the park or Botanical Gardens. In the winter there were practically always a few to see, and he drove a short round. He was in again shortly after ten, and began to see patients. Often it was three and even four o'clock before he finished, and he had only had time to snatch a hasty lunch brought to him in his consulting room. His patients gone, he rested for a short while either dozing in his chair or reading quietly, but not to be disturbed till the hour named for tea. He was very particular about his tea, which was always made watch in hand. For a long time he took it *à la Russe;* with lemon in it. During the hurried lunch and the tea, over which he loved

to linger for a short time, there were always
two or three of the family with him, telling him
of their doings, their plans and all that was
happening that concerned them. Tea was the
pleasanter of the two, he had no one to hurry
him, but little time was lost, and between half-
past four and five he started off on his rounds,
which generally lasted nearly four hours.
Dinner came on his return, the ceremony of
dressing being usually conducted with his family
round him. When work was in full swing, it
was only at such odd times they could be with
him. Dinner to him was a simple meal, and he
drank only the weakest sherry and water. In
former days, when he was a great smoker, his
cigar seemed more important than anything to
eat, but of late years he had only smoked
stramonium cigarettes. After dinner came
a chat and a glance at the evening paper,
and then more work, reading, dictating, or
correcting proofs, which lasted late into the
night.

"I need not speak of his capacity for work,
but, perhaps, it is worth while mentioning that
he always laid great stress on the proverb ' It
is good for a man to bear the yoke in his youth,'
and he was very much inclined to think that the
men who succeeded most, were those who had to

struggle against surroundings. Being one of the most energetic of men, he always impressed energy on those around him, and I often remember his applauding the remark that, a man should never be a schoolmaster when he had ceased to go upstairs two steps at a time. He had an extraordinary faculty for interesting himself in the doings of those he loved. When we were children he always liked to hear the minutest details of our work, and, however busy he was, could always make time to help us. Once when we were learning one of the scenes out of *Macbeth*, he sat up half the night reading various authorities and critics, and rose early for several mornings in order to coach us personally. Later on when we each had our separate occupation, he would help each of us individually. His general information was wonderful. He knew something of everything. He was very keen on all connected with art, and there was nothing he enjoyed more than taking us round the famous galleries of Europe, teaching and explaining. He was very much imbued with the idea that all women should have a profession or business, and watched us anxiously for an indication of a special gift in order to determine what he should make of us. He had a very great dread of our becoming frivolously dependent on amusement, and always urged me to spend two or three hours a day in "solid" reading, apart from my regular work, and was always eager to discuss all I read. He had a very deep sympathy with all women who work, and was very liberal-minded with reference to their entering the professions. He thought there was a great field for women as doctors, and with his great belief in specialism considered that they should be particularly adapted to the delicate specialities like the throat, eye, and ear.

"The reported saying of the Emperor Frederick to his son *Lerne zu leiden, ohne zu beklagen*, is very characteristic of my father. He had an extraordinary capacity for bearing pain and discomfort. Fortitude was one of the qualities he most admired. He always expected us to make the best of things, and I remember his being quite hurt with me—I can scarcely recall an instance of his being cross—on one occasion when we were riding, because I complained of a pain in my side brought on by a long quick trot, after partaking of home-made ginger beer. Riding was his favourite exercise but he was also formerly very fond of lawn-tennis, when he was an excellent player 'up at the net.' He would stand with his racquet right over the net, and hit the balls before they came over. After the rules were altered to prevent this he lost his fondness for the game, for he could not take much violent exercise, though ten or twelve years ago he would occasionally join in an energetic game of hide-and-seek or "tiger," and do long pulls on the river. But, of course, this was when his asthma was much less severe ; of late any exercise tried him, and when he was riding he would constantly have to smoke stramonium in order to ease his breathing. He was also very fond of driving.

"Building was one of his chief delights, and for the last twenty years of his life he was either building or altering one or other of his houses. He entirely rebuilt those at Wargrave and superintended every detail himself. His life at Wargrave was very quiet. He would wake early—for five or six hours' sleep, disturbed only twice or thrice by the necessity of inhaling, meant an unusually good night to him—and would write or read till breakfast. After breakfast he would work for two or three hours, and then stroll in the garden, where he knew every flower and had arranged for the planting of each shrub and creeper, or else play chess under the trees till lunch. Lunch over, he would ride or go on the river in the gondola, after

which he would take another stroll and then
read till dinner. The evening was always
devoted to chess if there was anyone to play
with; if not he would read. He was very
much attached to his garden, although actual
gardening was too much exertion for him, with
the exception of "spudding," and he would
daily enlist the aid of his family and friends in
his crusade against the plantains, daisies and
dandelions that marred the beauty of his
lawn. In spite of his efforts, however, the
weeds did not greatly decrease. He took such
a pride in his garden and in the result of any
improvements, and often spoke of having blocked
out a view of some unsightly cottages by a
row of thriving poplar trees as ' one of the successes of my life.' He had a great desire to
possess every kind of ivy, and nothing pleased
him more than to acquire a new variety. He
was extremely abstemious, and the plainest
possible food pleased him best.

" For a man who had been constantly deceived
in those on whom he showered kindness he had
a great belief in humanity. But of all men
with whom he had come in contact, his greatest
admiration was for the Emperor Frederick.
There was something of hero-worship in his
devotion to him, and he thought him the finest

character he had ever known. The inscription which he placed under the Emperor's photograph which always stood in his room, 'I shall not look upon his like again,' was an expression of his deep belief."

VIII.

THE EMPEROR.

VIII.

I NOW come to the most important and critical episode in Sir Morell Mackenzie's professional life. It is one in which his personality stands out before the whole civilized world, his reserve of power reveals itself for the first time, his self-control is put to the severest test, his firmness triumphs, his skill culminates, and his high devotion to duty shines out amidst considerable misrepresentation, jealousy and libel, like the sun when he goes forth in his strength.

In the autumn of 1886, the Crown Prince of Germany " *Unser Fritz*," afterwards Frederick III., had taken cold whilst driving out with the Crown Princess in the north of Italy. The coachman lost his way, the prince had no great coat with him, and as he afterwards said to Mackenzie, " I felt as if I had taken cold, and my throat has never become quite well since that evening."

On Wednesday night, May 18th, 1887, Mackenzie was just retiring to rest after a hard day's work when Dr. Reid was announced, who came direct from Windsor with a message from the Queen requesting Mackenzie's immediate presence at Berlin to examine the Crown Prince's throat. Our great specialist, thus summoned, started by the first train for Berlin.

It will now be my duty to condense Mackenzie's statement of what took place between May 18th, 1887, and June 13th, 1888, the day of the Emperor's death, to refer to the sort of criticism which the German doctors thought it appropriate to make, and to the principal views, favourable and the reverse, which have been taken of Sir Morell Mackenzie's conduct of the whole case.

If I venture to point to any definite conclusions which may fairly be gathered from the evidence in outline now placed before the reader, it will be merely as the foreman of a jury in consulting with the jury who have sat through a long case might attempt to formulate their verdict and the general grounds on which it is based, before re-entering the court and delivering it to the judge ; and if it be objected that I have not had the previous benefit of special "direction" from a competent judge, I might answer that not only has every news-paper in the kingdom (including the medical journals) sat on the Bench, and delivered judgment, but that the case has been carried from court to court, and that the High Court of Appeal now threatens to be nothing short of posterity itself, for whose verdict it might no doubt be desirable (had it been possible) for us all to wait patiently.

At that great assize many a premature decision may be reversed, many innocent proclaimed guilty, and some guilty declared innocent. Mean-while we have the present generation to deal with.

And here let me say that the simplicity and intelligibility of Mackenzie's book " Frederick the Noble," which makes it most distasteful to experts, also makes the task of simple analysis easier than I had anticipated ; we have merely to deal with a clear straightforward narrative of facts recorded from day to day in a private note-book.

I am told the artists for the sketchy illustrated papers produce their effect by drawing in full detail, and then striking out all the superfluous lines. This will be my method, the only one consistent with the proportions of this biogra-phical sketch. It is one which will, of course, render the account as incomplete from a technical point of view, as are the *Daily Graphic* pictures from an anatomical or microscopic standpoint, but as in those pictures the clear and truthful suggestion, so in this exciting case, the main drift is what the general public cares for, and about all it knows how to appreciate.

Of course I shall be at once met by the objection that only a medical expert should touch such a narrative as this. That no one can state or estimate a surgical case requiring special knowledge without having made a special study of surgery and hygiene. The answer is : Such is not the view of an English law court. There case after case comes before judge and jury, and neither judge nor jury are expected to be experts on the various matters discussed, they are assumed, nevertheless, to be able to form a fair opinion on the discussion, and to come to a pretty definite verdict on the case, after hearing the evidence *pro* and *con*, although they know no more of the matter than just what counsel have thought fit to put before them. And that is my only reply to the medical objection which declares that no one out of the profession can understand the drift of the plainest alleged facts, simply because they happen to be *medical* facts.

My carpenter may know a great deal more

about making chairs than I do, but when I sit down on a chair and it collapses, I am a good judge of whether that chair has been properly made, and when an "expert" explains to me that the reason it came to pieces was because it was left out in the rain and had only been glued instead of pinned or tenon-joined, I can estimate the force of that explanation as well as the carpenter. And so if I am told that a large metal tube is beyond dispute put into a man's windpipe, and causes irritation because it presses against one side,[1] or that excessive cautery has set up an irritation favourable to the development of cancer, or that a certain operation by statistics, which in this case cannot mislead,[2] is usually fatal, or that the laryngoscope requires special experience, which some who have attempted to use it have not possessed, that a great analyst examines tissue manifestly, and by his own admission, taken from the seat of disease, and does not find cancer, I maintain that the general bearings of such facts, if such are the facts, is broadly intelligible to everyone, just as intelligible as that a chair which is glued and not pinned may hold in dry weather, but is liable to come to pieces when it gets damp.

[1,2] Affirmed by Mackenzie, denied by the German doctors, but see Appendix E.

K

And now "*á Berlin.*"

Mackenzie arrived at the palace of the Crown Prince in the afternoon of May 20th, 1887. He was hardly allowed time to change his travelling dress when he was hurried into the presence of his illustrious patient.

The same thing happened to Lord Salisbury when he arrived worn out with fatigue to attend the Berlin Conference. Bismarck would take no denial, and his lordship had to dine with the man of blood and iron that same night. The same thing, oddly enough, happened to old Sebastien Bach when he was sent for by Frederick the Great; the famous composer, by Royal mandate, was hurried into the august presence, great coat, muddy boots and all ! The Hohenzollerns, it seems, brook no delay, and the Crown Prince (who spoke in a gruff whisper) was for immediate action, instant examination.

The wary English specialist, however, declined examination until after a formal interview with the German doctors in attendance. He retired into a side room and met the men with whom he had to deal during the next few terrible months. His rapid analysis of his medical companions, is characteristic and significant. I reproduce it from "Frederick the Noble" for what it is worth. Whatever its truth or value it is extremely characteristic of Mackenzie. (" Frederick the Noble," p. 10.)

There was GERHARDT, an experienced physician, who had given *some attention to diseases of the throat.*

VON BERGMANN, a military surgeon who had accepted the chair of surgery at Berlin (declined by Billroth, of Vienna, and Volkmann, of Halle).

TOBOLD, one of the earlier German throat physicians, but little more than a *nominis umbra* now.

Mackenzie adds that he was naturally surprised not to find one of the leading German specialists on throat diseases present, and at once assumed that whatever was the matter with the Crown Prince, there could not be much the matter with his throat.

First Scene.

Gerhardt reads a paper and makes a general statement in the presence of his colleagues, from which Mackenzie gathers that there is a small growth about the size of a pea on the Prince's left vocal cord.

K 2

Second Scene.

A darkened room. Mackenzie seated opposite the Prince, wearing on his forehead the laryngoscopic reflector, which flashed from a burner in front a stream of light down the Prince's throat. That light is caught on a small circular looking-glass about the size of a shilling, which, being introduced deftly into the open mouth to the back of the patient's throat, at once illumines and reveals what is going on in the vocal cords, and even some way down the windpipe. The whole is reflected upon the little hand mirror.

Mackenzie now saw, for the first time, the small tumour, the size of a split pea, which was partly attached to the under surface as well as the side of the vocal cord. This excrescence prevented the free play or vibration of the vocal cords which enables them to generate sound, they could not come together. This fully accounted for the Prince's " gruff whisper."

In the medical debate which followed, in another room, Gerhardt and Tobold, and more guardedly Bergmann, pronounce the tumour CANCEROUS.

Mackenzie denies that the presence of cancer can be *certified* without a microscopic examination of *some part* of the growth itself. *The doctors acquiesce.*

How to remove a piece?

" Will you try? " says Mackenzie to Gerhardt. *Answer : " I cannot operate with forceps."*

To Tobold : " Will you try ? "

Answer : " I no longer operate."

Mackenzie's astonishment was perhaps ill-disguised, but hardly unnatural. He then offered himself to perform an operation which he admitted to be delicate, but which they seemed to think was impossible.

Third Scene.

Again the darkened room, and Mackenzie seated with the laryngoscopic mirror, but this time armed with a borrowed forceps in his right hand, introducing the little circular mirror to the back of the Prince's throat with his left. The reflected image of the tumour appeared ; the cup-like blades of the forceps being then applied, the operation was seen to take place in the reflection upon parts otherwise out of sight.

Knowing nothing of the case before his arrival, Mackenzie had not got his own forceps, and was unaccustomed to the French pattern, with which he now attempted to operate. The first introduction of the cup-like blades failed to close upon and secure any fragment of the tumour, but the second attempt, the result of which " was greeted with a look of amazement, followed by one of annoyance and disappointment," brought away a bit of the growth. Dr. Wegner alone seemed pleased, and congratulated the English operator with sincere professional enthusiasm.

The fragment was at once despatched to Virchow, the admitted prince of analysts ; and then came a pause in the fateful drama.

Speaking to me of these operations, the last of which resulted in the complete removal of the warty growth with the forceps, Mackenzie said, with one of his lightly satirical smiles, " There was really nothing much in the operation, although all the German doctors about the Prince seemed to think it impossible. Why, I could name half a dozen German specialists who could have done it as well as myself. It wouldn't have done for me to say so, and at the time I hoped to manage the susceptibilities of the men who were about the Emperor. The operation, though one requiring, no doubt, special technical skill, is one which I have frequently done at the Throat Hospital, and which passes without comment. The patient comes in, sits down, and it is all over in a minute. It was the august nature of the patient, and the chance of possible failure, and not the perilous or impracticable nature of the operation which gave the matter so much importance." And he added, " The Crown Prince would have had a much better chance, had he presented himself as an ordinary patient at the Throat Hospital and been treated *incog.* He would have got the best attention throughout, and no mistakes would have been made. What happens with these great people is, that so many doctors have a finger in the pie, that the right thing (1) either cannot be done at the right time through interference, or (2) is marred in the doing, or (3) is not done at all. I need not say to which of the above cases the Crown Prince's belongs."

Virchow's analysis of the fragments removed had to arrive before the case could be carried one stage further.

Mackenzie now had an opportunity of in-specting the Royal farms, and of coming into closer personal relations with his illustrious patient, who, from the first, seems to have taken much pleasure in his society.

In his first walk with his English doctor the Crown Prince complained that Gerhardt had been openly saying he had cancer, and asked if it were correct professional etiquette for doctors to speak to "*other people*" about their patient's disease, especially "*when the patient's own wife*" had not been told. "And," said the Prince, "*if he thought I was suffering from cancer, was he right in sending me to Ems?*" Mackenzie had never heard of Ems being good for cancer, but waived the discussion, saying that no doubt Gerhardt would explain it all satisfactorily if he were personally interrogated.

It was in this conversation that the Prince denied that he had ever been a great smoker—excessive smoking notoriously predisposing to cancer.

It was then that Mackenzie first learned that a fearful operation had been decided upon by Bergmann, to take place on the 21st of May—that nothing but his timely arrival had stopped it. Bergmann was going to open the larynx just to see what was the matter, with a view to removing the whole growth and its ramifications if possible. This was only to be an "exploratory" operation, but one which would almost invariably lead on to a more radical one.

The arrival of Virchow's first report soon absorbed the Prince's entourage to the exclusion

of any other topic. Virchow was positive on
two heads :—

(1) That the fragment *was a portion of diseased
tissue.*

(2) That *it was not cancerous.*

This is important, because an early attempt
was made to float the theory that what had been
seized by Mackenzie's forceps was a bit of
healthy tissue, and, therefore, no guide to the
Prince's disease, but a wanton or clumsy wound
inflicted on a healthy part of the throat, either
for the purpose of proving the non-existence of
cancer, or from mere bungling. It is also right
to state that, *according to the German doctors* (who
always assumed that cancer was present from
the first), Mackenzie's operations were rendered
futile by his never being able to reach the
cancerous part with his forceps.

Scene IV.

The removal of a portion of the tumour was accompanied by an immediate improvement in the
royal patient's voice. In spite of some catarrhal
congestion of the throat, a second attempt was
now made to remove some more of the tumour.
It failed. And this gave rise to a pseudo or
melodramatic incident of some importance.

After the attempt, on looking into the Prince's throat, Gerhardt started back with horror.

Mackenzie, he declared, had injured the vocal cord !

Mackenzie takes the trouble (" Frederick the Noble," p. 25) to explain how technically absurd this accusation was. He, however, looked at once, and could see nothing but the catarrhal congestion before mentioned. Wegner looked at once, and he could see nothing, but Bergmann and Tobold sided with Gerhardt. The Prince himself seemed to have been much puzzled at this new diagnosis, and he said his throat "felt quite comfortable, and what was it that had so alarmed Professor Gerhardt ?"

Mackenzie assured him that there was nothing the matter, and that he thought that Gerhardt must be under some misconception. He adds, " His Imperial Highness said nothing more, and I clearly saw the plot had failed."

This was only a foretaste of what the English doctor had to expect at the hands of his German colleagues.

Mackenzie had left London May 18th ; he returned May 29th. What had he done in that ten days, and what had he said ?

1st. He had prevented an " exploratory operation," to ascertain whether another operation could be performed, which is usually fatal at once, but which, if successful, prolongs life a very little, after making that life absolutely not worth living.

2nd. He had removed with the forceps a piece of the tumour by a skilful operation, which the German doctors not only could not perform, but declared to be impossible.

3rd. He had obtained from Virchow, the greatest living analyst, an assurance that the portion of tissue removed was *diseased*, but distinctly *not cancerous*. And now what had he *said*, and *not said?* He had said that cancer was "*non-proven.*" He had *never* said, he never did say "the *disease was not cancer.*"

The second Act of this strange, eventful drama opens with Mackenzie's return to Potsdam on June 7th.

Scene I.

The congestion attributed by Gerhardt to Mackenzie's forceps, and by Mackenzie to the results of Gerhardt's excessive cautery (he had attempted unsuccessfully to remove the growth) having subsided, Mackenzie at once seized the opportunity to attempt the further removal of the growth with the forceps. A large portion was this time neatly brought away and dispatched to

Virchow, who stated in reply, " that although it was proved that the operation had reached the *deep parts*,[1] yet in no part could an ingrowth of the epithelial formation into mucous membrane be detected—nothing was brought away which would be likely to excite the suspicion of wider and graver disease."

Mackenzie dwells much upon the fact that all the German doctors in attendance were parties to Virchow's examination, and endorsed its results. If in spite of these results they were still *certain* there was cancer, they should have withdrawn and issued a separate report ; they did nothing of the kind, and thereby accepted solidarity of responsibility for the treatment along with Mackenzie ; Bergmann himself admitting, as late as October, 1887—an admission never denied by Bergmann—that Mackenzie had been *quite right* in the course recommended and adopted in the summer.

The scene of action now shifts to London.

Scene II.

On June 21st, as our Queen drove through the streets of London, to and from Westminster

---

[1] Thus it would seem directly traversing the opinion that Mackenzie had *not* reached the deep seat of the malady.

Abbey, where had taken place the solemn cele-
bration of her jubilee, no figure amongst her
body-guard of princes excited more attention and
admiration than that of her august son-in-law
the Crown Prince Frederick. Bursts of spon-
taneous applause broke from the crowd as he
passed by ; they hailed him " king of men by
gift of Nature as well as by right of birth."

" Few could have thought," writes Mackenzie,
" on seeing him there that behind the hero of
Königgrätz, Wörth, and Sedan, there rode on that
day of triumph a grim conqueror, who before
another year had passed would have laid that
stately form in the dust."

I need not dwell upon the attempt to control
Mackenzie by sending to England with Wegner
a young doctor, whose name I have no desire
to mention, because I have no wish any further
to injure his reputation. (See " Frederick the
Noble," pp. 39-55).

On June 28th, the Crown Prince was operated
upon at 19, Harley Street, in the presence of
Dr. Wegner and Dr. Norris Wolfenden, of the
Throat Hospital. All that remained of the
tumour on the left vocal cord was successfully
brought away, and immediately dispatched to
Virchow. The results of this third examination
were quite as negative with regard to cancer as

any of the previous examinations had proved to
be.   The last portion of the wart removed " gave
not the least support for the idea of a new formation penetrating inwards (*a distinctive sign of
cancer*) ".   (Virchow.)

Soon afterwards the Crown Prince goes to the
Isle of Wight; ugly symptoms announce themselves, and Mackenzie warns the Crown Prince
of probable danger.   At the same time the warty
growth threatens to recur.   This, however, is successfully and finally stopped by judicious cautery.

Scotland is the next move, whither the Crown
Prince went attended by Mackenzie's assistant,
Mr. Hovell, with whom the august patient expressed himself as quite satisfied.   The Queen
was delighted to hear the Crown Prince's
" natural voice again."   In September the
Crown Prince returned to Germany.

Let us again inquire, between June 21st and
August 31st, what Mackenzie had *done ?*

(1) He had removed the last portion of the
warty growth.

(2) He had obtained from Virchow a statement that it contained no more cancer than the
two previous pieces.

(3) He had finally stopped by cautery the
threatened recurrence of the warty growth.

What had he *said?*

(1) He had declared that with regard to cancer, Virchow's analysis must again be accepted. Cancer was *non-proven.*

(2) On the appearance of new symptoms he had warned the Princess that there were breakers ahead. This is what took place. At the end of August, before the Crown Prince and Princess left England, Mackenzie made the following frank statement :—

(1) Although at this time the disease does not seem to me malignant, *it may, nevertheless, turn out to be so (sic) ;* and, he added, these were the alternatives to reckon with :

(*a*) The tumour having been destroyed may not grow again, the affection being thus practically cured.

(*b*) The tumour may sprout up again, and require to be removed or destroyed more than once.

(*c*) A condition known as "multiple papillona" might result, which was dangerous if not properly treated, but not necessarily fatal.

(*d*) *The disease might be cancerous already, or that disease might develop later on.*

I can see in all this neither the *suppressio veri* nor *suggestio falsi* of which Mackenzie has been industriously accused. This seems the right place to introduce the following remarkable letter written to Mackenzie by the Empress Frederick :—

In 1888, I took care to tell all eminent German medical men with whom I came casually in contact, that you had said to me the first time I saw you that, though what you saw was innocent, yet you could not be sure until the fragment had been examined by Virchow, and that a malignant disease might be present somewhere out of sight, but that there was no proof of it. The most unfavourable element of the case being my husband's age at the time. You told me that a benign growth and a malignant growth were seldom found together, and that you thought the growth you could see on the vocal cord was a benign one ; you also said that you could not hold out any security to me that a malignant growth might not appear some day.

You said then, the operation proposed was running too great a risk, that it was exposing life, and that should it succeed the condition of the patient after would be so terrible that his chances if let alone would be more favourable. I have since heard that different German medical men think this a reasonable and sensible view, and say that under the circumstances no one could have done much better.

You also said, I think, that you would not have laryngotomy or laryngo fissure performed on your own throat, on the surmise or supposition of a malignant affection of the larynx without very positive proofs, and not even then, the tendency of malignant disease being to re-appear in other places. Consequently there would be a possibility of having gone through that operation, and yet losing one's life after all, and by the reappearance of the disease. Furthermore, you said, I think, that you did not know whether the Crown Prince's constitution would stand so serious a shock as that inflicted on the whole system by so important an operation. (*Nineteenth Century,* November, 1888.)

As this does not profess to be a detailed

account of the Crown Prince's illness, but only of Mackenzie in his relation to it, I may be pardoned, if I arrest the rapid stream of my narrative only at those critical points where Mackenzie's nerve and forbearance were put to the utmost test.

It will be seen that the time during which the Crown Prince was in England and Scotland is the only time when he could be really said to be under Mackenzie's sole charge, until the subsequent management or mismanagement of the tracheotomy operation at San Remo again made it needful, after many aggravating circumstances, to place Mackenzie in sole charge of a very damaged case. It was then according to him too late.

That the Prince's life might have been further prolonged, if not saved; that cancer was a later development, which might have been avoided, but which was possibly induced by Gerhardt's excessive cautery, and furthered by Bergmann's subsequent rough handling, this, rightly or wrongly, was undoubtedly Mackenzie's opinion, and his unpardonable sin consists in having put that opinion on record much to the disadvantage of his German colleagues. It seems to be regarded as unprofessional, however much you may be criticized, or saddled with the con-

L

sequences of other's mistakes, ever to say that there has been any *mismanagement* on the part of those who have *called you in*, even though you yourself may be accused by them of the gravest blunders.

Mackenzie had now to stand by, and see some things done of which he approved, and others which he was powerless to prevent. The third and last decisive Act opens at San Remo, whither the Crown Prince had come in search of a milder climate.

Scene I.

On November 6th, Mackenzie joined his royal patient there.

Again he takes his seat opposite him, wearing the laryngoscopic mirror. One glance is sufficient, and Mackenzie removes the reflector. The Crown Prince who was quick to read the truth, said " Is it cancer ? " to which Mackenzie replied immediately, " I am sorry to say, sir, it looks *very much like it*, but *it is impossible to be certain*."

The Prince quite understood and grasped Mackenzie warmly by the hand; he was grateful for his candour and his caution.

" I have lately," he said, " been fearing something of the sort; I thank you Sir Morell, for being so frank with me."

Soon after this, Drs. Krause and Schrötter are summoned at the request of Mackenzie, and all three agree that the disease is cancer, Mackenzie still maintaining that whilst that was also his own opinion, microscopic evidence alone could absolutely confirm the diagnosis.[1]

Matters having reached this point, Mackenzie invited Dr. Schrötter to make a formal announcement to the patient. It was a solemn moment, and a scene followed which must have left an indelible impression upon those present.

All the doctors stood round in a semicircle, in front of the august patient. The Prince also remained standing, and listened with the utmost calmness to what was practically his death sentence from the lips of Dr. Schrötter, who performed his painful task at Mackenzie's request, in German, but with great tact and feeling.

The operation of tracheotomy was next decided upon, and a young doctor Bramann, in

---

[1] The German doctors were never weary *after the event* of descanting on the untrustworthy character of microscopic analysis for purposes of diagnosis. Yet, they were parties to three separate analyses by Virchow for the purposes of diagnosis. See *Medical Journal*, i. (1888), p. 1360.

the absence of Dr. von Bergmann, was selected
to operate.

Mackenzie was present, and expressed himself
well satisfied with Bramann's performance, even
giving his method of procedure in some respects
the preference over the English one.   But there
his commendation ceased.   He now had to stand
by, and see a tube in his judgment much too
large thrust in.   He had to watch the irritation caused by this tube rubbing against the
side of the wind-pipe;[1] nor could he prevail
upon them to alter it until a suppurating wound
had been made.   Such is Mackenzie's statement.

He then, he says, had to substitute a tube of
his own, which, coming too late, disappointed his
expectations.   All through this trying time every
conceivable debate was raging round the Crown
Prince.   Mackenzie was watched with lynx eyes;
not only were his suggestions postponed, but
even his examinations were occasionally objected
to.

Alarmist views of cancer in the lungs now
got abroad, which, although summarily denied
by Mackenzie, were only allayed by the great
lung expert, Kussmaul, declaring that Mackenzie's opinion was correct.

Mackenzie's tube was taken out; one of

---

[1] This wound is denied by the German doctors.

Bergmann's put in. It was apparently bungled, causing the Prince great irritation, till he said, " *Send for Hovell*," who immediately put it right.

Hovell's turn came now, and he was threatened with imprisonment for not adopting antiseptic measures.

" If Mr. Hovell is sent to prison," said the Prince smiling, " I shall have to go too ! "

The cannula or tube continued to give trouble, till at last Mackenzie was permitted to have another made by a San Remo silversmith, which proved at last perfectly comfortable. Thus, according to the narrative I am resuming, was Mackenzie, hampered, " cribbed, cabined, and confined."

Scene II.

On the 4th March, 1888, just four days before the old Emperor's death, the decisive microscopic test of cancer for which Mackenzie had stood out was produced by Professor Waldeyer, and immediately after this the five doctors in attendance signed jointly with Mackenzie a document stating that *there were no differences of opinion among them regarding the nature of the disease*, and *restoring* (?) the case to the *sole charge* of Mackenzie.

In one damaging paragraph of his book, " Frederick the Noble," p. 122, Mackenzie strikes the key-note of the Emperor's forlorn hope, and indissolubly connects it with what he considered to be the mismanagement of the German doctors.

" The case was now formally restored to me, but in what a different condition was the illustrious patient from what he had been when I had given him over to the care of the German surgeons. On the day that he was operated upon, he felt " perfectly well," except that his breathing was difficult : he was now a confirmed invalid. Besides this the disease in the larynx, which had previously been progressing very slowly, had, through the coughing caused by ill-fitting tracheotomy tubes, been stirred into extreme activity. Greater destruction was probably occasioned in three weeks in this way than would have occurred in a year, had the illustrious patient not been subjected to such injudicious treatment."

Between August 31st when the Crown Prince returned to Germany after the Jubilee visit, and March 8th, when he was summoned to Berlin to attend, if possible, the death-bed of his father, what had Mackenzie *done?*

On being summoned to the Emperor—

(a) At San Remo, November 6th, Mackenzie had examined the throat, and decided on the operation of tracheotomy.

After at last getting rid of Bramann's large cannula—

(b) He had provided two tubes, the second of which proved a great success.

(c) He had been invariably able to alleviate the Prince's sufferings by local remedies, for which the Prince frequently expressed his gratitude.

And what had Mackenzie *said?*

(a) He had told the Prince on November 6th, 1887, his disease, " *looked like cancer.*"

(b) He had " *recommended* " that this information should be formally communicated to the Prince by his own doctor in German which was done.

(c) And four days before the Crown Prince became Emperor, he had " *agreed* " with all the doctors that the microscopic evidence for which they had all waited and which arrived some days before the old Emperor's death was quite conclusive as to cancer.[1]

---

[1] Had there been any real law or power preventing an heir apparent suffering from cancer from ascending the throne, there was plenty of time to have put it in motion.

(*d*) And he had signed a document to the effect that all the doctors were, including himself, of one and the same opinion.

I still fail to see the signs of prevarication and disingenuousness—the *suppressio veri* or *suggestio falsi*, so recklessly imputed to the English specialist.

The analysis of the narrative must now draw quickly to its close "as the rapid of life shoots to the fall."

The case was indeed "*restored to Mackenzie.*" It may well have suited the German doctors to hand over to the English doctor a patient now *for the first time authoritatively* declared to be suffering from a malignant and incurable disease. It would always henceforth be possible to say that Mackenzie had not been able to cure it.

The fourth and last act of this harrowing tragedy may now be said to begin.

Scene I.

On March the 10th, the Emperor, still prostrated with grief for the death of his father, decided to take the risk of setting foot for the first time in his own dominions. He did so at the earnest

representations of Bismarck, although that distinguished minister, and at that time hot
partisan of the grandson (William), not the son
Frederick, well knew the danger of such a
journey for such a patient in such weather.[1]
At Leipsic, on the way, Mackenzie had an
interview with Bismarck, who expressed himself
desirous to save the sick Emperor all unnecessary fatigue and danger; but it does not
appear, contrary to the Chancellor's expectations, that the Emperor was materially the
worse for his journey, and down almost to the
day of his death he was never inclined to
shirk any of his official duties, nor indeed was
he unable to perform them. He had now begun
in good earnest his brief reign of ninety-nine
days.

[1] *Serious news from Berlin, March 8th.*—News reached San
Remo that the aged Emperor was in a critical condition, and a
despatch was received from Prince Bismarck urging the immediate return of the Crown Prince. "His Imperial Highness
sent for me," writes Mackenzie, "and asked, ' *Will there be any
danger in my returning at once to Berlin?*' I answered, ' *Yes,
sir, there would be some danger.*' He then said, ' There are some
occasions when it is the duty of a man to run risks, and such
an occasion is now before me. I shall return the day after
to-morrow. I shall be obliged to you to make whatever
medical arrangements you think necessary, and to confer with
Count Radolinsky on the subject. I look to you to take all
steps possible in order to reduce the danger of my journey north
to a minimum." (See also Appendix F.)

He habitually rose early, and occupied himself steadily and effectively every day with the business of the State.

On now to Charlottenberg which was reached in a blinding snowstorm, yet the Imperial patient seemed still to bear the journey well, and to be little affected by the weather. The baiting of the English doctor too now began in good earnest.

The instant he had again set foot in Germany, in attendance on the Emperor, the wildest rumours were set afloat.

He had, so it was declared, done the Emperor no good; he had stopped an operation which would have saved the Emperor's life, and even now he was preventing his medical attendants, especially Bergmann, from treating him effectively. Tobold was the real operator (who "*no longer operated*"), who had brought away the fragments for analysis. Mackenzie was really a Polish Jew, and his true name was "Moritz Marcovics" and a highly imaginative biography of the "English Jewish horror" was got out, with a portrait in proper style, embellished with an unmistakably long nose.

A band of fanatics threatened him with assassination, and obligingly gave him to the 17th of May to clear out. Even so respectable a journal as the *Kölnische Zeitung* risked a remark, since become almost historical, that Mackenzie dared not show himself *Unter-den-Linden*, because if his face were seen the people would tear him in pieces or stone him to death.

This fine picturesque writing received a rude check when Mackenzie refused the police protection offered him, walked about the streets freely, and was cheered and respectfully saluted by the people whenever he appeared in attendance on the Emperor.

A body of German artisans sent him a special address of sympathy and confidence. There was never anything but gratitude and admiration for Mackenzie in Germany, except on the part of the reptile press, and a certain official clique biassed by political motives and a medical clique biassed by professional jealousy.

In spite of the gross misrepresentations which prevailed at this time and up to the date of the Emperor Frederick's death, there is no reason to suppose that the general public in Germany failed to grasp the substantial facts of the case, or failed to do substantial justice to the very great services rendered by the English doctor to the dying Emperor.

Meanwhile the crumbling away of the windpipe, the result according to Mackenzie of the wound at the back made by Bramann's first large tube, went on, whilst the sufferer was occupied unweariedly, interviewing foreign Princes, consulting with his ministers of State, or engaged in discharging those monotonous but essential duties, which consist chiefly in attaching signatures to documents after either perusal or at least a general mastery of their contents.

Mackenzie now seldom left him for very long; he had always to be within call. He regulated his hours, his meals, his interviews and his airings, and the Emperor with his martial instinct submitted with the docility of a subordinate officer in the army.

Only once did the illustrious patient seem on the verge of revolt; he had set his heart in the bitter weather on attending his Imperial father's funeral; but Mackenzie was this time peremptory, and the Prince gave in reluctantly; but he was restless and agitated all the day, being often heard to say, " I ought to have been there, I ought to have been there," and indeed that historic scene was incomplete without his noble and commanding figure.

But Mackenzie had the tact to watch the Emperor's wishes and gratify them whenever it was possible to do so without danger. One Sunday he said to his royal patient :

" A fortnight ago, sir, you asked me if you might drive into Berlin to pay a visit to her Majesty, the Empress Augusta, and I felt obliged to tell you that it would be dangerous for you to leave the house. To-day I think you may safely go."

The Emperor's face, says Mackenzie, beamed with satisfaction as he shook me warmly by the hand, saying, " I am indeed delighted."

Mackenzie was in attendance in a carriage following the Emperor's, and on being recognized by the crowds that lined the way, he writes, " The men took off their hats to me and the ladies bowed in a friendly way." The reptile press was not " in it " on that occasion.

I am permitted, by his friend, Mr. Parkinson, who knew him intimately,[1] to give his friends an eye-witness glimpse into his life at Berlin and Potsdam at that trying time of high pressure. I am glad to be able to do this, as some may imagine that I have exaggerated the severe and disastrous strain put upon him by his arduous duties as well as by the pitiless

---

[1] See also Appendix II.

persecution which dogged his footsteps and
thwarted his activities. His friend writes as
follows :—

" One fine morning in the spring of 1889, I put
myself in the train at Victoria, bound for Berlin
by the Flushing route. I had engagements to fulfil
in another and distant part of Europe, but my
visit to the German capital was wholly and
solely to see Mackenzie, to whom I gave only a
few hours' notice of my intention. A German
gentleman known to both of us met me at the
Berlin station, with a warm message from
Mackenzie thanking me for making the journey
to see him, and begging me to lose no time in
coming out to the palace of Charlottenberg, where
the late Emperor was then lying. Our meeting
was cordial, enthusiastic, affecting. I found him
in a huge barrack-like chamber, to which I had
been conducted by a private staircase, and
which was in direct communication with the
Imperial sick room. The suffering Emperor
had only to touch a string and the tingle of a
bell brought Mackenzie to his side ; and judging
from what I saw and heard, that string could
have been seldom out of the Imperial
patient's hand. There was an indescribable
' behind the scenes ' air about the palace.
All interest was concentrated upon the sick
room, and the daily routine of court life, the

sentries on guard, the minsters with their
portfolios, the mounted soldier messengers,
continually arriving and departing ; the officials
of high degree, the representatives of the press
from every part of the world ; the professors and
scientific doctors, and their consultations and
controversies ; the solemn officers of the house-
hold, and the servitors of lower degree, nay the
Imperial family itself and its august connections
seemed one and all to be mere subordinate
accessories in the terrible drama being enacted
in that inner chamber, a drama in which
Mackenzie was playing the leading part, next
to the suffering Emperor himself. Into the
merits of what has been made matter for controversy I cannot enter. I can only testify to
Mackenzie's personal devotion to his task, and
to its painfully arduous and exhausting character. If ever a man had nervous strain
almost to breaking point written on his face, it
was Mackenzie at Charlottenberg. His personal asthmatic ailment compelled him to keep
the temperature of his room abnormally high.
The personal needs of the Emperor kept him
perpetually on the move ; he was beset by
inquirers of all kinds, from whose pertinacity he
seemed to me insufficiently protected, and as a
huge table piled up with unopened letters
showed, his correspondence was of a magnitude

impossible to grapple with. It is true he had with him his friend and fully qualified assistant, the English surgeon Mr. Hovell, who relieved Mackenzie turn and turn about for night and day duty, but the weight of responsibility was Mackenzie's own, and *his appearance and demeanour frightened me.* Never of robust appearance, he had grown much thinner, and was haggard-looking to a degree ; with a troubled *hunted* look as if he never enjoyed a night's rest. It was obvious that the strain and anxiety of the position were almost unbearable ; and when an Imperial personage graciously expressed a desire to accord an interview to Mackenzie's English friend, I determined to express my fear that unless some alleviations were provided and insisted on, the Emperor would lose Mackenzie's services, as the latter would infallibly break down. This I carried out faithfully without, so far as I know, Mackenzie ever learning that I did so. The case was too serious in my eyes to mince matters, and in as courtly phrase as I could muster, which I fear was after all but blunt, I further pointed out the peril Mackenzie himself was in, declaring that the alteration I noted in his appearance and manner seriously alarmed me, and imploring that some means of changing the current of his thoughts, and insuring him regularly some fresh air and exercise should be insisted upon.

"This interview and conversation with the Empress was at her gracious instance an absolutely private one, and no one else was present or within sight. Mackenzie having first presented me, retired altogether, so that if I erred in my plain speaking no one knew it but the Empress herself, whose kind consideration for Mackenzie and grateful acknowledgment of his services were as unaffectedly sympathetic and outspoken as language could convey. Her Majesty recognized warmly the necessity for giving Mackenzie some extra relief to mind and body ; and graciously expressed the wish that other of his English friends would .come over to visit him, adding that when she saw us together from her window, in the park of the palace that same morning, when I was being shown around, she had felt instinctively that the change of companionship and intercourse with an Englishman fresh from his home, were the very things he needed.

" Something was said about horse exercise, and the difficulty of providing efficient change of scene for the doctor while the Emperor remained so ill, and so dependent ;

M

but the impression left on me by my interview
was that my very outspoken representations had
not been without their effect, and this was
confirmed by what I learnt from Mackenzie
later, of what had been suggested for him with
regard to relief in occupation and recreation as
a change from the terrible sick room routine.

"From Vienna, I wrote Mackenzie as strong
a letter as was possible from a layman to a
physician ; and felt my own presumption in
prescribing for him even while I did so. If
that letter, by any chance, be in existence
it will show far more clearly than I am able
to do now, what I felt and what I feared for
Mackenzie. My feeling was that the poor
fellow was killing himself, and that there would
be either a disastrous break down immediately
or *permanent injury inflicted on his constitution.*

"Mackenzie kept up until long after the
Emperor's death as all the world knows, but
how far his health was broken, and his power
of resistance impaired by the cruel strains of
that terrible time, and the anxieties following
it, is for experts to say. I know he impressed
me so painfully that I could not return to England without visiting him again, to see how
far my urgent and affectionate personal remon-
strance from Vienna had borne fruit. Ac-

cordingly, a week or two later I made a détour from the latter city and again visited Mackenzie, this time at Potsdam, where the Emperor had been moved a day or two before. I found Mackenzie looking a little stronger and I thought in more equable spirits.

" He had infinitely better quarters at Potsdam than at Charlottenberg, in fact at the Empress's own command, and selection, Mackenzie's rooms were one of the finest suites in the palace ; and he showed me over them, and told me stories about the pictures in them, and the decorations and fittings of the rooms, with a good deal of the boyish zest and frank sympathetic humour which made his society so delightful."

But now the Emperor's malady increased rapidly. The whole structure of the windpipe in the neighbourhood of Bramann's alleged wound was falling to pieces.

On returning home the Emperor asked Mackenzie to postpone his flying visit to London; and the great specialist, though at much inconvenience and loss to himself and his patients in town yielded, gracefully adding, when his Majesty remarked that the London patients would " hate him," "All English people take the deepest interest in your health, sir ; there is

M 2

no one who would not make sacrifices to be of service to you."

That night the Emperor sent for Mackenzie before he retired to rest, and handed him the cross and star of the Hohenzollern order, together with an autograph letter which ran thus :—

Charlottenberg, April 10th, 1888.

My dear Sir Morell,

You were called to me by the unanimous wish of my German medical attendants. Not knowing you myself, I had confidence in you in consequence of their recommendation. But I soon learnt to appreciate you from personal experience. You have rendered me most valuable services, in recognition of which, and in remembrance of my accession to the throne, I have the pleasure to confer on you the " Comthur and star of my Royal order of Hohenzollern."

Yours truly, Frederick, I. R.

At the same time Mr. Hovell received the second class of the " Kron " order.

Scene II.

The Emperor's breathing becomes worse, the crumbling of the windpipe continues, the

cannula no longer fits comfortably; at last
Mackenzie makes a provisional one of lead, but
before inserting it, out of courtesy, invites Dr.
Bergmann to be present. Then follows an episode unparalleled, I should think, in the annals
of surgical experiment. Had not Mackenzie's
daily note-book registered calmly, day by day,
with his well-known scrupulous technical accuracy, events which happened, the deplorable
catastrophe of April 12th, 1888, would be hardly
credible; but the details are so circumstantial
and the subsequent condition of the Emperor so
confirmatory of Mackenzie's plain statement,
confirmed by Mr. Hovell who was present, and
also by the American dentist, who had assisted
in the making of the tube, that I feel in duty
bound to register the unvarnished alleged facts
as they stand recorded.

Something had happened. Whether the
" orderly " (in attendance on the Emperor), had
influenced his employer's mind by some fresh
narrations of the " Jewish English horror's "
presumption and plain-speaking, or whether the
German doctors, especially Bergmann, who, as
Prince Radolin told Mackenzie, *was much trusted
by the official classes*, felt the Emperor, the case,
and everything in the way of reputation slipping
entirely out of his hands, it is difficult to say;

but when Bergmann arrived, in answer to Mackenzie's courteous summons, he seemed so excited and angry that he could hardly attend to Mackenzie's explanations. In his own report he transfers his excitement to Mackenzie, and says he was sent for because Mackenzie was "at his wits' end." [1]

Bergmann now proceeded to act in a way entirely inconsistent with the standing agreement that the case was to be left *solely in Mackenzie's hands* ("Frederick the Noble," p. 147), for he sat down in front of the Emperor, quickly undid the bandage, pulled out the cannula, tried to thrust one into the hole, but only thrust it into the *flesh;* pulled it out, took another, thrust that *further* into the flesh with considerable force down the same "false passage." These extraordinary proceedings were not unnaturally followed by violent coughing and *streams of blood,* upon which Bergmann thrusts his finger right into the wound, and then tries to hit the hole in the windpipe with another tube ; fails, then at last sends for Bramann, whom he has left in his carriage at the door, who, immediately on arrival, passes the cannula properly into the

---

[1] Bergmann describes the Emperor as nearly suffocated when he arrived. It can be proved that the Emperor was sitting writing quietly.

Emperor's throat, an operation which really presented no difficulty at all. Such is Mackenzie's amazing narrative.

Mackenzie professes to be able to throw no light upon these extraordinary proceedings on the part of an alleged skilled operator, except by suggesting the charitable hypothesis that something had so upset Bergmann, that he really did not know what he was about. His behaviour is described as "unaccountable," "extraordinary," a "state of great excitement," "over-excitement," "wits disordered through nervousness."

When it was all over and the Emperor was left with a new wound in his neck, he asked Mackenzie, "Why did Bergmann put his finger into my throat?" "I don't know, sir," was the reply. Then his Majesty added, "I hope you will not *allow* Professor von Bergmann to do any further operation on me." Mackenzie answered promptly, "After what I have seen to-day, sir, I beg most respectfully to say that I can no longer have the honour of continuing in attendance on your Majesty if Professor von Bergmann is to be permitted to touch your throat again."

The Emperor repeatedly referred to Professor Bergmann's "roughness" and has *left behind him an autograph statement* written only a few days before his death, in which he records his unfavourable opinion of Bergmann's "rough treatment of him."

The astounding account of this lamentable episode, given by the *Kölnische Zeitung* was that Hovell (!) had tried to adjust a cannula and had injured the windpipe, and pushed a mass of diseased tissue right into the lungs (which the *post-mortem* revealed to be quite healthy). This nearly suffocated the Emperor, but at last Bergman arrived just in time to snatch the Emperor from the jaws of death, by putting in a new cannula (*Bergmann*, according to Mackenzie, could not even find the hole ; *Bramann* at last put in the cannula) and so forth. I hasten to add that Bergmann had the grace to deny that he had caused this monstrous and absurd statement to appear. I merely cite it as a fair specimen of the calumnies with which even the respectable press rang during this period of unparalleled excitement and suspense.

Still so extraordinary a charge as that brought by Mackenzie against Professor von Bergmann, that he had actually made " a false passage " in attempting to force the cannula into the Emperor's throat, at once suggests the question, what has Von Bergmann got to say in reply ? This is what he says, after quoting the *British Medical Journal*, as follows :—" As the Professor von Bergmann has not contradicted this statement (viz. that he had made a false passage) it may be accepted as true, that is to say, because I am silent in the face of a statement of facts and of personal attacks, it shows they must be well founded. If the *British Medical Journal* were not a journal whose scientific value I prize very highly, I might still remain silent in the presence of such an accusation, but under the circumstances I must defend myself. I am not silent because I am in the wrong, but because I, like every other honourable British or German physician, do not talk publicly about what goes on at the bedside of my patients."

The fact is that Professor von Bergmann never has cleared up that fatal episode of the cannula and the false passage, and his explanations, which have invariably taken the form of an attack upon Mackenzie, have proved as little satisfactory to his medical *confrères* and compatriots as they have to Mackenzie and Mr. Hovell. The *Vossische Zeitung* records that at a meeting of the Berlin Medical Society, the members were anxious to hear Von Bergmann's explanation, and, having full confidence in him, intended to offer him a vote of confidence; but when his letter was read, it was received astonishment and dead silence, and no one had a word to say in support of him! " His explanations did not make a favourable impression; it was felt that he had used the Society to make a personal attack on a distinguished man at a time and place where he could not be answered;" and there the matter rests. If ever the question is reopened, the following truly appalling passage in Mackenzie's " Frederick the Noble " will have either to be met or cancelled :—

" If it was merely a question of credibility between Professor von Bergmann and myself ; if there was nothing more than my word against his respecting this matter, it might be difficult for the public to decide which version to accept. Fortunately, for the sake of truth, there are objective facts in the case which cannot be explained away.

" It can be proved that there was no bleeding whatever before Bergmann's arrival.

"It can also be proved that his forcible attempts to introduce the tube were followed by profuse hæmorrhage, the blood running out of the wound in the neck, and also down the windpipe, causing violent coughing. Three days after the Emperor had a shivering fit. A day or two later an abscess is noticed in the tissues into which Von Bergmann thrust his cannula. The abscess extends downwards, ounces of pus are secreted daily, the patient is harassed by constant coughing from the pus finding its way into the windpipe, and his strength is reduced by the profuse and continued discharge of matter. At last he sinks, and an immense abscess-cavity is found after death just in the place where Von Bergmann made the false passage. The logic of these facts is irresistible."

Soon after this, Professors Leyden and Senator, of whom Mackenzie speaks most highly, were added to the staff of physicians gathered about what was now, virtually, the Emperor's death bed.

As Bramann's cannula had produced a wound which broke down the back of the windpipe, so Bergmann's finger and performance with an *unprotected* cannula, according to Mackenzie's narrative, had set up an abscess.

Matters looked very grave indeed, and Mackenzie informed his Majesty that if he had anything to settle he ought not to delay. The Emperor answered quite calmly,—

" I am much obliged to you for telling me ; I hope I shall get better, for the sake of my people."

He was thinking, no doubt, of pacific reforms and the peaceful development of the country, and all the wise measures which he desired to carry out. Later in the day he said to the Crown Prince William,—

" Lerne zu leiden ohne zu klagen."

" Learn to suffer without complaining."

A few more airings, a few Imperial signatures, a march past of the Imperial troops, a Royal wedding, and a last visit to his father's tomb, and the pageantries of this world closed for ever upon the eyes of Frederick the Noble.

Scene III.

On the 9th of June, Mackenzie, observing that the Emperor was sinking, thought it his duty to say, as he had always been perfectly frank with his Royal patient,—

" I am sorry to tell you, sir, that you are not making progress."

His Majesty replied pathetically enough, like one putting in a last plea for life, and the sunshine of this world,—

" I feel pretty well to-day."

But he seemed to brood silently over his physician's words, and wrote, some hours afterwards, these few heartrending words which seem almost

to crave some last little word of encouragement
and hope in response,—

" I am very sorry that I (have?) made no
progress."

The handwriting is not quite so steady as usual
—how should it be ; it was the cry for life sent
out into the future which sends no answer back
again.

On the 11th the dying Emperor was sitting
up writing his diary (*where is that diary?*),
signing documents, and transacting a great deal
of business. He felt that night was coming on
apace in which no man can work, and Mackenzie, well knowing that it now mattered little
what he did, never checked him again.

On the 12th the Emperor actually received in
audience the King of Sweden. As he went out
King Oscar turned to Sir Morell and asked him
what he thought of the Emperor. The reply
was, " It is scarcely necessary to point out to
you, sir, that the Emperor is in a most critical
condition, from which I think it is almost impossible for him to rally; should he, however,
get over this attack, his life might be spared for
a few weeks."

This is Mackenzie's simple statement in reply
to an absurd account of his interview with the

King of Sweden, which appeared in the reptile press.

Scene Last.

At three o'clock in the morning a change came over the face of the Imperial sufferer. Mackenzie, in accordance with her Majesty's request, knocked at her bedroom door. She was awake, and answered immediately. She then went at once to the bedside of her dying husband, and never again left it, except for a very few minutes, until his death. On the morning of the fatal day, just before daybreak, Mackenzie came in to change the cannula. He was himself coughing with asthma, brought on by passing along an exposed balcony which gave him quicker access to his patient's room.

At this almost supreme hour, the Emperor then being unable even to speak, laid his hand once or twice affectionately on Mackenzie's breast as he bent over him, and looked up in his face with a glance of earnest sympathy for one whom he perceived was a fellow-sufferer—partly on his account—and who was destined in less than four brief years to follow him to the grave.

That last token of affectionate regard moved, more than any other token of friendship he received, the sensitive doctor, who himself felt so acutely for, and ministered so lovingly to the sufferings of such numbers who could pay him back with nothing but their gratitude.

At four o'clock on the morning of the 15th Mr. Hovell relieved Mackenzie, who was now almost worn out by his prolonged vigil at the Emperor's bedside, and his head sank for a few minutes in snatches of urgently needed sleep as he reclined in an armchair close by.

In an hour he was roused, and fed the Emperor, who then fell into a deep sleep; but the end had come at last. Mackenzie closely watched the Emperor's eyes languidly following the beloved form of his wife as she moved silently about the room tidying and arranging every-thing for his comfort with her own hands. Suddenly, at 11 a.m., the Emperor's eyes became fixed with the glaze of death, life flickered for a few minutes longer in the respiratory organs, and then Mackenzie turned to the widowed Empress with the announcement that life was extinct.

"Thus passed away," adds Mackenzie in a burst of genuine grief and admiration, "the noblest specimen of humanity it has ever been my privilege to know. . . . Only those who had the privilege of constant intercourse with the Emperor Frederick know how much poorer the world is for his death. No one could know him even slightly without loving him; no one could be more intimately acquainted with him without remembering him as one of the most large-minded and noble-hearted of men. . . . He has gone down to his grave leaving us the memory and example of a stainless life and a beautiful death."

The plots against Mackenzie in Germany did not cease with his august patient's death.

Worn out with a hurried and a fatiguing journey, he had been suddenly confronted in consultation with the staff of doctors in attendance on the Crown Prince Frederick in May, 1887. And now in June, 1888, exhausted with no less than a sixty hours' uninterrupted vigil, Mackenzie had no sooner thrown himself on his bed to sleep, when he was almost instantly aroused by a message from the new Emperor William that he wished to speak with him. Truly these Hohenzollerns cannot wait. The wearied specialist found the young Emperor, who received him courteously, with Prince Bismarck sitting in the adjutant's room.

Prince Bismarck then took Sir Morell aside, and requested him to draw up a brief report on the Emperor Frederick's case. The Chancellor seemed rather pressing.

"Will you do so before you leave?" he said.

"Well, your Highness," replied Mackenzie, "I shall leave on Monday, and I will certainly draw up the document before then."

The very next day, somewhat to Mackenzie's surprise, an official arrived and wanted to know if the report was ready.

"No?"

"Will you dictate it to me?"

"So important a document cannot be dashed off like that."

"But it is most important to get it done at once. The Ministers are waiting for it."

"In that case I will sit down and write it now," and within half an hour Mackenzie presented this singular emissary with the following report as below :—

"*Schloss Friedrichskron, June 16th,* 1888.

"It is my opinion that the disease from which the Emperor died was cancer. The morbid process probably commenced in deeper tissues, and the cartilaginous structure of the larynx became affected at a very early date. A small growth which was present when I first examined the late Emperor was removed by me by several endolaryngeal operations, and though all the portions taken away were submitted to Professor Virchow he was unable to detect in them any evidence of the existence of cancer. Examinations of the sputa made at the

N

beginning of March by Professor Waldeyer, however, led that pathologist to believe that cancer was then present. Whether the disease was originally cancerous or assumed a malignant character some months after its first appearance, it is impossible to state. The fact that perichrondritis and caries of the cartilages played an active part in the development of the disease and no doubt largely contributed to make it impossible to form a decided opinion as to its nature till quite recently. (Signed) MORELL MACKENZIE."

"In so far as my observations since last August permit me to form an opinion, I concur entirely with Sir Morell Mackenzie's views. (Signed) T. MARK HOVELL."—(Page 180.)

What did it all mean ?

This. It was known to Mackenzie that the Empress had besought that there should be no post-mortem. It was known that the young Emperor had ordered that his mother's wishes should be respected, and this was supposed to be all that Mackenzie knew.

Within an hour or two of the lying-in-state, however, great official pressure having been brought to bear upon the Empress, she had consented to an autopsy.

Now the great charge (a completely false one) against Mackenzie was, that he had always stood out against the disease being *cancer*, and it was hoped that in the presumed absence of any autopsy, he would commit himself to some doubtful phrase which would give colour, down to the last, to the current charge of his ignorance and incapacity in diagnosis.

The first line of Mackenzie's report defeated this little plot against his professional reputation, for it ran thus : " *It is my opinion that the disease . . . was cancer ;* " the rest of the report confirmed everything that he had ever said about the matter, and no syllable of it has ever been refuted.

When Mackenzie rises from his desk with the written report in his hand and goes into the next room to deliver it to the official, the cat suddenly jumps out of the bag, *mirabile dictu !* in the shape of Von Bergmann. There is the official in close converse with the Herr Professor von Bergmann who, above all things would wish to demonstrate that the English physician's diagnosis was not only as the German doctors complained, " slow," but also " shifty." Bergmann was not to have this last solace. The plot having failed, Wegner is obliging enough to put his head into the room half-an-hour afterwards and call out, " A post-mortem is going to be made " (as if it was quite an unexpected but agreeable little afterthought). " Do you care to come ? "

. " Do I *care* to come ! " exclaimed Mackenzie, with ill-suppressed and conflicting emotions,

N 2

"Do I *care* to come! how can you ask such a question?" and he immediately, accompanied by Mr. Hovell, went to the room where the Emperor's body was lying.

When they entered they found Virchow, who was charged with the performance of the autopsy, already there, and Professor Waldeyer, who had supplied the crucial proof of cancer by his late analysis.

Upon the painful details of this closing scene it is not necessary for me to dwell. Had Mackenzie been as keen to expose what he considered to be the professional mismanagement of his colleagues as some of his colleagues were to convict him of ignorance or duplicity, or both, he would have left that post-mortem chamber exultant.

There was the great gangrenous wound, alleged to have been created by Bramann's first large tube. ("Frederick the Noble," p. 183.)

There was the site of the fatal abscess caused by Bergmann's tube which had been forced into the flesh of the neck instead of into the tracheotomy passage, which he could not find, but which Bramann found immediately.

There were the lungs, which Bergmann had deemed cancerous, filled with air to their extremities, and as Mackenzie had always said quite free from cancer.

But it is time to draw a veil over these distressing details ; and I, for my part, sincerely
wish that any biographer of Mackenzie could
afford to pass over lightly or in silence those
amazing comments and accusations which the
German doctors subsequently hurled against
Mackenzie's plain statement in " Frederick the
Noble," of which I have now given a sketchy,
but not, I hope, an untrustworthy analysis.

IX.

THE GERMAN DOCTORS.

IX.

THE charges both before and after the publication of " Frederick the Noble " came tumbling in pell-mell.

But the book itself was provoked, or rather rendered necessary, by one of the most virulent and, according to the Empress Frederick (see p. 211), mendacious attacks ever levelled at distinguished genius and heroic conduct by professional jealousy, and I must add political rancour.

Before commenting on the form which Mackenzie's much criticized reply assumed, and the peculiar circumstances which justified the matter, and at least excuse the manner of that very remarkable literary performance, it may be well to put succinctly before the reader the chief points urged by the German doctors against their English *confrère's* conduct of the Emperor's case. We must remember that the great charge was that Mackenzie had stopped a salutary operation at a time when it could have been performed easily, and would have saved the royal patient's life. To this Mackenzie rejoins :—

(*a*) That the operation of thyrotomy, proposed and nearly carried out on the Emperor, is a dangerous procedure soon leading to death.

(*b*) That it does not afford a fair prospect of eradicating a malignant growth, but is frequently followed by recurrence.

(*c*) That the presence of cancer was not ascertained even with approximate certainty until November, 1887, if indeed, it really existed before that date.

These are technical points which by a perfectly conclusive, technical, and statistic reasoning, Mackenzie proves up to the hilt, nor has his argument ever been shaken—although an unsuccessful attempt was made to show that the Emperor's case was much simpler than the cases cited by Mackenzie, and that his statistics of disaster would consequently not apply. Yet Hahn himself was prepared to dissuade an operation. (Appendix E, and p. 202, " Frederick the Noble.")

Let me here remark that it seems all along assumed, that the admission of cancer must carry with it thyrotomy or perhaps the excision of the larynx.

As Dr. Koch, a great German authority says of this last operation that "it is a triumph for the operator, if the patient does not die under the knife," even had Mackenzie been certain of cancer all along, there are moralists alive as well as dead authorities like Jeremy Taylor, who would acquit him of all guilt in prevarication, on the plea that he did it to save a valuable life. But no one can read Mackenzie's systematic and reasoned statements, together with Virchow's pronouncement on the subject of the possibility of a benign growth existing with cancer (p. 34 and 199 of " Frederick the Noble "), without feeling sure that exactly what Mackenzie stated and adhered to from the first,[1] is exactly as much as he felt certain of and no more, and that in a case of

---

[1] In my opinion the clinical symptoms have always been entirely compatible with non-malignant disease, and the microscopical signs have been in harmony with this view. I need only add that, although in nearly every case of laryngeal disease it is possible at the first inspection to form an accurate opinion as to the nature of the disease presenting itself, yet in a few rare instances, the progress of the complaint alone, permits its character to be determined. Unfortunately, the case of His Imperial Highness is among the latter number, and at this moment medical science does not permit me to affirm that any other disease is present, than chronic interstitial inflammation of the larynx combined with perichondritis.

San Remo, February 12th, 1888.

(Sir Morell Mackenzie's Report, pages 97—98.)

life and death, he did not feel justified in making or countenancing a dogmatic statement, upon which disastrous action would probably have been taken, when in fact probability of cancer was all they had, even upon their own showing, to go upon.

I fail to see in this the slightest shadow or sign of that duplicity or dishonest playing into the hands of the Crown Princess, with which our great specialist has been so insolently charged.

Of the more personal charges I had better cull a few choice specimens. I do not suppose that any one of them is now seriously believed in Germany or anywhere else.

1. That Mackenzie had deceived the Emperor as to the nature of his disease. This has been amply refuted in the foregoing narrative. (See "Frederick the Noble," page 202.)

2. That Mackenzie used forceps without disinfecting them, the fact being that he drew his forceps out of a silk bag lined with carbolized wool.

3. That he could not flash the light on to the laryngeal mirror—(*risum teneatis ?*).

4. That he tore away a piece of *healthy* vocal cord on purpose to mislead Virchow; but Virchow says it was diseased, and Hahn, the great-

est operator on the larynx, who was actually engaged to guide Bergmann when it was proposed
to carry out a serious operation on the Crown
Prince—Hahn, himself, had said to Wegner
significantly *that unless Virchow found evidence of
cancer* (which he did not find) *in the portion of
growth removed, he would not recommend an external operation to be performed.* (" Frederick the
Noble," p. 202.)

5. That Mackenzie had promised the Royal
Family that he would cure the Crown Prince in
a few weeks.

The Royal Family are perfectly aware that
Mackenzie never promised anything of the kind,
that he merely said *if* the disease was not cancer
he thought he could cure it, but mentioned no
limit of time.

(6.) That Mackenzie recommended the Isle of
Wight as a suitable place for the Prince's complaint. The circumstances under which the
Prince went to the Island are perfectly well
known, and had nothing to do with any special
advice given by Mackenzie.

(7.) That Mackenzie was surrounded with
fourteen press correspondents who enabled
him constantly to float his own version of what
was going on; to which Mackenzie replies that
so far from this being the case, although he

would willingly, had he had time and been at liberty to speak out, have primed 1400 correspondents instead of fourteen, to contradict the unscrupulous lies that were appearing about him every day, as a matter of fact, he had no time for this, and confined his press interviews to the narrowest limits, and notoriously subjected himself to systematic misrepresentation, by refusing to listen to the overtures of one of our leading English newspaper correspondents.

" Why," asks Mackenzie, " does not Bergmann add what was really the case, that my alleged injudicious relations with press correspondents were laid before the Emperor as a serious charge against me, and that His Majesty not *only treated it with silent contempt*, but being fully aware of what were my real relations with the press, condescended personally to advise me in the most important journalistic episode of my life ? "

It must be confessed that Sir Morell's exceedingly smart style of controversial writing has laid him open to severe criticism both in Germany and in England, but we must remember that before he replied he had been stung to the quick. The following is a good specimen of the way in which he hurled back,

with a damaging *tu quoque*, such a charge as
that made by Von Bergmann, of his having
primed the Press :—

Dr. von Bergmann's virtuous indignation on the subject of
coquetting with the press is edifying even if not altogether
convincing. Methinks the Professor doth protest too much
when he is not accused, and not enough perhaps when he is.
At any rate he has never answered my challenge in the *British
Medical Journal* of May 12th, 1888, p. 1032, where I openly
charged him with having been in frequent communication with
journalists, and mentioned specific instances in which this had
taken place. Professor von Bergmann, who was so eager to
reply to a remark in the same journal not long before, has
never attempted to traverse the statements made by me in that
letter.

If he held himself as scrupulously aloof from the papers as
he would have us believe, the faculty of "thought-reading"
with regard to him which seems to have suddenly become
developed in several "able editors," is little short of miraculous.
Not only did they know by intuition what Von Bergmann had
said in consultation with his colleagues, but they were able to
record measures as having been actually adopted, which had
been proposed by the Professor without, however, having been
carried into effect.

Thus on the morning of April 19th, Dr. von Bergmann
brought with him a piece of elastic tubing which he intended
to pass through the cannula. He then intended to withdraw
the cannula and leaving the elastic tube in the throat, afterwards
to thread another cannula over it, and pass a second one into
the trachea. As it happened there was no occasion for this
apparatus, Mr. Hovell having changed the tube without any
difficulty during the previous night. The Professor's ingenious
device was however described in the *National Zeitung* on the
following day as having been adopted with the greatest advantage.—(Page 219.)

When the Emperor was at Charlottenburg the *National Zeitung* published the minutest details concerning His Majesty; not only was the exact diet given, not only the frequency of the pulse, but even the number of respirations per minute. By a curious coincidence, when Von Bergmann retired from the case, these details no longer appeared in the *National Zeitung.* —(Page 220.)

But the power of divination shown by this enterprising journal, with which Von Bergmann "had no relations whatever," was even more remarkable in November, 1887. At that time the details of a conference between Professor von Bergmann and Professor Gerhardt, which took place at the Haus-Ministerium in Berlin, were reported in the *National Zeitung* with such amazing accuracy that the official report of the conference which now appears in the German pamphlet, is identical in its language !—(Page 220.)

Nor is the following retort a bad specimen of the way in which Mackenzie, when he had his back to the wall, could face two of his most implacable opponents and hit back :—

These facts are, I think, sufficient to show the value that should be attached, not only to Professor von Bergmann's own protestations, but to the disclaimers of the various editors, who, "of their own accord, declared in the most solemn manner that (Bergmann) had never had any relations, direct or indirect, with them." There is a refreshing simplicity about the dilemma propounded by von Bergmann, viz., that either these honourable gentlemen have "lied intentionally, or their solemn statement aforesaid must be received as gospel truth." I, at least, have no difficulty in deciding which of these alternatives is to be accepted.—(Page 220, 221.)

The mystery which he seems to think underlies the fact of Gerhardt not having come to England in the Crown Prince's suite, may of course appear as insoluble to Bergmann as it does to Gerhardt himself.

I cannot profess to be able to dissipate the Cimmerian darkness in which this important matter is involved, but it strikes me as just within the bounds of possibility, that the Crown Prince may not have cared to be accompanied by a man who had shown himself incompetent, indiscreet and obstructive.— (Page 221.)

Before I leave the German strictures on Mackenzie and his conduct of the royal patient's case, I must notice three plausible and apparently weighty criticisms to his disadvantage. All three of them, doubtless because of their extreme clearness and intelligibility, have fastened upon the public mind in Germany and to some extent in England, almost to the exclusion of others, and are repeated to this day with parrot-like pertinacy.

First Popular Charge.

It is said, " *After all, the Germans were right about the cancer and Mackenzie was wrong;* for did not Mackenzie run counter to the highest German authorities who declared for cancer from the very first ? Well, he was wrong, and he went wrong for a purpose, and has been justly blamed."

The very opposite is the case. Mackenzie

O

never denied that there might be cancer, and he was really blamed, not because he *ran counter* to the highest medical opinion, but because he *bowed* to it. He accepted Virchow's diagnosis that cancer was not proved. He accepted Hahn's opinion, who said that under the circumstances he himself would not venture to operate; yet even Bergmann (who was to have operated with Hahn's assistance) admitted that the course pursued by Mackenzie with regard to the operation was the *right one*, and all the doctors acquiesced *at the time*, and accepted solidarity of responsibility for the treatment adopted ("Frederick the Noble," p. 121). And yet they crowed over Mackenzie when cancer was at last proved, although all along Mackenzie had stood out for nothing but this very proof. Was it not entirely owing to Mackenzie that the proof of cancer was obtained? Why, surely, it is the German doctors, and not Mackenzie, who were wrong in proposing to treat as a certainty what was and continued for some time to be only a probability.

Bergmann proposed an exploratory operation on the strength of a speculation, and Mackenzie was blamed, and would have been blamed whatever he might have done or counselled; but he was right and not wrong in refusing, without the least dogmatism or denial, to accept a speculation as proven, so long as it remained " *non-proven.*"

Second Popular Charge.

That Mackenzie denied cancer (which he never did), because by the Hohenzollern law no Crown Prince affected with cancer could succeed to the throne, and high Imperial interests affecting the status of the present widowed Empress, made it of the utmost importance that her husband should become Emperor before he died, or as some one coarsely put it : His accession made all the difference to her of a Crown Princess' state allowance, and the income of an Empress relict.

This Hohenzollern fiction was exposed at the time in some of the English papers, which pointed out that the German Empire and Imperial Crown to which the Emperor Frederick succeeded was only set up in 1870, and that the *Imperial* Constitution contains no such condition. But even supposing cancer had been a real legal or constitutional bar, *four full days*, as I have already pointed out, before the old Emperor's death, Professor Waldeyer's analysis establish-

o 2

ing the existence of cancer *was in the hands of all the doctors, and fully subscribed to by Mackenzie*.

It was notorious that the Bismarck faction would have been well content to skip the Emperor Frederick.[1] Had the doctor in favour with that faction operated, Frederick would never have come to the throne : could action of exclusion have been taken when cancer was proven, it would certainly have been taken four days before the old Emperor died ; but cancer or no cancer, Prince Frederick could not be excluded constitutionally, and Mackenzie's real crime was that he had *stopped his scientific if not his political assassination and prolonged his life*. And so the famous Hohenzollern bugbear as a whip for Mackenzie's back, vanishes finally from the page of history.

From out of this whirlpool of mutual medical recrimination two facts now emerge with tolerable distinctness :—

First, that had the procedure of the German doctors been allowed, the Crown Prince under extraordinarily favourable conditions might have survived the operation (for which the operating table was already prepared) a few weeks ; he would certainly never have come to the Throne.

. [1] See Appendix F., "Bismarck and the Succession."

This would have suited excellently well that political section, whose confidence Professor Bergmann undoubtedly enjoyed.

The other fact now accepted as most certain, is that Mackenzie by his procedure, although heavily weighted, as he believed, by other people's blunders, actually prolonged the life of the Crown Prince for several months, and enabled him not only to reign for ninety days, but also to transact the ordinary affairs of state, incident to his exalted official position, with promptness and ability.

The reader may well inquire, How could Sir Morell Mackenzie have more faithfully and skilfully performed his duty as a man and a doctor ? If he did amiss, how could he have done better ?

The etiquette of humanity teaches us to alleviate suffering, to spare pain, and sweeten existence, whilst I have always understood that the etiquette of the medical profession is not always to operate, especially when success is doubtful, but rather to keep the patient alive as long as possible. In closing this part of my subject, I cannot refrain from quoting what Mackenzie himself has called his consoling reflections ; they seem to me even now, after all I have read upon the subject, the soundest and most satisfying comment upon the whole case:—

"In looking back on this sad case, there are one or two matters which will always be a source of deep satisfaction to me: one is that through the mild and painless operations performed by myself, the dangerous methods recommended by Gerhardt and Von Bergmann were prevented, and that I thereby not only prolonged the life of the Emperor, but also saved him much suffering. The other point which affords me some consolation is that I was able to prevent His Majesty suffering any actual pain during the long course of his distressing complaint. Even in February when he was put to so much trouble and inconvenience, when he passed weary days and sleepless nights, whilst Von Bergmann and Bramann were in charge of the case after the performance of tracheotomy, the Emperor experienced no actual pain. Except at the moment when Von Bergmann made the "false passage," and forced his finger into the wound, I do not think he ever had a moment of severe pain. Occasional slight neuralgia in the head, and mild muscular rheumatism was his worst trouble in this respect."—(Pages 186—187.)

I do not think I could better cap this entirely feeling and sincere passage than by quoting some words which Dr. Krause, one of the ablest of the German doctors in attendance on the Emperor, has been good enough to send me. It proves that in the heart of the enemy's camp Mackenzie, in fair fight, had won warm admirers and friends, and be it observed that Dr. Krause here is the mouthpiece of many other doctors throughout Germany, who have not had an

opportunity, and might not possess the courage
and fairness which he here shows :—

" The Emperor's disease was cancer. It is supposed that
Sir Morell from the beginning likewise conjectured that it was
a case of cancer. But he demanded, as every conscientious
physician in such a case would, that the clinical diagnosis from
the microscopical examination should be made convincingly
clear. If this demand was not complied with by the doctors
who had till then managed the case, it was probably because,
on account of the peculiar situation of the tumour, the removal
of a small particle for the purpose of microscopic examination
appeared too difficult or altogether impossible. Sir Morell
also did not succeed in taking away parts from the depth of
the tumour ; on that account the examination by Virchow was
unsuccessful. After this result of the anatomical research all
the doctors determined to await the further course of the
disease. At the particular desire of the Crown Prince, Sir
Morell had the sole responsible conduct of the treatment. By
the then still very uncertain inferences from the statistics of
the results of operations on laryngeal cancer, and by the still
wide-spread objection among doctors against such operative
encroachments, one is justified in thinking that Sir Morell
from the first had determined to deprecate, or to hinder, any
operation which had for its object to cut out a part of the
diseased larynx. He feared endangering his patient's life by
this. The German doctors, however, insisted on the operation,
because they themselves considered it without danger, and
hoped to be able to keep the Crown Prince longer. In this
antithesis lies, I think, the central point for understanding the
medical strife which has arisen on this question.

" Any one who has closely observed Sir Morell during the
time of his medical activity on behalf of the Crown Prince and
Emperor, must admit that he at all times was completely
conscious of the range of his responsible treatment. Every
moment he stood under the severe supervision of the eyes of

his enemies. In spite of this he has never wavered in his treatment; he placed his whole knowledge and his entire personality in the task he had undertaken, and for the good of his patient. He who assigns him any other object than that of helping his patient always, and in every way, *wrongs him.* But if a doctor, without any regard to the easily influenced public opinion, exercises his whole art to the best of his ability and knowledge for his patient, who has given him his confidence, then he *does the best a doctor can possibly ever do.* And Sir Morell possessed the confidence of his patient in the highest degree. Therefore his influence over his patient was also unlimited."

But I hasten to add that Dr. Krause was not the only eminent German medical authority about the Emperor who spoke out boldly in favour of Sir Morell Mackenzie's treatment. Dr. Schrötter, who visited the Prince at San Remo in November, declared frankly that—

" He would consent to the removal of the larynx being *postponed,* as the life of the Crown Prince could be prolonged for some time by other remedies, especially tracheotomy. By complete removal of the larynx the life of the Crown Prince might perhaps be saved, but the operation was *most dangerous.*"

"Dr. Billroth could not conceive that Mackenzie, with his vast experience, doubted cancer, but if he insisted on microscopic proof it must have been from pressure from above or *motives of humanity.* He did," adds this eminent German authority, "as a man *and a physician,* what was still possible to be done, when the unfortunate word ' cancer' had once been pronounced." (See for the above, *British Medical Journal,* p. 1360.)

I am glad to quote these far from partisan

but perfectly fair opinions, and I think I should cap them with these equally frank words of Mackenzie :—

"Theoretically it may be maintained that the practical results which are to follow an opinion ought not to influence the formation of that opinion; common sense demands a different conclusion. If action is to be taken—and especially if that action brings a human life into immediate danger—much greater certainty ought to be arrived at than if the opinion is not to be followed by any practical consequence. In a case of such transcendent importance as that in which I was engaged, I maintain, at the risk of reiteration, that before it would have been justifiable to perform an operation, not only highly dangerous in itself, but extremely uncertain in its results, the most positive evidence of its necessity was required. This, however, was not forthcoming. The pathological reports only show that scientific investigation has its limits. ("Frederick the Noble," p. 200-1.)

X.

THE BOOK.

X.

IF the professional and personal attack made upon Mackenzie by Bergmann and his nine co-adjutors raised the wind, Mackenzie's reply in " Frederick the Noble " raised the whirlwind.

It was of course translated, and then had the honour of being publicly burned, whilst the English edition ran through 100,000 in a short time. Few authors could hope for more than this.

The controversy raged briskly on both sides of the water. Mackenzie met with no more quarter from the medical profession at home than abroad. He had, as we have seen, his warm supporters in Germany ; he had his warm supporters in England ; but, whatever some of these individuals may have thought, few of them had the courage to speak openly, and the general feeling of the faculty expressed by the Royal

College of Physicians and the Royal College of
Surgeons was, that Mackenzie had violated professional etiquette by publishing the details of
professional consultations, and had overstepped
all the limits of fair controversy by exposing or
trying to expose the alleged mistakes of his
medical *confrères*, and by answering their charges
with counter-charges, their personalities with
counter-personalities, and, in fact, generally
paying them back in their own coin.

When summoned before the College of Physicians, the Emperor's English physician not
only declined to appear, but removed his name
from the roll, returned his diploma, and treated
both the Royal and awe-inspiring medical
corporations with an indifference and contempt
which many of his friends, and I amongst them,
deplored.

It is perhaps difficult and presumptuous for
an outsider to estimate at its right value the
vote of censure which was immediately passed
upon his book, " Frederick the Noble," by the
Royal College of Physicians.   To this vote of
censure Sir Spencer Wells and two other influential members were openly opposed, taking a
somewhat larger, less narrowly professional and
more temperate view of the whole case—but the
eloquence of Sir James Paget prevailed, the un-

failing appeal to professional *esprit de corps* told, and a stigma was put by these great authorities upon Mackenzie and his book, which no doubt clung to him to the day of his death, and has doubtless prevented many people from reading " Frederick the Noble " with that impartiality and general all-round consideration which so extraordinary and exceptional a literary performance doubtless deserved.

The instant it was clear which way jumped the orthodox medical cat, many even of Mackenzie's friends forsook their guns, or at most exchanged championship for apology.

They went about saying that Mackenzie was sick, overwrought—had dashed off the book in a hurry under great excitement ; that of course the book was inexcusable, but allowance ought to be made ; that Mackenzie himself, in his calmer moments, would regret what he had written, and perhaps even to some extent consent to withdraw and apologize.

Four years passed, but Mackenzie neither withdrew nor apologized. Perhaps he thought that *rôle* would better become the German doctors.

To the outside public who took the trouble to look at the matter all round, the weak point in the medical censure appeared to be the theory upon which it was based, viz. that it was just, or even possible, to judge such a book apart from the circumstances which had called it forth, and the varied social, professional, and political considerations without which it is in many places hardly intelligible at all.

But with all that—the opinion of the Imperial patient himself, the views of the Empress, the complex interests involved, the jealousies ignited, the truth or untruth of the libels hurled at Mackenzie, to which the book was a telling reply —the Royal College had nothing to do ! " Was or was not the language of the book, under any conceivable circumstances of provocation, justifiable or in accordance with medical etiquette ?" That, so they said, was the only real question before them. They decided that both as to matter and manner, as to form and tone, the book was not justifiable.

'Put case,' as Browning used to say.

The *form* was unprofessional. " Well," said Mackenzie to me, " that is what they say. They wanted a clinical study of the case addressed to experts, which of course would have been unintelligible and therefore unread by the general public. But was that the form adopted by the German doctors ? No ! They intentionally put forward a popular statement, a popular attack,

a public libel. This at once removed the case
out of the region of a mere professional discussion or controversy.

"Remember, up to the time of their attack I
had practically kept silence—they chose the
weapons. Now if a duellist chooses pistols, does
he expect his adversary to fight with buttoned
foils? It might have been a question whether,
under the special, and I may say abnormal, circumstances, I should fight at all; but if I were
to fight, I could only fight in one way. People
said that I had the alternative of speaking or
keeping silence when attacked, and that I ought
to have kept silence. They are mistaken, I had
no such alternative."

I then said, "Why did not you explain this
at the time? It might have excused the popular
and polemical form of your book, which had
mainly brought down the censure of the Royal
College of Physicians."

"My lips were sealed," he replied; and I
could see the firm control he put upon his features, whilst I well knew the strong excitement
under which he was labouring.

Presently he said, "The fact is the *form* was
decided for me. It became not only a medical
but almost a State question, as to what should
be done after the preposterous statements put

P

forth by the German doctors, I could not say
that the Queen and Lord Salisbury both agreed
that the reply should be not of a merely technical
and clinical nature, but that as the attack had
been made with an eye to the general public, so
ought the reply to be of the same nature and
addressed to the same general public."

So Mackenzie, to the day of his death, having
the trump card in his hands, never played it. He
simply stood and was fired at with his pistol
down, giving no return fire.

Now that Mackenzie is in his grave the time
for such reticence seems passed. " When the
question of reply or no reply," said Mackenzie to
me, " was submitted to Her Majesty, the Queen
with her unfailing intuition and invariably correct judgment, said : ' I think that a reply ought
to be made, and Lord Salisbury thinks so too.' "
But Mackenzie was not only silent to the public
about what might seem to amount almost to a
Royal command, which would have gone far to
clear him in the eyes of thousands, he even re-
frained from using material in his hands which
he might have used with full Royal permission.

At an interview which Sir Morell Mackenzie
had with the Empress Frederick at Windsor
Castle on February 23rd, 1889, from seven to
eight o'clock, Her Imperial Highness said,—

"*You are at liberty to tell everybody* that I consider the German doctors' pamphlet was a *collection of untruths* and personally insulting to me, and that your book has been a great consolation to me." The Empress added shortly afterwards, "When your book arrived it was read by all the people at the Palace, and no one saw anything *the least objectionable* in it ; on the contrary, they all said it was most careful and *particularly moderate* under the circumstances."

February 23rd, 1889.

I may here add a telegram from His Royal Highness the Prince of Wales, which, though brief, is perhaps the best reply that could be given by one very accurately informed of all the circumstances of the case to the critics of Mackenzie's general treatment of the Emperor's case.

The Prince of Wales' telegram to Sir Morell Mackenzie, which arrived at Berlin soon after the announcement of the Emperor's death, was as follows :—

" *To Sir Morell Mackenzie.*

" I thank you from my heart for your constant care and attention and for having pre-

P 2

served so long my ever-to-be-regretted brother-in-law.

"ALBERT EDWARD."

And now a word or two about the general tone and the kind of material which Mackenzie thought fit to import into his reply. Is it possible to judge either fairly—the occasional passion, the scarcely-veiled indignation, the satire, the scorn, the medical and sensational incidents, the disappointment, irritation, and at times almost despair, that glow and throb in these pathetic and often scathing pages—without considering the man and his surroundings and the momentous responsibilities which were at last forced upon him single-handed?

In spite of the Royal College of Physicians' view, which is entitled to every respect, but which cannot be final, it seems to me but fair to consider what Mackenzie's position really was, then how he was treated, and then—if you will—what he wrote.

An able American thus sketched the general situation, and I could not improve upon his very telling words :—

" Sir Morell Mackenzie's position at Charlottenberg was strangely interesting—even pathetic.

It was the most brilliant a physician could hold. All Europe was watching him. His patient was an Emperor. Yet it was by no wish of Sir Morell Mackenzie's that he was there or remained there. He had asked more than once to be relieved, but neither the Emperor nor the Empress was willing he should go. They believed in him, and in him only. It is easier to understand their feelings after reading the few lines *fac-simile* of the Emperor's handwriting, reproduced in Mackenzie's book, referring to the April crisis, '*when Bergmann ill-treated me.*'

"At Charlottenberg Mackenzie had rooms close to those of the Emperor, and scarcely half an hour passed without his seeing his patient. He was a prisoner, not with a sentinel at his door, but with a dying Emperor in the next room. He was like a soldier on a forlorn hope—perhaps still more like one of those singular beings of the Middle Ages, whose ideal of devotion to duty was monastic. The stern plainness of the rooms, the lean, ascetic face and figure of the English doctor, the fire in the grey eyes, the simplicity and the sincerity of his manner and talk, all lend themselves to this notion. That, at any rate, was the impression he made at the time—of a man entirely absorbed in one task, which he accepted at a heavy sacrifice, and was performing to the end amid difficulty and danger, and with the certainty before him of what his enemies would call disaster. He knew the Emperor could not live —he knew he would die in his hands—and knew he himself would be held by his enemies responsible for the failure to save a life which no human power could save."

Such was the situation. Under these circumstances, how did the German doctors speak of Mackenzie in their pamphlet, his reply to which has been so much criticized?

Some insinuations in that pamphlet are too gross to be alluded to even in the elaborate analysis of the German pamphlet given in the *British Medical Journal;* others were of a character calculated to sting to the quick a man of far less sensitive temperament, whilst if believed, or not refuted, they would injure him professionally, whilst destroying for ever his reputation as a man of honour.

It was boldly declared that he introduced into the Emperor's throat dirty, uncleansed instruments; his manipulation was uncertain; he made a dishonest use of Virchow's microscopic analysis; he gagged the press; he could not focus the laryngoscopic mirror; he tore healthy

tissue out of the Emperor's throat in order to dis-
prove the existence of cancer ; he destroyed the
Emperor by preventing an operation until it could
no longer be safely performed; he lied persistently
about the cancer ; he refused to see what was
evident to the youngest German medical man in
attendance, and only very reluctantly confessed
to point after point when the skilful gentlemen
about the Emperor forced them, one by one,
upon his notice. A critic called Guttmann,
however, excelled even these ingenious assertions, by asseverating that Mackenzie doubted
to the end, and "vacillated without diagnosis,"
whilst at the same time representing the Emperor's disease most confidently in the most
hopeful light ! In point of fact, he did neither
the one nor the other ; but it is evident that in
no case could he have done both, for, if confident and hopeful, he could not be vacillating
and without diagnosis, and *vice versâ*.

And now, when all these secrets of the consulting-room had been not only blurted out in a
pamphlet, which has been (p. 211) characterized as "*a collection of untruths*," and paraded
on platforms, in public lecture-halls, and at
private assemblies, Mackenzie is expected to
sit down quietly and say nothing, or, when he
speaks, to confine himself to a dry statement of

medical facts couched in technical language, and dedicated perhaps to the Royal College of Physicians or the Royal College of Surgeons !

Under the circumstances, we can understand such advice being given to Mackenzie, but the utmost stretch of sanguine imagination could hardly anticipate its being taken.

It would have suited the German doctors down to the ground, no doubt; it might have saved the great specialist from the official censure to which he affected to be so indifferent, and which some people think he so little deserved, but it would not have suited Mackenzie, or Mackenzie's friends, or the cause of truth, nor would it have satisfied the commonest instincts of justice and fair play.

XI.

THE RESPITE.

XI.

THE breath was no sooner out of the Emperor Frederick's body than a cordon of soldiers was drawn up round the palace, and all egress or ingress strictly regulated. The object of this was to prevent any documents of a compromising nature being taken out of safe custody. Amongst these was undoubtedly the Emperor's diary. With that diary Mackenzie had a great deal to do—how much, perhaps, no one will ever know. That diary, could it have been destroyed, would have been destroyed. This much was known, that it was terribly compromising to the German doctors and a complete justification of Mackenzie.

In the eyes of the medical world, however, such testimony would be absolutely valueless. It seems to be a rule of medical etiquette that the patient's opinion about himself is of no value. As the *British Medical Journal* remarks, when

alluding to the Emperor's opinion that Bergmann had " *ill-treated him*," the opinion being
that of the "patient" would have merely a
" psychological interest ! " But as the majority
are patients and a small minority only doctors,
such an opinion would no doubt have some
weight with the many, and we can hardly
wonder that the diary was so well watched that
—it disappeared.

There is reason to believe, however, that it
did get through the cordon, and that our Queen,
who throughout took the most tender interest
in her Imperial son-in-law, has seen it. It probably got back to Germany, but where it is now
nobody seems to know.

The policy, and it is no doubt a wise one, from
some points of view, seems to be to let all sleep-
ing dogs lie, but the duty of a biographer is not
only to manage susceptibilities but to record the
main facts of a life, and place them, with the
assistance of any side lights at his disposal, in
their right perspective.

" Some day," as an illustrious personage, who
was acquainted with the contents of that diary,
remarked, " when we are all dead the truth will
be known."

Worn and haggard, the shadow of his former

self, Mackenzie at last passed out of the palace
of Charlottenberg. He had accomplished his mission, but he was himself a wreck. He had prolonged a life which, but for him, it is now generally admitted, would have been sacrificed. He
had saved an Emperor and enthroned an Empress. This exploit, whether it be considered
from a political or a medical point of view,
whether the means adopted be approved or condemned, remains unprecedented in the annals of
medicine or surgery. It has fallen to the lot of
no other physician on record to have created at
once so startling and so pathetic a page of history.
Neither the annals of British surgery nor German politics can be written without a reference
to those terrible months at San Remo and
Charlottenberg, where, in the full blaze of that
fierce light which beats about a throne, the English physician, surrounded by treachery, and
watched by envy, with the eyes of the whole
civilized world upon him, fought a hand-to-hand
fight with cancer, and kept the enemy at bay,
until at last death was in some measure deprived
of his sting, and the grave robbed of its political
victory.

Mackenzie now seemed to labour under an im-
perious and almost morbid need of self-efface-
ment. Every place through which he passed

was ringing with his .name. Every paper had paragraphs, stories, or speculations about him. Wherever he went he was liable to be accosted; people at hotels would sidle up to him and open indirect conversation; some would have the effrontery to stop him in the streets, whilst letters and wires followed him relentlessly from town to town as long as he could be identified or tracked by name.

His patients too were clamouring for his return. Mackenzie was never insensible to their claims, but the moment had at last come when he *could not* respond to the call.

I remember when Garibaldi came into Naples ; he had the same hunted, anxious, worn look upon his face that stamped itself on Mackenzie's countenance after the Emperor's death. Garibaldi said he felt that, when all was over and the king had fled, leaving Naples in the hands of the Garibaldians, the prolonged strain had been such that he felt he could have " *slept for a month ;* " he wanted to lie down anywhere and forget life.

This was also Sir Morell Mackenzie's mood. There was nothing for it but to vanish. For some weeks no one knew where he was except his family and his intimates.

His daughter Ethel (now Mrs. McKenna) was

with him, and both went to Venice, but he travelled *incog.*, and his luggage was labelled " John Morell."

It was June—the weather was intensely hot, but Mackenzie could seldom be too warm, and the delicious respite and sudden freedom from grinding anxiety, vigilance and suspense seemed almost immediately to tell upon him favourably.

Venice is at once a great healer as well as a slayer. She is insanitary, but she is inspiring, and the chosen spirits of the earth seem to resort to her with a kind of romantic instinct as though she afforded them the readiest and most perfect escape into the Ideal—away from the routine of care and the commonplace of life.

At Venice George Sand wrote in a fortnight that marvel of pathos and passion, " Leone Leoni," whilst suffering herself from one of those psychic revulsions of feeling, which seemed to be at once the consequence of her errors, and the stimulating cause of her *chef-d'œuvres.*

At Venice Byron, alone with the MSS. of "Manfred," " Parisina " and " Don Juan," sat up in his Palazzo on the Grand Canal, which beneath his windows was all ablaze with the reflexion of innumerable wax candles, making the Venetians as they floated past wonder and speculate.

Here Alfred de Musset dreamed of his vanished
illusions and his wasted loves on the green
sward of the funereal Lido—

" Où vient sur l'herbe d'un tombeau
Mourir la pale Adriatique."

Here Wagner, carrying with him the score of
the " Parsifal," fled in contempt from the noisy
acclaim of a world that, after forty years of persecution and ridicule, was beginning to hail him
as the greatest composer that ever lived—too
late ; for he was on the brink of the grave, and
never left Venice alive.

"Ah !" he would say, as he sat in his gondola,
and took in long draughts of soft and balmy
air, " No smoke, no dust ! " We can easily
understand what *that* must have meant to
Mackenzie, who was a martyr to asthma.

Here came Paganini in broken health, and
Liszt " about sunset," and Robert Browning—
who, like Mackenzie, " was ever a fighter," yet
who sent forth his " Swan " song from the city
of the sea, full of peace and contentment.

" How gratifying ! " were almost his last
words, when they told the dying poet of the
success of his latest book, " Asolando," which
appeared only just before he breathed his last.
Certainly there is a sweetly soothing influence,

and a consoling and bounteous charm about
Venice, which must have indeed formed a grateful contrast to the " bare barrack-like " apart-
ment—the military discipline—the harassing
entourage—the sleepless imprisonment, and the
bedside of the dying Emperor at Charlottenberg.

Mackenzie's old delight in picture galleries
revived ; he was never tired of visiting them
whenever he could with his daughter, and he
found in Ethel an appreciative companion, an
intelligent critic, a ready listener, and a model
sight-seer.

The year 1889 was chiefly engaged by Mackenzie in picking up the threads of his long-
neglected practice, for which the very large fee
of 12,000*l*., given him for his attendance on the
Emperor cannot be said to have altogether compensated him; but it must be remembered that
no sum of money whatever, and no additional
Court honours showered upon him, could ever
have compensated him for the strain which
shortened his life, by so weakening his powers of
resistance that he was almost bound to succumb
when smitten again and again by a disease
which habitually undermines the strength of the
most robust.

Mackenzie himself considered that he had
been liberally treated, and always expressed the

Q

utmost reverence and affection for the two Imperial personages in whose destinies he had played so important a part.

In 1887, in one of those brief respites which he enjoyed in the earlier stages of the Emperor's illness—he had gone to Balmoral to visit the Queen. The Emperor, under his care, had at that time entirely recovered his voice, and boundless hopes (which Mackenzie thought might have been realized under better conditions) were entertained, both by Her Majesty and the Empress Frederick, of the august patient's ultimate recovery. The Emperor had written to the Queen, requesting Her Majesty to confer the honour of knighthood upon his English physician. His Imperial Majesty's letter is as interesting as the Queen's reply. The Emperor wrote at the same time these few lines to Sir Morell :—

" I wish to give you an Order in grateful recognition of your valuable services to me, and in remembrance of my accession to the throne. I shall therefore ask the Queen whether she will make an exception in your case, and allow you to accept and wear the decoration."

Mackenzie remarks upon this with a touch of pardonable pride :—

Balmoral Castle.

den 28 Aug: 188[illegible]

Theuerer Fritz,

Ich [illegible]
[illegible]
[illegible]
[illegible]
[illegible]
[illegible] hat [illegible]
bitten zu [illegible]
Herrn Dr. Morell Mackenzie
[illegible] ernstlich [illegible]
[illegible]

"I know of no other instance in which a foreign monarch has before conferring an honour on an Englishman—not only taken the trouble to ascertain whether the distinction would be pleasing to the recipient's own sovereign, but obtained leave for him to accept and use it."

The Queen's reply to her son-in-law's request is equally characteristic :—

¹ Balmoral Castle, August 28th, 1887.

" Dear Fritz," wrote Her Majesty from Balmoral, " I shall have much pleasure in conferring a knighthood on the physician who has rendered *you and us* such great services, for Dr. Morell Mackenzie has indeed treated you with the greatest skill. I am so pleased that you have derived so much benefit from staying in England and Scotland. I am glad that you can come to luncheon again to-morrow, and help us ladies to entertain the handsome and amiable Rao of

¹ Balmoral Caſtle, am 28ſten Auguſt 1887.

Theurer Fritz,—Ich werde mich ſehr freuen den Arzt der Dir und uns ſo große Dienſte geleiſtet hat zum Ritter zu ſchlagen, denn Dr. Morell Mackenzie hat Dich wirklich mit größter Geſchicklichkeit behandelt. Wie freue ich mich, daß Du in England und Schottland Dich erholt haſt. Ich bin dankbar, daß Du wieder zum luncheon kommſt morgen und uns Damen helfen wirſt den ſchönen und liebenswürdigen Rao von Rutſch zu empfangen. Ich habe Vicky bereits telegrafirt wie wohl ich Dich gefunden habe und werde morgen ſchreiben. Auf Wiederſehen,

Ewig Deine treue Mama,   V. R. I.

Q 2

Kutch. I have already telegraphed to Vicky how well I have found you, and I shall write to-morrow.

"Always,
"Your affectionate Mother,
"V.R.I."

Hand-in-hand with these honours went, as we know, the continued and sustained attacks upon Mackenzie by the "Reptile" Press in Germany, and by a section of the medical profession in England. And here I should like to say, bearing in mind the vote of censure and the official attitude of the Royal College, that it must be always remembered that many men will do in their corporate official positions (boards of directors, for instance!) what they would shrink from doing in their private capacity. Sir Spencer Wells, himself a distinguished member of both colleges, not only opposed the vote of censure at the Royal College of Physicians, but he was permitted to read various extracts from the Empress Frederick's letters which, in Sir Spencer Wells' own opinion, rendered such a vote entirely unnecessary and unjust. And I venture to affirm that many medical men in London and throughout the country were of the opinion of Sir Spencer Wells, Dr. Langdon Down, Mr. Critchett, and others—who nevertheless were not strong enough or did not think themselves obliged to endanger their professional prospects by open disagreement with the official decrees of the Royal Medical Colleges.

A similar thing happened in my own profession, the Church, some five and twenty years ago—when Bishop Colenso was condemned by both Houses of Convocation, and an attempt was made to deprive him of his See—there were hundreds of clergymen of the established Church who sympathized with the persecuted prelate, but very few thought it wise to incur the displeasure of their own Bishop by saying so.

Dean Stanley was almost the only eminent dignitary who defended Colenso, although I have reason to know that the Venerable and enlightened Dean of St. Paul's, Henry Milman, disapproved of the Colenso persecution. One day, at Fulham Palace, at a Saturday garden party, given by Bishop, afterwards Archbishop Tait—the celebrated Australian Emu, that used to be one of the Fulham attractions, and which many of my readers will remember, was chased by several cows in an adjacent field, greatly to the amusement of the Bishop's guests. " There goes poor Colenso," said Dean Milman, " and all the bishops after him ! "

An official censure may not deserve the con-

tempt with which Mackenzie met it, but it
certainly does not necessarily carry the public
and popular weight which some people propose
to attach to it.

And this soon became evident in Mackenzie's
case. When he went north, he found the
greatest indignation prevailing with regard to
a medical policy which was characterized as
the "boycotting of Mackenzie." The medical
students at the Edinburgh University made
their class-rooms the scenes of boisterous protest, and when Mackenzie lectured in 1889 at
the Philosophical Institution, he received an
ovation which was intended to be a popular
snub direct to that section of the medical profession which had taken an unfairly harsh view
of his practice and his book.

And here I willingly surrender my pen for a
short time into the hands of my friend, Archdeacon Aglen, the doctor's brother-in-law, who
sends me the following interesting memoranda
of the Scotch visit of 1889 :—

"Mackenzie never forgot his Scotch descent,
and whenever he crossed the Border he went
with the intention of being pleased with everything and everybody. It was an additional
gratification to him that when he was knighted

the Queen happened to be at Balmoral, and that
he received the honour on Scottish soil. On his
way home, on that occasion, he paid us one of
his short visits, in Perthshire, and the con-
gratulations he received in broad Scotch from
the homely people in the village, to whom
he was introduced and exhibited as the great
throat doctor, seemed to give him especial pleasure. Among them was a local celebrity, a
political shoemaker, well known for his oratory
and eccentricity, who, shaking hands warmly
with the new knight, exclaimed, ' I congratulate
you, Sir Morell ; and hoo did you lave them a'
at Balmora ? ' Sir Morell fell into the humour
of the thing, and explained that he had left Her
Majesty and the Royal family in good health and
spirits, and that he had had a very agreeable
visit. And it was plain that the quiet possession
the Scotch seem to take of their Sovereign during
her autumn stay among them interested him
greatly, appealing, as it did, to his own inherited
feelings. Apart, then, from other considerations,
the invitation he received to lecture in Edinburgh
in December, 1888, was a source of gratification.
In spite of professional etiquette, which, of
course, would keep the doctors, as a class, aloof,
he had no fear of the welcome he would receive
in Auld Reekie, and the fact that he was to be

the guest of Mr. J. R. Findlay, the proprietor of the *Scotsman*, insured at once, not only the warmest hospitality, but access to all that was most worth seeing and hearing in the Northern capital. At all events, I found him in the best of spirits when I joined him in Rothesay Terrace, full of delight at the works of art and objects of interest with which Mr. Findlay has adorned his town house, and evidently prepared to enjoy his visit. We were chatting in his room—I mention this to bring out a trait in his character—when I noticed a novel-looking object on his dressing-table. It was a safety razor, lately patented in America. He had a passion for new inventions. I believe he became the possessor of the first type-writer that came over from America, and I remember well the enthusiasm with which he exhibited it, and the saving of labour he promised himself from its use. The promise was not, how-ever, fulfilled. He must have used it at first in his correspondence, for it got about that Dr. Mac-kenzie had so much game sent him that he had a printed form of thanks ; but it was soon handed over to his hall-porter, Bowden, who also gave up the use of the machine because of its rigour in the matter of spelling. 'With a pen,' he said, ' it did not matter where you put the *e* and the *i* in words like *receive*, but with the type-writer it was necessary to be exact.' It was partly a keen interest in the powers of invention that first drew Mackenzie to the laryngoscope, to the manipulation of which he owed so much of his success. I had another glimpse of character given me during the same interview. He asked me to take charge of the manuscript of the lecture he was to deliver that evening, that I might put it into the reporter's hands. I suggested that it might be safer for him to keep it about him till the end of the lecture. 'What! Do you suppose I am going to break down?' he exclaimed, with a burst of laughter that showed how intense was his own confidence in himself. I suppose he never in his life was visited with that misgiving which to some minds is torture. I do not mean only that he was free from nervousness. He had absolute faith in his own powers. I once asked him what he would have done to make a career if he had not been a specialist. 'I should have written,' he said; 'I would have made myself known somehow.' And he would. He was so constituted that he would no more have broken down in anything he had undertaken than he did in his lecture that evening.

" The large music hall was crowded to suffocation, and the reception accorded to the lecturer by the great audience was calculated to put him in good spirits for his work. Standing there with the Order of the Hohenzollern on his breast, Sir Morell could not mistake the meaning of the prolonged cheers that greeted him, and he began his address by alluding to Charlottenburg. It was there, he said, the invitation of the Philosophical Institution had first reached him, and he had accepted it because of the proof it gave of sympathy with him in the difficult duty there discharged, and approval of the way in which he had discharged it. The lecture that followed, on 'Speech and Song,' finds a place in Mackenzie's published works, and will always have a value as coming from the greatest authority on vocal chords; but the audience felt, as Sir Morell himself expressed it, that they were present that night chiefly to show that in this trying time 'dear old Scotland,' the land of his forbears, 'stood by him.'

"In his opening address, Mr. Findlay, as Vice-President of the Institution, said that Lord Rosebery had spoken of the Philosophical Institution as a 'magnet which drew to Edinburgh all that was best in the intellectual life of the nation,' and remarked that the presence of the eminent physician who was to lecture that evening showed that the magnet had lost none of its attractive power.

" The address delivered on the succeeding
evening to the University students showed that it
was much more than the specialist that had been
drawn north on this occasion. The students,
through their Representative Council, were in-
augurating a series of addresses to provide funds
for their contemplated ' Union,' and they seized
the occasion to press Mackenzie into their service.
It was very gratifying to him. The meeting
would show how the young men, hundreds of
whom would themselves become doctors, viewed
his conduct in the matter of the Emperor, and it
afforded himself an opportunity of using his
powers outside the professional range. The
subject he chose was the importance of culture
for professional success, and his treatment of it
gave occasion once more to his friends to wonder
how, in a life which had been necessarily so busy,
and with an education which had been so rigor-
ously restricted to the requirements of his calling,
he had been able to assimilate such varieties of
knowledge. To those who knew how much he
would have valued a University training, and
what he would have made of it, there was a
pathos in the well-chosen sentences in which he
told the students in Edinburgh that, while the
individual study of books might do much, they
must, if they would aim at the highest type of
culture, avail themselves to the uttermost of op-

portunities of intellectual communion which
only a University could supply. The address
struck the right chord. It was throughout a
noble appeal to a higher ambition than that of
getting on in the world and making money, and
the speaker did not fail to drive his moral home
by allusions, as pointed as they were apposite, to
the careers of distinguished Edinburgh men,
especially her great physicians. The audience
was fairly carried away, and every point
was vociferously cheered. The enthusiasm
of the students especially was unbounded,
and it was with the greatest difficulty they
were induced to forego their desire to take the
horses from the carriage and draw the lecturer
home.

"Our kind host had taken care that my
brother-in-law's short visit to Edinburgh should
not lack interest and amusement. He filled his
elegant house with the people he thought Sir
Morell would most like to meet, and we have it
from his own lips that he had never known of
so much anxiety in all sorts of people to be introduced to a celebrity as in the present case. He
also arranged a trip to the wonderful Forth
Bridge, then just approaching completion. I
was one of the party who visited the bridge, but
was too occupied with my own novel experiences

to notice how it affected the others, and cannot describe the impression produced on the doctor. All that I can remember is that he was determined to see every detail of the great work, and to climb up and down wherever the engineer, under whose guidance the inspection was made, would allow us to venture.

"An account of the Scotch visit of 1888 was all that the editor of this 'Memoir' requested from me, but I may perhaps be forgiven if, with the recollections of this occasion, there mingle those of other visits paid to myself in Scotland. I like to think of the man as he was in those brief holidays snatched from his busy life. He was so genial, so happy, so ready to be pleased. He would praise a country life, and, to the peril of his thin London boots, would climb our hills and ramble over our moors. He would pretend that he never got any dishes in London to compare with Scotch broth or hotchpotch, and laughingly ask us to exchange cooks with him. Our local practitioner was, of course, eager to get the great specialist's opinion on any difficult throat case on hand, and Morell was always at his service. I believe the gratuitous cures he made brought him more pleasure than all the rest of his professional success. He was essentially a kind man."

In the same year, 1889, Sir Morell Mackenzie, suffering from an attack of an old internal disorder in addition to his chronic asthma, and evidently able less and less to resist disease without the assistance of a climate unlike anything to be got in England, set off with Harry, his eldest son, Ethel and Hilda for Teneriffe.

Sir Morell has himself written so charmingly about his respite at Teneriffe, that the island, its inhabitants, its woods, with its valleys and villas, pass before us like a moving panorama. The expositor seems to stand close by and point out from time to time whatever it may be interesting for us to know, and he speaks with a condensation and a selection of careful detail which leaves nothing to be desired.

On reading some of these glowing and flowery pages,[1] so graphic and so clear, we can well understand his own surmise—that he would have made for himself a name in literature had he devoted himself to writing instead of operating.

In his remarks on Teneriffe he seems to have selected, with the practical instinct of a physician, and described with the heart of a poet and the eye of a painter, the things which it

[1] See Mackenzie's "Essays" (Sampson Low, Marston, & Co).

most concerns those to know who have any idea of seeking health in those favoured climes.

Teneriffe, chief of the Canary Islands, is but five days' steam (which might be easily reduced to three days') from Plymouth. Landing at Santa Cruz, which our travellers found somewhat relaxing, they pushed on up-country about twenty-five miles to the capital, Oratavia, and there Mackenzie met his old friend and quondam patient, Dr. Douglas, who had set up a sanatorium at Salamanca, about a mile from Santa Cruz. Everywhere he was astonished and delighted with the loveliness of the foliage and flowers; nothing escaped him; the volcanic soil, favourable to the fig, the cactus, and the aloe; the shrubby euphorbia; the verandahs, gay with the purple bougainvillea and creeping bignonia, "with its rich yellowish-brown clusters of flowers"; the laurus indica, which here grows to the size of a forest tree; walks flanked with rose-trees; the gardens, stocked with New Zealand flax and sub-tropical plants; the vines, the palms, the oleanders, and, up among the hills, the creamy apple-blossom, the golden gorse and broom, and the resplendent forests of chestnut-trees, the groves of laurel in the mountain valleys, and the heather, in bright contrast with the dark Canarian pines ; and, highest of all, the barren waste of rock, covered with lava and pumice.

The climate, he tells us, has three great merits—(1) relative uniformity of temperature, (2) dryness, (3) variety within a small area. It is better to go there before Christmas ; November and December are perfect months.

No fires or any ways of generating artificial heat are used by the natives, but the English often like a small fire, even at Oratavia.

For phthisis, Vilaflor, 6000 feet above the sea, is the favourite resort. There consumption is simply unknown, and the death-rate is said to be lower than in any other part of the world.

As a health resort, in Sir Morell's opinion, Teneriffe bears off the palm—superior to and cheaper than Madeira or the sister Canary Isles.

The rose-leaf, however, even at Vilaflor, is a little crumpled. Mosquitoes cannot be entirely ignored, neither can the crowing of matutinal bantam cocks, and those who demand poultry for the table have to put up in bed with the chanticleer at early dawn.

The stillness of the towns, owing to the almost complete absence of vehicular traffic, is very soothing to the nerves ; and the following picturesque description gives a very good idea of Sir Morell's graphic powers of observation :—

"The natives of Teneriffe struck me as particularly fine specimens of the human race. The men are strong, well grown, and healthy looking, and many of the women very beautiful ; but those of the lower class, owing to their being so much occupied in field labour, become old and worn in appearance at a comparatively early age, while the ladies, from want of exercise, soon lose their slimness of figure. Dark eyes and complexions prevail, but a trace of the extinct Guanches is often seen in light-coloured eyes and ruddy hair. The peasantry wear a light cotton jacket and short trousers, but each man has a thick Witney blanket, which is worn as a cloak when the weather is wet or cold. Everybody smokes, urchins of five or six seeming to find as much relish in their cigarettes as their fathers. The outdoor life," adds this indulgent physician, " which is led in these privileged regions makes this apparently excessive indulgence in tobacco harmless."

The first thing a reader of Sir Morell's essays on Teneriffe and other health resorts will naturally look for, is some guidance as to how far the climate of the Canaries may be regarded as a panacea for pulmonary diseases. Sir Morell's words on this point give no uncertain sound with regard to Teneriffe, and the same remarks apply very largely to the sister isles and to Madeira :—

"No climate can cure a patient in an advanced stage of phthisis whose lungs are riddled with cavities and whose vital

.R

power is exhausted by hectic. No patient should ever be sent abroad who is obliged to keep his bed."

But he also admits that when the disease is in an early stage, or when there is only some "delicacy" of the lungs, "a stay at either Madeira or the Canaries for a length of time will, in all probability, ward off the danger, and perhaps permanently cure the patient," and in some cases "the fiend of tubercle seems to have been, by such timely measures, completely exorcised."

We are not to suppose that climate in itself possesses any specific quality by virtue of which it cures disease.

"Climate only helps those who help themselves."

And again—

"Climate cannot overcome disease; it only removes one of the exciting causes of the mischief, and so far leaves nature a fair field for the exercise of her healing influence."

It will thus be seen that our great specialist was never less idle than when taking rest, never more thoughtful for others than when treating himself; and that everywhere his first idea was to avail himself of all opportunities of accumulating knowledge which would be helpful to others, as well as technically useful to himself and his professional brethren.

The busiest men are always those who have time to undertake new things. The idlest man I ever knew never had time for anything. It is said that Lord Brougham was always at leisure. Walter Scott always had time to take his grandchildren on his knee and tell them stories. Lord Palmerston could always gossip with callers.

I remember visiting Mr. Cleveland, the President of the United States, at the White House on the morning of the opening of Congress, 1885. He swung himself round in his rotating chair as he sat at his bureau, and seemed delighted to chat for half an hour. "Rather a relief to have a chat," he said, as the wires and telephones and special messengers kept arriving every minute.

"You and I," wrote Sir Morell Mackenzie to Mr. Stead in 1890, "are probably among the busiest men in London ; but as it is always the busiest men who undertake fresh work, I am willing to serve with you on such an experimental committee in connection with Count Mattei's cure for cancer as is suggested, should it be formed, and if no abler and younger member of the profession can be found willing to take my place."

R 2

Sir Morell had no faith in the Mattei system, but he was willing to give that, and everything else, what he considered a fair trial; and he went so far as to place a ward at the Throat Hospital at the committee's disposal for experimental purposes. The results obtained were, to say the least, negative; but the problem was by no means a simple one, and possibly hinged on conditions and had to deal with elements perchance not dreamt of even in Sir Morell's own large and liberal philosophy.

I have no reason to suppose that he had any leaning towards the occult. The habit of his mind was not at all that way; though I am equally certain he would not have denied to any occult problem, intelligently and intelligibly brought before him, an impartial and experimental consideration. He was, however, a man of practical action first and foremost, and he favoured results rather than speculations.

Sir Morell was ever full of public spirit, and the volunteer forces commended themselves to him as excellent in every way, both as a physical training for young men and as a popular expression on the part of England's youth of their love for their country and of their willingness to undergo sacrifices, and, if need be, peril

of life and limb in its defence. The following
letter from Colonel Howard Vincent, M.P.,
himself a distinguished member of the volunteer
forces, throws a pleasing light on Sir Morell's
connection with the movement :—

Some mention ought to be made, I think, of the public spirit
Mackenzie showed when, despite his tremendous engagements,
he at once accepted an offer I made to him about 1887 of the
surgeonship of the Queen's Westminster Volunteers, under
my command. Nor did he only accept the commission; but
he worked at the duties it entailed, and even in 1890 submitted himself to an examination by an Army Medical Board
into his knowledge of field surgery.

He went into camp with the regiment, took great interest
in its welfare, subscribed liberally, attended parades and
festive gatherings, and whenever he met with or heard of a
regimental case of sickness he could not deal with at once, the
sufferer was welcome at Harley Street before waiting-rooms full
of paying patients, and so the best advice in Europe was
gratuitously at the service of the Volunteers.

I have not yet been able to replace him.

Three weeks before he died Lady Helen Vincent went to see
him. She said she had a bad cough. He blew a powder down
her throat, and she was well! He asked after me. I called on
him, found him full of interest in the corps, but saw the hand
of death was on him. I urged him to go off at once to the
sunny South. " Yes," he said, " I will go, but not until after
the distribution of prizes to the corps."

Such men are rare, and you do well to take a cast of their
footprints on the sands of time, for the sake of those who are
left still to run their course.

Yours sincerely,
C. E. HOWARD VINCENT.

It was in 1890, when London society was much occupied with Sir Morell Mackenzie and his book " Frederick the Noble," that I asked him to deliver at my house one of a course of "lecturettes" undertaken by a certain number of distinguished men, such as Prince Malcom Khan, General Booth, Justin McCarthy, Holman Hunt, and others who, for different reasons, were occupying public attention at the time. Of course, I tried to induce him "to speak a piece" about the late Emperor and the eventful months at San Remo and Charlottenberg, which had left so deep a mark on the history of his own time, and in which he had played so important and dramatic a part. This he absolutely declined to do.

"Mackenzie on the Throat" was obviously the next best subject. And although at the time he was beset with patients, besieged by editors and journalists, harried by doctors, and immersed in every conceivable epistolary controversy, he at once agreed to take a lecturette, and brought with him the most interesting diagrams, exhibiting the vocal cords, coloured and magnified in such a manner as to render his explanations intelligible to the least enlightened of his audience.

These personal glimpses of Mackenzie, a bare

two years before he died, seem now to assume, in my eyes, an importance which I little dreamed at the time they could ever possess.

I can see him enter our drawing-room with something of his old cheeriness and elasticity, glance round at the company rapidly, and recognize here and there a friend.

He was anxious to begin at once, all introductions had to be postponed till afterwards; he then went to the furthest end of the room, and we propped up the large diagram showing the interior of the larynx and the vocal cords, which, I am bound to say, presented rather a painfully surgical appearance, but any passing shudder was soon lost in the interest of his popular exposition, a style in which he was certainly a master.

The séance opened with a little characteristic trait. I had told Mackenzie that our lecturettes did not usually extend beyond half an hour, though of course we would not venture to limit our distinguished speakers, but the idea of the lecturette was an informal reception and talk, and afterwards such introductions to the lecturer as might be mutually agreeable, followed by a general *conversazione*.

Before Mackenzie began his lecture he could not resist the temptation of giving me a little satirical side-thrust, and in alluding to the half hour limit, which he had received from me, he begged to inform the audience that I did not myself observe in the pulpit the rule which I laid down for my lecturers. When I rose to offer him the thanks of the company for his interesting exposition, I could not help saying that I deeply regretted to have to inform the audience that Sir Morell's exceedingly irregular attendance at my church entirely disqualified him from passing any judgment on the average length of my sermons. Sir Morell received this as a legitimate hit, and laughed heartily at getting his *quid pro quo*.

The last year of Sir Morell's life was characterized by extraordinary literary activity. He revised and completed his great work on the throat and nose. I well remember the proof-sheets of this truly monumental work for months lying about his inner sanctum in various stages of revision, addition, and correction. "When do you find time for this?" I asked, as he pointed to a pile of proofs. "All times," he said, "but chiefly at night. I have to sit up to finish it." Of this work Dr. Norris Wolfenden writes :—

" Of Mackenzie's great work on ' Diseases of the Throat and
Nose,' it is impossible to speak too highly. The first volume,
which appeared in 1880, comprising diseases of the larynx,
pharynx and trachea, was quickly out of print, and but little
remains of the first edition of the second volume, which com-
prised diseases of the œsophagus, nose, and naso-pharynx, and
which was published in 1884. In these volumes was presented a clear and concise treatise on the subjects of which
they treated, and the work was universally regarded as of
great value. It is a classical treatise, which must for years
remain the model for similar efforts of the kind. It is replete
with clinical material, and every chapter bears the impress of
its author's individuality and unrivalled experience in throat
work. It is not merely a book for the specialist, but one that
ought to be in the hands of every practitioner, and its practical
character makes it all the more valuable. The labour expended
upon this work by its author must have been immense, especially when one remembers that every minute had to be
snatched from the most exacting professional duties. This
work was translated into German by Semon, formerly one of
Morell Mackenzie's assistants, and also into French by E. J.
Mouré, assisted by Berthier and Charazac."

But this was only the crown of a long series
of articles and a few books which have attained
a general circulation unusual for books on strictly
medical subjects. The " Laryngoscope," for
instance, published in 1865, passed through
three editions, and is still, in spite of subsequent advances in laryngology, said to be an
admirable introduction to the study of throat
surgery.

" Diphtheria," 1879, also reached three editions, and contains a good deal of original and what at the time was new matter.

"Hoarseness and Loss of Voice," 1868, was sufficiently in touch with the common experiences and needs, as to run through two editions, whilst such works as "Growths in the Larynx," 1871, and "Leprosy of the Air Passage," and "Hygiene of the Vocal Organs, 1888," although full of popular elements such as an account of the vocal organs of Nilsson, Albani, Foli, Brandram, Anna Williams, &c., appealed naturally to a more strictly professional circle.

The now famous Pharmacopœia of the Hospital for Diseases of the Throat, is said to be almost "as indispensable to the dispensing chemist as it is to the British Pharmacopœia."

But the essay on "Hay fever" achieved a remarkable popularity—largely, no doubt, on account of the extraordinary success achieved by Mackenzie in alleviating and even curing this intractable affection.

It is not safe for a living biographer to dabble in estimates of the technical value of medical writings. Fortunately, there is a very general consensus, both at home and abroad, as to the general value of Mackenzie's clinical writings. His published works are also useful, as preserving a record of the many special inventions to which he might lay claim. In his inventive ardour, however, he was never keen upon claiming for himself this or that method of treatment or modification of instrument. In the laryngoscope essay, he describes many such methods first adopted by himself, but since become common property, such as the *rack-movement lamp*, employed whenever gas is the illuminant, the *epiglottic pincette*, to grasp and hold back the epiglottis, the *eclectic inhaler*, the *laryngeal lancet*, the *laryngeal electrode*, the *tube forceps*, the *guarded wheel ecraseur*, laryngeal brushes, etc.

" He it was," writes Dr. Wolfenden, " who introduced the method of making all laryngeal instruments bent at a right angle instead of the curve at which all German laryngeal instruments are bent—an apparently small, though really a very great and lasting improvement. He himself never attached much importance to claims for recognition for the introduction and invention of instruments, but there is no doubt that he possessed a great degree of mechanical ingenuity, and was very often able to devise improvements in existing instruments and mechanical contrivances necessary to deal with cases difficult of operation by the means already at hand. Everybody knows his insufflator, and his modification of Physick's tonsillatome, and his æsophagoscope was an ingenious contrivance for obtaining a direct view of a tract not amenable to direct observation."

He was also the first to suggest the use of volatile oils (pure juniper, thyme, cassia, cubeb, calamus, aromaticus) as a means of medical inhalation, and to devise the formulæ which now are employed for their suspension in light carbonate of magnesia.

He was also one of the earliest to employ the steam spray.

The following high praise is only one of the many official medical tributes to his ability, which flowed freely enough wherever the demon of personal jealousy or professional partisanship could be exorcised.

The *Medical Times,* speaking of his great work on the throat, remarks :—

" We cannot but admire the splendid industry and perseverance which have combined to place before the profession so complete and scholarly a summary of such a wide and varied field of research."

And another distinguished authority writes :—

" It is the fate of most books upon scientific subjects to become, within a short time, antiquated, and their matter ancient history. This is not the case with Mackenzie's work, and this is due, not to the fact that laryngology has ' lagged behind ' in the advance of knowledge, but to the circumstance that everything that Mackenzie wrote was of eminent practical value ; his opportunities for clinical observation were unrivalled, and his written work is replete with the results of such clinical study. In many instances, as has been remarked by a distinguished laryngologist, Mackenzie was prophetic in his utterances. To properly estimate the value of his scientific writings, we must carry ourselves back to the periods at which his earlier works appeared. Compared with such writings as were then existent his own marked a gigantic advance, and when we reflect that to-day there is little to be added to what he wrote years ago, the solid value of his scientific work will be duly appreciated." (*Wolfenden's Pamphlet.*)

The well-known saying about genius that it is merely all-round ability specially developed and directed by the pressure of circumstances, seems to find some justification in Mackenzie's case, although it has always seemed to me unsatisfactory as a general statement,—it is what might be called a wide-meshed definition which lets many cases slip through. But in Mackenzie's life one cannot help being struck with the fact that he showed himself able to do so many things, and that he did everything which he attempted to do so well.

A consummate surgeon, an admirable physician, an ingenious mechanician and inventor, a good entertainer, an excellent talker, a fine rider, a good athlete in earlier days, excellent at games, appreciative of art, a great organizer, an effective disciplinarian, an excellent soldier, a capital lecturer, an omnivorous reader, a remarkable writer—in how many things could he and did he actually excel !

I have given in an appendix a proximately

correct list of his known writings, but there are numberless essays, letters, and paragraphs, some of which might still be collected and arranged for publication. They are scattered about in medical journals, encyclopædias of the day, and the magazine press of England and America. Probably Messrs. Sampson Low's volume of essays include most of those suitable without further setting for the general public, and they certainly give a very good idea of Mackenzie's range of culture, acumen, controversial ability, wide sympathy, or what Confucius used to call "humanity."

One of these essays on the use of tobacco and its effect on the speaking and singing voice is an excellent example of Mackenzie's agreeable, and yet singularly condensed style, and a lesson to all those medical and scientific writers who are of opinion that anything to do with hygiene or medicine must not only be technical, but likewise dull and dignified at the risk of being deemed medically valueless.

To combine instruction with amusement is doubtless not a common gift, but it was one possessed in an eminent degree by Mackenzie both as a lecturer and a writer.

His grace and facility with the pen is apt to conceal from the reader the solidity of his literary performance. In the amusing and pointed paragraph which opens the essay on smoking only the vigilant reader will observe that in the first *twenty-eight* lines there are no less than *ten* quotations, showing an acquaintance with Greek criticism, French and Spanish literature, English medical books, proverbial philosophy, Athenian history, Shakespeare, Calverley, etc. ; yet all these witnesses to a full brain and a ready memory are so woven into the fabric of an entertaining and instructive disquisition that they pass almost without notice.

In these days of aggressive sanitation, tobacco, like nearly every other gift of God to man, has been denounced by well meaning fanatics as the cause of numberless ills both to soul and body. I am inclined to think that to this indiscriminating anathema the practice of smoking owes, at least in some measure, its present all but universal diffusion. A French *dévote* is reported to have said of some innocent pleasure that it would be perfect if it were sinful. In the same spirit, no doubt, the " average sensual man " feels that indulgences in themselves almost indifferent gain additional relish from the fact that they are regarded as wrong by the " unco' guid," or by truculent sanitarians as hurtful.

The gospel of health is an excellent thing, but, like the poor, it is perhaps a trifle too much with us, and the relentless zeal of its preachers wearies men of ordinary mould as the just Aristides bored the Athenians. I say this out of no irreverence towards Sir Edwin Chadwick, Dr. B. W. Richardson, and the other apostles of hygiene, whom I honour on this side idolatry as much as any, but because it seems to me that they are apt to forget that physical well-being is not the sole end of existence. I wish it to be understood that, though a doctor, I do not consider it to be my function to stand at the feast of life, and, like poor Sancho's physician, condemn everything on the table. I am not a member of the Anti-tobacco League, nor do I believe that all those who seek solace from the "herb nicotine—

> "Go mad and beat their wives;
> Plunge, after shocking lives,
> Razors and carving knives
> Into their gizzards."

On the contrary, I am teleologist enough to think that as tobacco is supplied to us naturally from the bounteous bosom of Mother Earth, it is meant to be used, and if used in the right way it is often helpful rather than injurious. I have no sympathy with the famous "Counterblast" downwards, who would deprive poor humanity of one of the few pleasures which tend to make our way of life, in however small a degree, less desolate than it otherwise would be.

Whatever padding there was in Mackenzie's more popular writings, it was certainly of the very best kind, and in every sense he brought out of his store house "things old and new." As smoking has vastly increased, especially cigarette smoking, in these last days, a few more allusions to the essay on tobacco may not be out of place.

Mackenzie, after making the utmost concessions which a physician could conscientiously make to the smoking fraternity, undoubtedly held that smoking in anything like excess affected—and not for good—both the singing and the speaking voice. That Mario smoked incessantly he holds to be the exception proving the rule rather than example for imitation. That Tennyson drank a bottle of port every day for fifty years, and died quietly at a good old age, is no proof that port wine prolongs life.

Use and wont may do a good deal. The throat and vocal cords may become inured to tobacco, but at the risk of losing a certain muscular sensibility and quality of *timbre*, which are most valuable to vocalists. Those who sing well in spite of tobacco might have sung still better without it, and he quotes an admirable saying of Balzac's concerning great men, who had been great although victims to the tender passion, that "there was no knowing how much greater they might have been had they been free from that weakness."

Sensitiveness to cold and even chronic congestion are due to the abuse, and in some cases even the moderate use of tobacco. The insidious weed acts on the nervous centres and the heart; it relaxes the muscles—that is why men must not smoke whilst in training. Not only dimness of sight or *Amblyopia*, but dulness

S

of voice or Tobacco "*Ambhyphonia*" (a word coined by him) is due to smoking. Its tendency to develop or excite cancer of the tongue is well known; but Mackenzie thinks this only results from the abuse and not the moderate use of the weed.

The worst form of smoking is the cigarette; the least injurious is the Turkish method, in which the hot smoke is cooled by passing through water. The Turk, it seems, is our master even in cigarette-smoking, as he always throws half of it away.

Clergy, we are told, generally give up smoking when they find it is injurious, and actors do not.

"Most of the leading actors in London suffer from a relaxed condition of the upper part of the throat, brought on entirely by smoking."

Actresses, as a rule, only toy with the poison in a " Platonic sort of way," " puffing out innocuous blasts of dry smoke," as Charles Lamb says.

It seems almost as bad to expose yourself often to a tobacco-laden atmosphere as to smoke yourself. Many Spanish ladies, who do not smoke, suffer from the men smoking inordinately in their bedrooms.

" Smoking concerts should be *anathema maranatha* to the vocalist who has any regard for his voice."

The two evil things in tobacco are (1) the poisonous nicotine ; (2) the high temperature in which the smoke strikes the palate.

" To sum up," writes Mackenzie, in his most winning and temperate mood, " I believe that most people can smoke in moderation without injury, and that to many tobacco acts as a useful nerve sedative.

" I would say to any one who finds total abstinence too heroic a stretch of virtue, let him smoke only after a substantial meal ; and if he be a singer or speaker, let him do so after and never before using the voice. Let him smoke a mild havannah, or a long-stemmed pipe charged with some cool-smoking tobacco. If the charms of the cigarette are irresistible, let it be smoked through a mouthpiece, which should be kept clean with ultra-Mohammedan strictness. Let him refrain from smoking pipe, cigar, or cigarette, to the bitter and, it may be added, rank and oily end. Your Turk, who is very choice in his smoking, and thoroughly understands the art, always throws away the *near* half of his cigarette. Let the singer who wishes to keep in the " perfect way " refrain from inhaling smoke, and let him take it as an axiom that the man in whom tobacco increases the flow of saliva to any marked degree is not intended by nature to smoke. Let him be strictly moderate in indulgence—the precise limits each man must judge for himself—and he will get all the good effects of the soothing plant without the bane which lurks in it when used to excess."

The recently published volume of " Mackenzie's

s 2

Essays," in addition to some very smart criticism under the title " Reform of the College of Surgeons," contains some very pregnant observations on " Specialism in Medicine," and " The use and the abuse of Hospitals." We find also a carefully prepared report of the now almost historical lectures at the Edinburgh Philosophical Institute in 1889, entitled, " Speech and Song," and a delightful account of his trip to the Mediterranean on board the *Chimborazo* in 1890.

A notice of this, and a sadly prophetic and suggestive last essay on " Influenza," must close my allusions to Mackenzie's writings.

It would be quite possible to collect and edit a second volume of such remains, and I hope that a perusal of the present book, as well as the pleasure and instruction to be derived from the published essays, will inspire Mr. Alfred Mackenzie or some other competent editor to seek out and arrange a second volume for publication.

XII.

THE LAST VOYAGE.

XII.

"In the middle of August last year (1890)," writes Mackenzie, "after an exceptionally fatiguing season, I was still busy in my consulting room, though sighing for release, and half inclined to say to my servant, 'Tie up the knocker, say I'm sick, I'm dead.'"

Within a year of writing these words Mackenzie was dead.

The coming events were indeed casting their shadows before them, though, perhaps, few years of his life were more full of happy and joyous experiences than were his last.

In these more than in any previous years— half forced and half persuaded—Mackenzie left his London cage, and, like a bird set free, speeded away to summer climes and sunlit seas.

The *Chimborazo*, with its company of tourists, all bent upon health or pleasurable change, and the delight of travel, was bound for the Mediterranean.

> "And take me away,
> And take me away,
> And take me away
> To the blue water."

In the essay called the "New Yachting" we have a graphic account of his voyage and adventures.

The company set out from Plymouth on August 30th, 1890. The Bay of Biscay was kind, and the good ship *Chimborazo* passed Cape Finisterre in smooth water, giving a wide berth to the Boy Rock, off Cape Vilemo, where the *Serpent* met her fate a few months later.

No historical point was missed. There seem to have been numerous guide-books, as well as amateur cicerones, on board, anxious to impart information, and to point out *Torres Vedras* in connection with Wellington's lines; *Cintra*, where Don Manuel watched for the return of Vasco de Gama, and so forth. Mackenzie, in his lightest mood, proceeds to describe his fellow-passengers and their various tables in the dining saloon. One was the "high and mighty," another, "the select," a third, "the superior persons." He does not mention to which he belonged, but I have a shrewd suspicion that he shirked the " high and mighty."

As a philanthropist, he says he was pleased to notice the excellent appetites of the passengers. " The wines," he added, " were good, and by no means dear ; but it will comfort Sir Wilfrid Lawson to hear that the wants of total abstainers were amply provided for with ginger ale, soda water, and the other exhilarating fluids, in which they are wont to drown their sorrow for the sins of their less temperate fellowmen."

A controversy soon arose as to the inventor of the most popular drink on board—yclept " John Collins"—which seemed to have been at once claimed by the Americans. But Mackenzie gives them a taste of his encyclopædic knowledge, and warmly vindicates the honour of his country at the same time, by proving the mixture to be of British origin, against all adverse American opinions on board; quoting these weighty and convincing lines :

"My name is ' John Collins,' head waiter at Limmer's,
 The corner of Conduit Street, Hanover Square ;
My chief occupation is pouring out brimmers,
 For many young gentlemen bothered with care."

It is far from improbable that Mackenzie

himself might have been one of their number at the time when residing in George Street, Hanover Square, in complete obscurity—and casting about him for some opening which would enable him to emerge, with distinction, from the serried ranks of the faculty—he made the acquaintance of the head waiter at Limmer's, and possibly coined the distich which adorns the pages of his posthumous volume of essays.

The chief people on board all come in for some characteristic and genial allusion, with usually a slight, but piquant flavour of satire about it.

The captain is " obliging and courteous," but some of the passengers thought he might have been more "diffusive " in his " social attentions."

The purser was " dignity, tempered with affability," having evidently formed himself on the most " approved royal models—his urbane condescension in answering silly questions," is specially commended ; but a certain " commander " seems to have been the favourite, a sort of " delicate Ariel," at every one's beck and call, and generally invaluable for smoothing down difficulties.

Mr. Tristram Ellis, the artist, seems to have been on board, and his soubriquet was "the lightning artist of the *Chimborazo*." " The

Church was not represented, which was regarded as of good omen by the sailors." Of the thirty ladies on board, some "young," and others of "a certain age," only three seem to have made any definite impression on the light-hearted physician. One an Alpine explorer, one a young poetess, who recited her verses to indulgent and appreciative listeners in the gloaming— and what verses would not sound "all right," as the golden sun sank quickly from a pale green sky into the porphyrian blue of the Mediterranean, smitten, here and there, with wastes of blazing orange. Those who know what these effects, of almost raw colour, are on the Mediterranean about the time the electric stars begin to flash out in the heavens—before the dull monotony of the night extinguishes the sunset glories—can well believe that the young poetess had her audience well in hand "in the gloaming."

The most interesting snap-shot is, perhaps, "the lady whose many wanderings in many lands rivalled those of Odysseus. So great was the effect which the mingled dignity and suavity of this fair pilgrim's manners produced on the natives, whenever we landed, in the way of obtaining admission to otherwise inaccessible public buildings, that they gave her the name of the *Grande Dame*."

Mackenzie thus sums up cheerily :—

" When the frost of suspicion with which every free-born Briton at first regards those of his compatriots with whom he does not happen to be acquainted had melted under the genial influence of personal companionship, the travellers on board the *Chimborazo* proved to be as agreeable a set of people as one could wish to meet."

The opinion of the "travellers" on Mackenzie has already been recorded by " one of them " in an earlier portion of this book (p. 114).

Tangier was passed, Algiers was visited, so was Palermo ; thence on by Scylla and Charybdis to Syracuse and to Athens.

Here Sir Morell received the most courteous and flattering attention from the Duchess of Sparta, and indeed seems to have preferred a drive with her to the routine visit to the plains of Marathon, which he consequently missed.

In inspecting the shrine of Æsculapius he remarks that the treatment which has given that ancient leech such a celebrity seems to have been a judicious "mixture of devotion and hydropathy."

Athens was not left without a call upon Dr. Schliemann and his treasures :—

" The famous archæologist, whose explorations under ground almost rival Stanley's above it, invited several of our party to his house, where he received us with the greatest courtesy, and

interested us with remarks which showed a remarkable combination of Yankee' cuteness and German philosophy."

Pushing on eastward, Constantinople was
reached. The Mosque of St. Sophia, like Scylla
and Charybdis and the shrine of Æsculapius,
seems to have been a disappointment, "tawdry
in ornamentation," "ill-assorted colours,"
"badly patched mosaic;" the whole thing
"had a shabby-genteel look." The original
beauty of the temple seemed almost destroyed.

Mackenzie's description of his interview with
Rustem Pacha, the Grand Vizier, is interesting.
The Vizier said to him, "Yes, I do work very
hard. I have been doing so for five years
without any rest. I am not so fortunate as
Lord Salisbury or Mr. Gladstone, who go away
to their country houses. I can never leave my
post for a day."

He saw the Sultan, and thought the expression of his face "anxious" rather than disagreeable. He "looked more the soldier than
the student."

His luggage seems to have been detained at
the Constantinople Custom House, owing to some
informality, and nothing short of a direct appeal
to the Grand Vizier availed to release it.

"One tries," observes Mackenzie, "in vain to imagine what
would happen if a Turkish citizen were to call at the house of

an English Prime Minister, during the sacred hour of dinner, and ask him to make the Custom House authorities give up his portmanteau."

A visit to the battle-fields of the Crimea was amongst the last interesting episodes of this truly restorative voyage, which made the shattered physician, within a little more than a year of his death, almost believe that he had taken a new lease of life.

In the midst of so many and various scenes and interests the professional eye was ever on the *qui vive*.

Tangier is not recommended, on account of its dampness.

Algiers is preferable for pulmonary complaints. Malta is decidedly condemned.

" It is," writes Mackenzie, " the most windy place I have ever been in, and it is extremely dusty, whilst the glare of the sun is most disagreeable. It is further afflicted with one of the most disgusting harbours in the world, and has the questionable privilege of possessing a special fever of its own production."

The following passage will be read by many with interest in these days when pilgrims in search of health are more and more taking to the sea in order to visit, for relaxation and amusement, the Fjords, the land of the Midnight Sun, Japan, India, and even China :—

"In the new yachting there is no unpleasantness as to the choice of places to be visited, nor are carefully arranged plans liable to be disarranged at the last moment by the thoughtlessness or unpunctuality of friends. You have the pleasures of companionship without any of the responsibilities of a host or the obligations of a guest. You can enjoy the sea and the air —charged with ozone, which is the champagne of the lungs, and free from any taint of vegetable or animal corruption— just as fully as if you were an Alexander Selkirk on a floating island ; and you have many comforts which cannot be had even on the largest and best appointed yachts. I can strongly recommend what I may call the 'omnibus yacht,' if not exactly as a 'pentacle of rejuvenescence,' still as one of the best remedies I know for the effects of overwork or prolonged illness. Only, in order to get the full benefit of it, the traveller must change his mind as well as his sky. He must leave all his professional and other worries behind him, and give strict orders that no business letters or telegrams shall be forwarded to him. Let him say with Tibullus, 'Carry me through remotest peoples, carry me over the waves, where no woman [read ' client,' ' patient,' or ' constituent,' according to circumstances] shall know my way.' Then let him allow himself to be borne along, seeing many men and cities, and throwing himself completely into the life of the moment, absorbing new impressions and new experiences, as a plant draws nourishment from the surrounding air. Let him be content that the thing does him good, without troubling himself why it should do so, or insisting on having his sensations translated into scientific phraseology. The great benefit of such a trip is repose in a pure atmosphere with constant change of scene. Further, there is the important circumstance that in a voyage in a well-appointed ship, a man is amid ideal sanitary surroundings, where the bacilli (or a large proportion of them) cease from troubling, and the drain-afflicted householder is, or ought to be, at rest. Many people to whom ordinary yachting would be intolerable on account of sea-sickness, could defy the enemy on a large ship, and in case of accidental illness of any kind, the latter has advantages too obvious to need mention. On the whole, I can echo the sentiments expressed in the following classical lines which I had the pleasure of hearing recited by the author himself, the Honourable Member for the *Chimborazo*, as the Greek poets used to read their own verses at public festivals :—

> "'If you're sick of seeing patients, or of interviewing clients,
> Or have lectured quite sufficiently on politics and science ;
> If your legislative powers are in want of reparation,
> And you've spent a tedious session in the service of the nation ;
>
> .　　.　　.　　.　　.　　.　　.　　.　　.
>
> Then I stake my word upon it that the best thing you can do, sir,
> Is to take an ocean voyage in an Orient Company's cruiser.' "

Beyond a doubt, the astonishing buoyancy of Mackenzie's temperament was never more remarkably displayed than during this last memorable voyage. He even contrived to deceive himself as to his real condition. " I felt," he writes, " like Faust after his great transformation scene, ' from age to youth.' "

But it was, alas ! only a flash in the pan.

XIII.

LAST GLIMPSES.

XIII.

SOME may think I have dwelt at dispro-
portionate length on this tourist episode ; indeed
I have with difficulty torn myself away from it.
I have lingered wistfully over the pages. It
seemed like being with Mackenzie for the last
happy time before the sun went down and
the shadows fell. The light was even then fast
westering.

At a point in the morn the sky presents the
same appearance as it does at a corresponding
point in the afternoon ; the only difference is
that the sun is rising at one time and falling at
the other. I do not think that Mackenzie himself was really taken in. At any rate, soon after
he returned to England the truth must have
sometimes crossed his mind, perhaps when he
penned those words, written in 1891, describing

T 2

the happy voyage of 1890 : " Tie up the
knocker ; say I'm sick—I'm dead ! "

There have been men who, well knowing that
a catastrophe is impending, eagerly interpose
incidents, distractions, everything that seems to
belong to the ordinary course of daily life, trying
thus to cheat the mind for a little while, or at
least lift the strain and burden of the advancing
calamity.

It is with this feeling that I look about for
incidents—some of them even trivial—remembering the last time he stopped his carriage in
Wigmore Street and drove me whither I was
bound, as this was the only chance he had of a
few words in connection with a certain *Pall Mall
Gazette* article : remembering the kindly anxiety
which he expressed on my behalf, because he
thought I had not been quite courteously treated
by some members of the Hospital committee in
connection with the Samaritan Society, which I
superintended for many years.   He was for
going down and speaking warmly and indig-
nantly to the committee; but I checked his
ardour, thinking that the hospital interests would
be better served by avoiding discord, and I soon
after solved the question by retiring from a post
which I had long been anxious to resign owing

to other absorbing occupations, but which I held on to simply out of a desire to serve Mackenzie.

The last time I saw Mackenzie alive was late in the autumn of 1891. I was lunching at Harley Street one Sunday, and Mackenzie, who often lunched very lightly in his own consulting room, came in and sat down at the end of the table. He was looking very ill. Presently, when he saw me at the other end, he nodded, but made no remark, and did not come round, as was his wont, to speak to me. He was unusually silent, and, I thought, looked very depressed. He got up rather languidly (it was no longer the old elastic tread) before the end of lunch, and came round to where I was sitting, and laying his hand on my shoulder—a way he had—

" Do you want to see me about anything, my dear fellow ? if so, come into my room."

I am sure he meant to be cordial, but the words came out rather wearily.

" No," I said, " I won't. There's nothing the matter, and I dare say you've got lots of work."

In fact, I believe at that moment Henry Irving, who usually came on Sunday when he wanted advice, was waiting to see him.

Mackenzie turned and left the room, and I never saw him alive again.

If only we knew !

It is thus our friends flit across the stage of life, and one day they vanish, without warning, and we see them no more. What remorseful memories are revived by those words " the last time."

The last time I saw Tennyson—and he said " Are you going ? " as though he had said, " Will you stay no longer ? " and I went.

The last time I met Frederick Denison Maurice—and he was walking in Queen Anne Street on the opposite side of the road, and saluted me, and I never crossed over to speak to him.

The last time I saw Kingsley—standing with his back to the fire at Dean Vaughan's, and I never went up to him to say good-bye. The last time I took Jenny Lind down to dinner—and never gave myself the trouble to call on her before she left for Malvern, never to return.

The last time I saw Garibaldi—and although he left the next day, I never went down to the Quai at Naples to see him off.

The last time I parted with Archbishop Tait —standing on the damp lawn at Fulham, and thought how reckless a proceeding for a man in his state of health, and not long afterwards he passed away, and I had refused his last invitation.

The last time M. Renan accompanied me to the door of his rooms at the College de France, and bade me return without delay—but I never returned; nor delayed even a day to meet M. Taine at his house—and now both are dead; and had I known that when Mackenzie invited me that Sunday into his room—it was my last chance—how fain would I have been to accept that farewell call; how long and lingeringly would I have sat and talked with my friend, and how loth would I have been to go !

I record now but one more incident in the public life of Sir Morell Mackenzie, and although it took place the year before the yachting excursion in the Mediterranean, it seems a fitting crown to his professional life.

The Métropole dinner, at which about 200 guests attended, was the occasion of presenting Sir Morell with a handsome piece of plate ; a donation list of 2000l. was also handed in for the Throat Hospital, Golden Square. This splendid tribute to the wide esteem in which he was held by the general public whom he served, formed a

sharp and almost dramatic contrast to that other
scene in which, with closed doors and in privileged
debate, many of the foremost doctors of the day
met and passed their ephemeral vote of censure
upon the man who, whatever may have been his
imperfections, had done so much for medicine
and surgery, and deserved so well of the two
greatest Empires in the world.

On that memorable evening I entered the
Whitehall Room of the Hotel Métropole, to find
myself surrounded by a very remarkable collec-
tion of men. First and foremost there was Lord
Randolph Churchill, who was to occupy the chair
that night, and who presented 25*l.* to the Hos-
pital; Lord Calthorpe, the true and tried friend of
Sir Morell and the Throat Hospital in storm and
sunshine; the Earl of Londesborough; the aged
Lord Crewe, since gone to his rest; Sir W. Ewart,
M.P., Sir R. Hanson, Sir Duncan Campbell, Sir
Bruce Seton, Sir Henry Isaacs, Sir John Monck-
ton, Mr. Jennings, M.P., Mr. Henniker Heaton,
M.P., Mr. Dixon-Hartland, M.P., Mr. T. P.
O'Connor, M.P., Mr. R. G. Webster, M.P.,
Lieutenant-Colonel FitzGeorge, the Rev. Canon
Barker, Mr. H. Irving, Mr. E. Yates, Mr. Augustus
Harris, Mr. C. Wyndham, Mr. Dadabhai Naoroji,
Mr. H. Marks, Mr. Mark Hovell, Mr. B. L. Far-
jeon, Mr. Potter, Q.C., Mr. Wheeler, Q.C., Mr.

J. L. Toole, Mr. Corney Grain, Mr. Mortimer Menpes, Mr. Passmore Edwards, Mr. Beerbohm Tree, Mr. A. Cecil, and others, over 200 in number.

Lord Randolph Churchill, in proposing the toast of the evening, said that this was the 26th year of the operation of the hospital. Its history was a remarkable one. During the first ten years of its existence it enjoyed the honour of being the only hospital for special treatment of diseases of the throat, and it had attracted students from all parts of the Continent and of America, anxious to derive from its teaching the special knowledge it was so well qualified to give. Since its foundation over 110,000 poor persons had received relief within its walls—(hear, hear)—and last year, while there were 314 indoor patients, 6500 new cases received treatment as out-door patients, and the total attendance of patients reached nearly 30,000. (Cheers.) This was the first hospital which established and carried into effect the principle of obtaining from the persons benefited payment for the treatment received, the absolutely indigent, however, not being asked for payment at all; the result was that out-patients last year paid some 2290*l.* (Hear,

hear.) As to expenditure, the hospital was not, and never had been, in debt; it contributed nothing to the debt of 100,000*l.* weighing on the London hospitals, a debt which to him appeared a scandal. The absence of debt in this case was due to economical management. (Hear, hear.) The hospital, however, required funds for the enlargement of its premises and the extension of its field of operations, and a unique opportunity now offered for the acquisition of two houses adjoining the hospital, so that he would appeal to their liberality for aid. For great professions owed much to specialists treating diseases of the throat; the clergy, the bar, the stage, and the politician. (Laughter.) Politics were a profession—(renewed laughter)—and an honourable profession, one to which he was proud to belong. (Hear, hear.) Those professions should contribute largely to such an institution as this. There was another reason which he did not hesitate to press upon them, and that was the confidence they reposed in, and the admiration they felt for, Sir Morell Mackenzie, the virtual founder of the institution. (Cheers.) Like all men engaged in the discharge of difficult public duties, Sir Morell Mackenzie had been exposed to a storm of criticism, but in connection with the late Emperor of Germany criticism had

sometimes degenerated into slander—(cheers)
—and Sir Morell had not always found his
warmest supporters in those to whom he was
perfectly entitled to look for help. Public
opinion, however, would not be led astray by
the counsels of rival authorities or the clamour
of competing parties. It was rarely the lot of
any member of the medical profession to influence the fate of a nation so directly as it had
been that of Sir Morell Mackenzie. By an
unequalled exercise of great moral courage, and
guided by pre-eminent skill, Sir Morell Mackenzie saved a life very precious to the world,
and by the same skill and care so prolonged
that life that Frederick III. was enabled to
succeed to the throne of Germany. (Cheers.)
Although the reign was all too sadly brief, it
was of incalculable importance to his own
country and to Europe. Party passion and
military ambition might endeavour for a moment
to obscure, but they could never efface or
diminish the lustre of the character of Frederick
III. (Cheers.) On the contrary, his memory
would shine forth like a beacon, brighter and
ever brighter, pointing out clearly to monarchies
and to men the true direction and only object
of an Imperial career. (Loud cheers.) In conclusion, he asked them to drink to the Hospital

for Diseases of the Throat, coupling with the toast the name of Sir M. Mackenzie. (Cheers.)

Sir M. Mackenzie thanked those present most sincerely for the manner in which they had received both the toast and his name. He would point out that there was no antagonism between general and special hospitals, and in this case this hospital had provided the general hospitals with the medical officers who attended there to these special diseases. The hospital was not in debt, and that was due to the efficiency of the medical staff and to the work of the committee, both bodies acting in harmony. As regarded the personal matters which had been alluded to, his friends, and his enemies, perhaps, would admit that he had been placed in a position of considerable difficulty and delicacy. It was not for him to say how he had discharged his duties, but he believed that the time would come when national jealousy, political rancour, and professional rivalry would subside, and he would receive fair and impartial judgment. (Cheers.) He was at any rate quite willing that his reputation as a physician and a man should be left to the verdict of history. (Cheers.)

Mr. Henry Irving, who was received with cheers, said that on behalf of a body of workers deeply indebted to the distinguished guest of the evening, he desired to say a few words. There had always been a special sympathy between doctors and actors. He did not know why, unless it was that doctors regarded the players as being a little mad. (Laughter.) Whatever the cause, the faculty had always treated the players with the most cordial fellowship, and many an actor had reason to be grateful for kindly help from them. (Hear, hear.) He was charged by his professional brothers and sisters to present to Sir Morell Mackenzie a small token of the great regard in which he was held by them all. (Loud cheers.) They were especially grateful to him ; for, but for his aid, many would scarcely at times have been able to make themselves heard at all—a state of things which some people would perhaps think advantageous. (Laughter and cheers.) He had heard many suggestions in regard to the interpretation of Macbeth, but had the physician in that play belonged to the clan Mackenzie, Macbeth would never have told him to " throw physic to the dogs "—(loud laughter)—nor would the raven who croaked have been so hoarse. (Renewed laughter.) Sir Morell was allied to the stage by family ties, his uncle, Mr. Henry Compton, had been one of the most distinguished and popular actors of the time—(hear, hear)—but he need not dwell on Sir Morell's kindness, he had rendered the players many services, and had often ministered to their wants ; he was a great physician and a great friend—(cheers)—and the actors would always speak of him with one voice and, he might say, with one throat — (cheers and laughter)—and wish him every happiness he might and could possibly desire.

The testimonial was then presented to Sir Morell Mackenzie. It consisted of a silver bowl of the time of George II., on which was inscribed—" To Sir Morell Mackenzie, M.D., a grateful tribute of admiration and regard from those whose names are inscribed on this bowl." Among the names were those of Mr. H. Irving, Miss Ellen Terry, Mr. Corney Grain, Mr. H. Neville, Mr. Marius, Messrs. J. L. Toole, Grossmith, Augustus Harris, J. Billington, J. Alexander, J. Brookfield, A. Cecil, C. Wyndham, H. Kemble, A. Reed, Wilson Barrett, Brandon Thomas, J. Hare, D. James, J. Fernandez, A. Stirling, C. H. Hawtrey, Mr. and Mrs. Bancroft, Mr. and Mrs. Beerbohm Tree, Mr. Bernard-Beere, Mrs. Wood, and Mrs. Kendal.

Sir Morell Mackenzie, in acknowledging the

gift, thanked them heartily for the valuable present. He had a great affection for the profession, which, as they knew, had been adopted by one of his sons, whom he hoped to see walk in the footsteps of the great-uncle to whom Mr. Irving had referred. He would rather have this as a gift than as a testimonial, for the best testimonial they could offer would be to pay him professional visits. (Cheers and laughter.) Very few people, except doctors, had the opportunity of realizing the conditions under which actors often appeared before the public. He could assure them that the beautiful bowl he had just received would be one of his most precious possessions. (Cheers.)

On this occasion Lord Randolph was admirable, speaking with a deliberation and an almost clinical authority, which might lead one to suppose that he had himself made a special study of medicine and surgery, and had been from the first most intimately acquainted with the Hospital for Diseases of the Throat. The speech was not only as carefully prepared as the closest parliamentary oration, but it had a sincere ring about it which fully convinced the assembled guests that in securing the presence in the chair of a distinguished nobleman, a fluent orator, and what Macaulay used to term, "a man of genius and sensibility," the committee had also had the good fortune to select an out-spoken admirer, and a sincere friend of Sir Morell Mackenzie.

I have heard Sir Morell himself speak better than on that night; he may have been a little in doubt about what to say and what not to say as he looked around him, and remembered the cross-fire of criticism which at that very moment he was being subjected to "outside the house." With a knowledge that every word he let drop at such a time would be analyzed and commented upon by friend and foe, perhaps he picked his words a little at the expense of that light-hearted spontaneity which makes the charm of after-dinner oratory. But the dinner, socially and financially, was a great success, and it is pleasing to remember that upon this last great public occasion of his life the interests of the hospital, which he had created, were not separated from his own personal triumph.

XIV.

THE END.

XIV.

THE END.

THE years 1890, '91, '92, will be long remembered as influenza years. More insidious than cholera, but in certain months little less fatal, this distressing malady left a deep impress upon the social life of England, sweeping away old and young,

> " The bearded grain, at a breath,
> And the flowers that grow between ; "

and cutting down especially those who were already enfeebled by any kind of chronic malady, especially lung-disease.

Even Art seemed smitten with influenza, and the Royal Academy frames of 1890 were full of invalids—children dying, young girls recovering or fading away, wives sickening and husbands dead. It was, perhaps, a very living artistic year for all that—for painters, instead of going hither and thither in search of a subject, and in that barrenness of artistic invention peculiar to the British nation, choosing at last perfectly inane subjects, or reproducing some one else's ideas, for once sat down and painted what they saw and sometimes felt—deeply, bitterly, and passionately. The result was, no doubt, dismal, but it was respectable, and sometimes touching and dignified.

One of Mackenzie's last writings is an essay on the "Influenza," to which he finally succumbed, and which already had its fatal grip upon him.

It is republished in his Essays, and is a most careful, brilliant, and, within its limits, exhaustive piece of medical writing, and a perfect model of what a medical essay addressed to the general public should be. All through the essay there is a pathetic, and perhaps prophetic consciousness of the danger of influenza

"to those of unsound constitution, especially in lungs or heart—an attack of influenza often quickens the smouldering embers of the complaint into a flame, in which the feeble remnants of life are speedily consumed."

He was of opinion that the scourge of influenza was a question of national importance, and deserved the attention of any government which considered it to be the first duty of a civilized power to provide for the safety of its own citizens, rather than for the scientific extermination of its neighbours.

The disease, it seems, is one of recognized antiquity, and from 1510 at least, to 1866 and 1890, we have its vagaries duly chronicled. There is a description of it in a letter by Randolph, English Resident at the Scottish Court in the days of Queen Elizabeth, so accurate, that Mackenzie thinks it would be hard even now to improve upon it. After a most exhaustive historical survey, Mackenzie declares that influenza is due to poisoned nerves, though he does not tell us what poison, and that it is certainly contagious. He recommends feeding up, and a judicious use of stimulant, " support, not depletion, is the secret of success." Bleeding he is dead against, and remarks succinctly—

" In the epidemic of 1557, in a small town near Madrid, some 2000 persons contracted the disease—they were all bled and all died."

He is also against overpurging, and is not afraid of high temperature, in what he called a " feveret," e.g. 103 or 104 degrees. In reducing temperature we must take care not to reduce the patient.

Painfully apposite to his own case are his closing words, when we remember that he relapsed after recovery—relapsed again—improved, and then at last succumbed quickly.

" After recovery the really dangerous time may be said to have come. The busy man will not be restrained (*sic !*) but will rush back to his work, and in a week or two he is in the deadly grip of pneumonia. For some little time after the most trivial attack of influenza the greatest care is necessary to prevent relapse, and it will be well if extra precautions are taken against catching cold for a considerable period afterwards. [N.B.—Mackenzie got out of bed with the influenza upon him, almost too weak to stand, to see a poor patient *gratis.*] Of the consequences of influenza it may be said with the most literal truth, that he that loveth the danger shall perish in it."

Such is Mackenzie's " *dernier môt* " on the influenza. In the autumn of 1891 he took his holiday, accompanied by his daughter Ethel, on the Lake of Como, Mr. Lasster having placed his villa at Bellaggio at his disposal. In this delicious retreat, where the grey blossom-crested rocks sink into the crystal waters of the lake, and the lemon blossoms and oleanders are reflected in its depths as in a mirror, Mackenzie seemed to imbibe health and refreshment.

On his return, only those friends who watched him narrowly could discern that the improve-

ment was superficial, and that his holidays now
seemed to have less "last" about them. The
London climate told instantly on his asthma,
and although otherwise quite capable of going
his rounds and receiving patients, his sleep was
more brief and broken than ever, and much of
the night had to be passed dozing in a sitting
posture. With so little sleep and so little food,
his medical friends often wondered how he could,
especially in the last year of his life, get through
such a prodigious amount of work.

He was in the habit of leaving town from
Saturday to Monday, and spending Sunday at
Wargrave on the Thames with his family.
These respites were always eagerly looked forward to by his wife and family, and they were
seasons of as perfect relaxation as Mackenzie
ever allowed himself.

One morning in November, 1891, he sent
word that he should not leave Harley Street on
Saturday as usual, having caught a slight cold.
Influenza was not suspected by the family, and
the precaution was thought very natural.
Mackenzie himself was always sensitively eager
not to alarm his family; when he was bad he
would go away into his room and suffer, and

smoke a stramonium cigarette, and so tide over an attack; then get into his carriage and disappear for hours; so that from day to day few, if any, knew what he endured—whether he was better or worse. "Lerne zu leiden ohne zu klagen," the Emperor's favourite motto, was certainly one which Mackenzie had adopted in practice all through his life of chronic suffering.

The next news was that his cold was "rather bad."

Such an admission from Mackenzie it was felt meant a good deal, and Lady Mackenzie immediately hurried up to town to find her husband prostrate with an attack of influenza.

For two days he consented to keep in his bedroom—not indeed before he was powerless to do anything else. Even then the thought of the incessant callers who needed his services worried him, and more than once he imprudently struggled out of bed to see them—paying as well as unpaying patients were treated just alike: sick or well he made no distinction down to the last. That tireless sympathy with the sufferings of others and eager readiness to alleviate them was, I think, one of the most beautiful features about Mackenzie's character, and I can speak from a personal experience of nearly thirty years, during which I have had singular opportunities of watching the crowds of all sorts and conditions of men, women, and children, that have come within the radius of his beneficial treatment.

In ten days Mackenzie was out again in the black November fogs; and on November 24th came the inevitable relapse. But he rallied suddenly, and displayed for a few weeks astonishing nervous energy—visiting the Prince of Wales about five or six times before the close of the year 1891.

His Royal Highness, who seemed to place great confidence in his skill, presented him on New Year's Eve with a token of his Royal favour and consideration, in the shape of a richly jewelled breast pin, which Mackenzie valued amongst his chief treasures.

He had himself a strong presentiment that the end was not far off. I remember, on one occasion, when we were discussing the probabilities of life, at a time when very unfavourable opinions had been expressed about the state of my own lungs, Mackenzie, after a characteristically rapid examination with the stethoscope, indicated exactly where the danger lay, and said,—

" You're all right ; you'll probably go off with bronchitis about seventy ; your life's better than mine—I shall probably not reach sixty."

Our conversation was only half serious, but it was instructive, because Mackenzie dwelt at some length on the great change of opinion that had taken place since the increasing facilities for travel had made it fashionable to go abroad and try new climates. "People," he said, "myself amongst the number, might prolong their lives indefinitely if they would only winter in Egypt or Madeira for a few years, when the first sign of delicacy in the lungs made its appearance. People delayed," he said, "too long. Most of us will not stir until we are forced—and then it is generally too late." Mackenzie had a strong feeling, which he imparted to a friend, that he would not live to see 1892.

As the last day of the year approached, those of his family who knew his presentiment suffered extreme anxiety. A prophecy so often fulfils itself !

The last day of the old year dawned. Sir Morell seemed fairly well. He, himself, was quite unperturbed—but his wife could hardly bear to let him out of her sight, and his children asked him if he would not sit up with them and

see the old year out. "Nonsense," he replied,
"I shall do nothing ridiculous. I shall go to
bed."

He latterly occupied a room by himself, as at
night the temperature was kept abnormally
high, and to others somewhat oppressive.

Mackenzie retired to rest about eleven.
Kenneth, his younger son, who knew of his
father's premonition, kept watch, as did also
Lady Mackenzie—and the tension of the situation had become somewhat extreme—when, at
the last stroke of twelve, Kenneth opened the
door softly, and said, "Good night, Father!"
Lady Mackenzie then came into the room, and
said, "A happy New Year, Morell!" He sat
up, chatted, and smoked a stramonium cigarette.

In six weeks from that time he had ceased to
breathe.

On the 18th January, 1892, he dined with his
family, and every one was very merry, Sir Morell
being unusually bright and cheerful, and full of
interest in everything that was going on.

On the 19th he had a relapse. Lady
Mackenzie then urged that he should at once
get out of London, but he said he was "too full
of business," and, ill or well, must be on the spot.

He added—and the words betrayed the fatal
undercurrent of his thoughts—"*If I am going
to get well*, I shall get well anyhow ; and if I am
not to get well, I may as well stop where I am."

The time now was indeed short. Lady
Mackenzie superintended everything in the sick
room and seldom left him. His chief anxiety
seemed to be that she should not over-fatigue
herself, and he was divided between his desire
to have her with him and his anxiety that she
should not suffer from her prolonged hours of
attendance. No one knew better than he did
what that meant, and he was affectionately
thoughtful for others down to the last.

As he said to his daughters, when he noticed
that his wife tried to monopolize and concentrate
in herself the whole service of the sick-room,—

" I don't want your mother to do all, but," he
added, apparently with a vague sort of appre-
hension of how it was going to end, " I don't
want her to go out of the room much."

At that supreme hour, the dying man, looking
perchance across the chain of years to the
happy nuptial period and early married days,
when there was yet time for constant companionship and interchange, and remembering, it
may be, how the inexorable demands of an

exciting professional career had often inflicted separation and robbed him of her presence, " I don't want her out of the room much," are words which have a pathos of their own.

So the time was come when she could remain, and there was at last—at last—no time left for anything now, but close—close companionship to the end.

Mackenzie's clinging to his wife as the shadow fell upon him, was, even then, free from any taint of selfishness, and noticing that she would hardly leave him for meals, he insisted on her always coming downstairs to dinner, and not having it brought up, " because she ought to have it hot."

From February 1st to February 3rd—the day on which he died—his wife hardly left his side for more than a few minutes at a time. So indomitable was his spirit, that he got out of bed and moved about his room on the very day of his death.

His mind was absolutely clear and bright to the last. He could direct ; he could sympathize ; he recognized ; he had a kindly word for every one, servants and all ; and none, but perchance

himself, dreamed that he would not survive the
evening of the 3rd of February, 1892.

Hilda had been reading to him a good deal in
the afternoon, and he was all attention, though
much troubled with the asthma.

Towards evening he fell asleep, and when he
woke about nine o'clock he sent for Ethel, who
gave him an egg beaten up in wine. Soon afterwards Lady Mackenzie, who had snatched a
little rest in an arm-chair, came in, and he then,
turning his head towards her with a look of
unusual disquiet, said, "I'm not at all comfortable." He was sitting in bed, propped up
with cushions, and his breathing seemed certainly very bad. He thought he would inhale ;
but he got less relief than usual from this, which
was his own favourite remedy.

He then asked for his stramonium cigarettes,
and smoked one after another. This seemed to
soothe him. Ethel re-arranged his pillows, and
putting her arm round him as he sat up, his
head sank on her shoulder and he seemed to
doze off.

Presently he roused up and wanted his pulse
taken. " Not as good ? " he said, inquiringly.
He inhaled again, and once more asked about
his pulse. Lady Mackenzie said, " It isn't as

good;" and, becoming suddenly alarmed at the appearance of his face, she added, " Shall I send for Stephen?" (that was his brother, who throughout had had the medical care of him, and who lived only a few doors off in Cavendish Square). " Yes," said Mackenzie, more faintly, but quite articulately, " *send for Stephen!* " He never spoke again. His wife put her arm round him whilst he once more inhaled about twice; then a little cough; his head fell forward. One broken exclamation escaped from his wife as she tightened her hold upon his body.

" Oh! Morell!" But it was the call of the living to the dead, and there came no reply.

Stephen Mackenzie arrived, but neither brandy nor artificial respiration were of any avail.

Stephen Mackenzie continued his manipulations for several minutes after he knew that it was useless, then he turned to Lady Mackenzie, and his look betrayed the truth.

" Are you sure it is no use? " she said.

" I am sure it is no use."

.   .   .   .

So died this singularly original, successful and gifted man; admired and beloved by many, misrepresented and envied by not a few, but recognized by all as one who was lifted up in his generation to play a great part, exceptional in its political importance, and supreme in its human and dramatic interest.

When the sad news reached me at Tangier I could only wire to place my church and the services of my assistant minister, the Rev. John Penfold, at the disposal of the family for such use as might be thought expedient or acceptable.

The Memorial Service at St. James's, Westmoreland Street, Marylebone, was attended by an immense concourse of persons famous in art, literature, and the drama, amongst whom might be observed Henry Irving, Mr. Toole, Miss Fortescue, Mr. and Mrs. Pinero; whilst the most magnificent wreaths were sent by the Empress Frederick, the Duchess of Manchester, the Marchioness of Ely, Sir Lionel and Lady Darell, Mr. and Mrs. Bancroft, Miss Ellen Terry, and a host more, to such an extent that when, later in the day, the body was conveyed to Wargrave Churchyard, where it reposes in the green place chosen by Sir Morell Mackenzie for himself, the wreaths and floral tributes were piled in such manner that no part of the enclosure could be seen for the flowers. The coffin bore the simple inscription :—

Sir Morell Mackenzie, Kt., M.D.
Born July 7th, 1837,
Died February 3rd, 1892.

The clergy, who officiated in my unavoidable absence, were—at St. James's, Westmoreland Street, the Rev. N. Oakley Coles and the Rev. Albert Cooke; the first, Sir Morell's brother-in-law, the second, his nephew, the son of his sister Agnes. The service at Wargrave was conducted by the Rev. A. H. Austen Leigh.

The chief mourners were Mr. Harry Morell-Mackenzie, Mr. Kenneth Morell-Mackenzie, his two sons; Mr. Theodore McKenna, his son-in-law; Mr. Alfred Mackenzie, Mr. Stephen Mackenzie, his brothers; Mr. Arthur Carey, his nephew, and Mr. Ben Hannen.

Amongst the numerous letters of sympathy received by Lady Mackenzie immediately after Sir Morell's death, were one from the Empress Frederick and one from the Prince of Wales. The Empress wrote that she was most sincerely grieved and deeply affected to hear the news of the death of Sir Morell Mackenzie, and that she would always gratefully remember his skilful and devoted services.

Sir Francis Knollys, writing to Lady Mackenzie about the same time, stated that he was desired by the Prince of Wales to say that he felt the death of Sir Morell Mackenzie to be a loss, in a personal sense, and that he had the fullest confidence in him.

X

EPILOGUE.

EPILOGUE.

I LAY down my pen with mingled feelings. Whether in the multitude of counsellors there is always wisdom may be doubted, but there can be no doubt whatever that I have been largely favoured with that wisdom, such as it is.

Had I followed *all* the advice given me, I should have compiled no memoir at all ; and that course would have gratified not a few.

Some, for instance, wanted the story of the Throat Hospital left out, others wished me to pass over the fatal illness of Frederick the Noble, others were for letting alone Mackenzie's private practice, and others wished to eliminate as irrelevant his family life. Then, as his social life was only indirectly connected with his profession, it was thought that also might be passed over.

We have all heard of *"Othello"* without the Moor of Venice, and *"Hamlet"* without the Prince of Denmark. An ingenious writer the other day

contrived to give an account of the rise and
progress of the *laryngoscope* without so much
as alluding to Morell Mackenzie; but how to
write a life of Morell Mackenzie without Morell
Mackenzie was a little beyond my powers of
comprehension. So, after listening to everyone's
advice, I was obliged to go my own way, making
a few concessions to prejudice, omitting a few
names, and altering a few phrases.

Valuable as is " Frederick the Noble " as a
fragment of autobiography, interesting as are
the few essays just given to the public as specimens of Mackenzie's lively observation and
charming style, priceless as are his medical
works, numerous and diverse as are the pam-
phlets, criticisms, and opinions which have been
bestowed upon him, it still seemed right that an
outside and not unappreciative picture should
be given to the world of a man who played so
prominent a part in politics, medicine and
surgery, as well as in the social life of London.

That this ought to be by a friend and not by
a foe seemed self-evident. To me it has been a
labour of love. Never until now have I quite
realized how great Mackenzie was, because never
before was I in a position to appreciate the difficulties of his position, and the consummate ability
and indomitable will which enabled him to

master one situation after another, as he rose higher and higher above his adversaries, until the loud thunder of their brawling seemed to have melted into a confused and faint murmur when he so suddenly passed

"To where beyond these voices there is peace."

APPENDIX A.

A.

SOURCES.

I AM indebted to the following persons for materials :—

To various members of the family, specially, of course, to Lady Mackenzie and her daughters, Ethel (Mrs. McKenna), Olga (Mrs. Hannan), and Hilda Mackenzie, and to his two sons, Harry and Kenneth.

To Alfred Mackenzie, whose excellently written narrative of his brother's life up to the foundation of the Throat Hospital I have largely used.

To Bessie, Agnes, and Fanny, Mrs. Aglen, Mrs. George Cooke and Mrs. Oakley Coles, for some charming early traits and anecdotes.

To Mr. F. C. Parkinson, for a most interesting account of Sir Morell's life whilst in attendance on the Emperor in Germany.

To Dr. Krause, for his most kindly, able, and

outspoken letter on Mackenzie's treatment of the Emperor.

To Mr. Shield Nicholson, for his charming account of Mackenzie on board the *Chimborazo*, the whole of which I was not able to use.

To Henry Irving, Lord Londesborough, Edmund Yates, F. C., Joseph Wright, C. R. Grindrod, Sir Spencer Wells, Plumpton Wilson, W. H. Brereton, Miss Ada Fielder King, S. M. Whitcom, James Ray, Miss Elsie Hinton Smith, Sir William Dalby.

To Alfred Dunning, Mr. and Mrs. Bancroft, John Lawn Stewart (from Colonel Stewart) for a graphic account of Mackenzie's school days, Mr. Prothero, Stephen A. Miall (for extracts), Dr. McCall Anderson, for a letter from Friedrichskron.

To Miss Ryley, T. G. Meyer, Miss Benedicta Stuart, for a most interesting anecdote in connection with the Throat Hospital.

To Mr. T. A. Churchill.

To Mr. T. W. Wheeler, for interesting school anecdotes, and a host of other correspondents whom it would be impossible to enumerate, and whose contributions I cannot particularize, and many of which I have been unable to use. I extremely regret that I have not been favoured with more of Mackenzie's letters.

APPENDIX B.

B.

THE HOSPITAL SUNDAY FUND AND ITS EARLIER METHOD OF DISTRIBUTION.

AFTER a long conversation with Mackenzie, I gathered from him the chief points of difference between him and the Hospital Sunday Fund Committee of Distribution, then sitting. I embodied them in a sermon, the following summary of which appeared next day in the *Echo* :—

"*Mr. Haweis on the Hospital Sunday Fund.*

"Mr. Haweis, of St. James's, Marylebone, in the course of his sermon on Hospital Sundays, stated his reasons for withdrawing from the Fund, and announced his intention to divide his collection between a general and a special Hospital. He pointed out that the contributions of the last three years had fallen below the first two years; and that last year 26,082*l*. showed a falling off of nearly 1000*l*.

"Hard times had been assigned as the cause; but commercial depression had not affected the Hospital Saturday Fund, which for the last three years showed a steady increase."

"The cause of the decline of the Hospital Sunday Fund is,

in his opinion, want of public confidence in the method and
the results of the Distribution Committee. First, the Distribution Committee had some bad rules and some good rules, but
they broke their best rules, and seemed averse to reconsidering
their worst.

" Rule IV. provided that no grant should be made to any
institution which was not managed by a committee duly
constituted. An excellent rule.

" What do we find this year ? A large grant made to the
Hospital of St. John and St. Elizabeth, which has no committee
at all.

" Again, Rule V. provides that in no case shall a grant be
reduced or withheld until a conference shall have been sought
with the Managing Committee. Another good rule.

" What do we find this year ? An award granted to the
Golden Square Hospital withheld (whether by the Council or
the Distribution Committee is of no importance), but without
any conference with the Managing Committee being either
sought or accepted.

" Now as to bad rules. Rule V., which bases the awards
made primarily on the total expenditure of each institution for
the last three years, after certain deductions—to some of which
exception might be taken—is entirely vitiated by a clause
which states that, after all, this numerical basis is to be really
subjected to a sliding-scale, introduced by a consideration of
the ' merits ' and ' pecuniary needs ' of each institution. This
mars the whole ; the fixed intelligible basis disappears altogether, and in its place we have awards made by the Committee
simply on the vague and undefined things called ' merits ' and
' pecuniary needs.' How such a clause can stand upon any
document headed ' Laws of the Constitution ' of this or any
other public fund is a mystery, but the mystery will have to be
solved.

" Are we to place unbounded confidence in the wisdom, as
we do in the honour, of the Distribution Committee ? Even
then we should have a right to know the numerical basis on

which each Hospital works out, and the numerical basis on which each receives a grant. An occasional statement concerning merits and needs would also be acceptable; yet in no single case is anything of the sort given us in the published Report of the Fund. Specimens, however, of 'merits' and 'needs' upon which awards have been determined will occasionally leak out, and are not reassuring.

" First—Case of 'Merits.'

" The Hospital of St. John and Elizabeth (before mentioned) has 120 in-patients, no out-patients. It received a grant of 135*l.*—i.e. over 1*l.* per head—for no reason that can be assigned except the economy of its management expenses, which amount only to 4 per cent.

" The North-Eastern Hospital for Children, with 350 in-patients and 135,000 out-patients, received a grant of only 7*s.* 6*d.* per head, for no reason that can be assigned except that 23 per cent. expenses of management was considered large. But in truth 23 per cent. is not higher than several other hospitals for women or children, and the real reason why the St. John and Elizabeth works at 4 per cent. is because the institution is managed gratuitously by a Roman Catholic sisterhood ! What merit is there in writing down 0 for what costs 0 ? Yet the merit of 0 is reckoned at 1*l.* a head by the Distribution Committee.

" Secondly—'Needs.'

" Last year a tank burst at St. George's Hospital. The tank cost 1600*l.* By an appeal to the papers this already wealthy hospital got 2600*l.* to repair their tank; and the Distribution Committee were for giving them a special grant of 25C*l.* more ! It is fair to say that this absurdity was stopped by the Council, but it was fought for and gallantly defended by the Distribution Committee.

" Now what does all this prove ?

" 1st. That ' merits and needs ' are calculated to confuse the judgment of an intelligent Distribution Committee.

" 2nd. That nothing short of putting ' merits and needs '

Y

out of ambush into the light of day—nothing short of publicity can justify the Distribution Committee in retaining such a clause in Rule V.

" This suggests the last point —*publicity*.

" 28,000*l.* of public money ought not to be annually distributed without either the public or the institutions concerned having the faintest clue given them as to the reason of the awards.

" We have a right to demand from the Distribution Committee—

" 1st. The numerical basis on which each institution works out.

" 2nd. The numerical basis on which each receives a grant.

" 3rd. When special merits or needs would justly modify the award made on a mere numerical basis, we ought to be told the nature of such 'merit' or 'need'—e.g. St. Elizabeth and St. John's Hospital, entitled to no consideration on the score of its cheap 4 per cent. management, because worked gratis by a sisterhood—e.g. St. George's Hospital, entitled to no special grant on the score of broken tank because a public newspaper appeal brought in 1000*l.* more than the cost of repairing tank.

" No one wishes to be hard on the Distribution Committee, no one will blame them for occasional mistakes; but let them admit that public criticism is their best and only safeguard. Year by year they will do better if they submit to it—year by year they do worse because they will not. Let us have a fair distribution-sheet, like that of the Hospital Saturday Fund, where the public can see the reason of each award—where the institutions can read and compare the results of each other's management and efficiency.

" A vast mass of valuable information pours annually into the Mansion House—this great educational influence is withheld from the public, this great corrective and experimental influence is withheld from the various hospitals and dispensaries—and why? All for the want of a few columns of figures, and a page or two of plain statement. And the consequence—widespread dissatisfaction and a falling-off from the Fund.

"Mr. Haweis, in conclusion, commented severely on the fact that fifty pages of the Report were devoted to the churches, clergy, and sums collected, and but four to the question of awards.

" Not a figure in connection with the numerical basis was published ; not a fact beyond the bare statement of the award was mentioned.

" He then pointed to the Saturday Hospital sheet, which, instead of three columns, gives twenty-two columns of statement to each institution, and which deals with 107—i.e. only twelve less than the Hospital Sunday Fund, which deals with 119 institutions.

"He was not comparing the two bases, but merely the publicity given to each, and he affirmed that, although a vastly larger sum had to be distributed by the Sunday than by the Saturday Fund, the publicity given in the one case was possible, and ought to be given in the other, and until this much, at least, was done, he intended to withdraw, not from the cause, but from the Fund."

APPENDIX C.

C.

Dr. Mackenzie's Defence of the Throat Hospital.

THE meeting, which began by being refused the charges as a matter of right and expediency, was gratified towards the close by a full and able speech, in which Dr. Morell Mackenzie met and refuted the charges *seriatim*, as follows :—

Dr. Morell Mackenzie, who on rising was received with applause, said,—

" When he saw what was the feeling of the meeting, it was evidently within his power to decline to enter upon the so-called 'Charges ;' but as there were many subscribers who were not present, and who might like to hear the whole story, he should, with the permission of the meeting, read the charges, and give the reply of the Committee to them. He must premise the charges, however, by observing that in the year 1876 some differences arose between the then chairman and the Committee as to the treatment of two patients. The matters in dispute were, in fact, whether two patients had been treated properly; whether in one case the Clinical Assistant had arrived sufficiently promptly, and whether in the other the Clinical Assistant had operated skilfully. These were perfectly *bonâ fide* subjects for inquiry. When, however, these matters were ultimately to be investigated, the late Secretary had thought it necessary to 'pad' the charges by trumping up fresh ones, and it would be found that many of these were repeated over and over again, only in different words, and all sorts of irrelevant topics were introduced. Some of these had reference to himself, others had no meaning at all. He would, however, read them, and give the answers of the Committee, only here and there making such additional remarks as might be necessary to render the facts clear. The document is headed:—

" *Subjects of Complaint against the Management of the Hospital for Diseases of the Throat.*

" (1.) That a Resolution passed by the Committee of Management in 1871, conferring almost absolute power on Dr. Mackenzie, was allowed to remain in force after Dr. Mackenzie showed by acts and orders issued by him to the Matron, and which were detrimental to the interests of the Hospital, that he could ignore the Committee of Management altogether.

" (1.) This is a mere assertion. The Committee are quite able to protect themselves against any encroachments of any officer of the Hospital. Dr. Mackenzie, the Hon. Medical Superintendent of the Hospital, has always shown himself most anxious to co-operate with the Committee in every way.

" As instances, the following may be quoted, viz.:—

" (a.) The taking away the Hospital Porter to take charge of his (Dr. Mackenzie's) own house.

" (a.) The Porter ' taken away ' by Dr. Mackenzie had previously been his private servant, and whilst employing him Dr. Mackenzie paid for a substitute. The arrangement facilitated some proposed changes as regards the Porters at the Hospital, and was sanctioned by the Treasurer, the highest Officer of the Hospital.

" This charge was only raked up a year after the event, and he (Dr. Mackenzie) was at a loss to discover that the Hospital had been put to any inconvenience by his employment of one of the Porters, as the substitute was far more efficient than the man temporarily taken away.

" (b.) The dismissal of the Porter at the shortest notice, without reference to the Committee.

" (b.) The Porter was not dismissed by Dr. Mackenzie, but had he been so dismissed Dr. Mackenzie would have acted entirely within his jurisdiction.

" (He might here remark that there was no more necessity for consulting the Committee when a Porter had to be discharged than there would have been for conferring with the Prince of Wales when a scullery-maid had to be sent away.) (Cheers.)

" (c.) The instructions given to the Matron not to telegraph to the Surgeon in cases of emergency, but to send a messenger for his (Dr. Mackenzie's) Clinical Assistant.

" (c.) The instructions given to the Matron to summon a Clinical Assistant (whose position corresponds to that of a House Surgeon at a General Hospital, only that the Clinical Assistants are, as a rule, men of higher standing than House Surgeons) was perfectly in accordance with By-Laws. (No. 4 Rules of Physicians and Surgeons is as follows:—' The Physicians and Surgeons shall treat all cases indiscriminately, whether surgical or medical, which come on their days. The Physicians shall have the right, if they desire it, to perform surgical operations, and the Surgeons to make medical exami-nations, but each shall have the power of inviting the other to assist and co-operate in the treatment of cases.') [Dr. Mackenzie here explained that some years ago, when Mr. Thornton was acting as his Clinical Assistant, telegraphic com-munication had, at his own expense, been established between his house and that of Mr. Thornton. Subsequently the Committee relieved Dr. Mackenzie of the expense of maintaining the wire. When Mr. Thornton became Assistant Surgeon he asked to be allowed to retain the office of Clinical Assistant. This was acceded to, and even after Mr. Thornton became Surgeon, for a time he acted as Clinical Assistant. When Mr. Thornton resigned the office of Clinical Assistant the telegraphic communication ought to have been discontinued, but it was allowed to go on for a year. At the end of that time Dr. Mackenzie, finding that the telegraph was only used for private communication between Mr. Evans and Mr. Thornton, suggested that the wire should be discontinued ; but Mr. Thornton expressed a great desire for it to remain, and accordingly undertook to attend whenever the Clinical Assistants were not accessible. Subsequently Mr. Evans and Mr. Thornton endeavoured so to arrange matters together that Mr. Thornton might be summoned instead of the Clinical Assistant, and thus break through one of the fundamental rules of the Hospital.]

" (2.) That the Committee passed an unmerited Vote of Censure on the Secretary on December 20th, 1876.

" (2.) The Committee did not pass any vote of censure on December 20th, 1876 ; but, on the contrary, although they did not consider the Secretary was justified in making certain suggestions to the Matron, they nevertheless exonerated him.

" (3.) That when the circumstances connected with the operations on Fanny Brooks proved how right the Secretary had been in making the suggestion for which he was censured, the Committee did not think fit to cancel the Vote of Censure.

" (3.) This is answered in No. 2. As no Vote of Censure had been passed, it could not be cancelled.

" (Several Subscribers here exclaimed that 'a censure ought to have been passed.')

" (4.) That Dr. Mackenzie instructed the Matron to summon

a Clinical Assistant by messenger in cases of emergency, and forbade her summoning the Surgeon by telegraph.

" (4.) This is answered in No. 1 above. Instance c. This is a mere repetition.

" (5.) That the Committee showed their approval of such instructions by allowing them to remain in force even after the occurrence of the case, when more than half an hour elapsed before a Clinical Assistant could be procured, and the patient died before his arrival.

" (5.) In the case referred to the Clinical Assistant ought not to have been summoned at all. The patient had been seen by Dr. Mackenzie and Mr. Stewart, and the case was 'given up' by the first-named physician at nine o'clock in the morning. He was, however, subsequently twice seen by the Clinical Assistant, the last visit having been paid at eight o'clock p.m. The Senior Clinical Assistant was subsequently summoned by the Matron between ten and eleven, contrary to orders, as the case had been given up, and no private person, under the circumstances, would have sent for a doctor. In fact, the summoning of the Clinical Assistant was simply a piece of vexatious annoyance adopted by the Matron, who was aware that the Senior Clinical Assistant was seriously ill. Having in the meantime been more acutely attacked (as can be shown by a certificate from Dr. Ord), the Senior Clinical Assistant was unable to go to the Hospital, and was obliged to send to the Second Assistant, who promptly attended. Although the visit was quite unnecessary, and although the gentleman first summoned was too ill to attend, it is admitted that assistance was obtained within "half an hour." It would be difficult to conceive any circumstance more clearly illustrating the excellence of the arrangements.

" (6.) That in the case of Fanny Brooks, the Clinical Assistant sent for was a gentleman not on the Staff of the Hospital, and, therefore, not a proper person to be summoned, as his position as a Clinical Assistant had

not been recognized by the Committee, in accordance
with the By-Laws then in existence.

" (6.) The Clinical Assistant was the proper person to
summon in accordance with the By-Law, the Clinical Assistants' appointments not requiring the sanction of the Committee, but being in the hands of the Medical Staff.

" (7) That he had never before attempted to perform tracheo-
otomy, unassisted, in the dead of night, and had only
once performed the operation at all, and had then not
completed it.

"(7.) That he had *previously* performed tracheotomy in the
presence of several physicians, and that in the case of Fanny
Brooks he performed it with great skill and perfect success—
the patient having made an excellent recovery.

" (8.) That to entrust such a dangerous operation to such in-
experienced hands, when the Surgeon (who had performed similar operations nearly fifty times) could have
been summoned by telegraph, showed a want of regard
for the interests of the Hospital, if not an absolute
disregard of human life.

" (8.) The Surgeon of the Hospital had only become experienced in performing the operation by previously acting as a
Clinical Assistant. The Committee consider that the 'interests
of the Hospital' and a 'regard for human life' require them to
carry out the By-Laws of the Hospital, which provided for the
instruction of a large number of practitioners in performing
tracheotomy, instead of confining the operation to the hands
of one person. The operation was most skilfully performed.

" (9.) That the statement of the number of patients treated
at the Hospital, published for the information of the
subscribers and the public, have been wilfully falsified.

" (9.) The Committee are not aware of any inaccuracy in
the statement of the number of patients treated at the
Hospital; but if there has been any 'wilful falsification' it
must have been effected by the person who has fabricated the
charge.

"The Committee declined to allow this charge to be investigated in the following words :—

"'As regards No. 9, the charge is of such a very grave character, involving, as it does, the personal honour of some officer, that before allowing the matter to be made the subject of inquiry, the Committee of Management would require to know the name of the person who is thus charged with '*wilfully falsifying*' the numbers of the patients treated at the Hospital, and the exact details of the falsification.'

"In conclusion, Dr. Mackenzie desired to call attention to the fact that not a single charge of want of care or attention had been brought forward by any patient of the Hospital, and he did not hesitate to say that these charges of mismanagement were entirely the result of the jealousy of an inferior man towards a distinguished young physician, his friend, Dr. Semon. (Loud and prolonged cheering.)"

APPENDIX D.

D.

ALFRED MACKENZIE'S ANALYSIS AND ACCOUNT OF
THE GENERAL PROGRESS OF THE THROAT HOSPITAL.

THE progress of the Hospital has been in all respects remarkable, and the more remarkable when we consider that it was
founded, fostered and fathered by one man. Of course, he
found many kind friends to assist, but it would be difficult to
mention any workers for the Hospital who have not been
drawn into it by either Sir Morell Mackenzie himself or his
personal friends.

Here is its growth in the first ten years of its existence.

1863. Donations 86*l*. 15*s*. 11*d*., Annual Subscriptions 24*l*. 3*s*.
1873.   „   4244*l*. 16*s*. 8*d*.,   „   „   579*l*. 5*s*.

This 4244*l*. 16*s*. 8*d*. included the proceeds of a Bazaar held
at the Hanover Square Rooms, and supported by Royalty, and
also an anonymous donation of 1000*l*.

During these ten years, a large number of medical men, both
in esse and *in posse*, enrolled themselves as students, and in
addition no less than 2308 practitioners "attended to witness
the regular practice." Indeed it would be difficult to mention
any throat specialist who, during those ten years, did not derive
some of his training and experience either from the Hospital or
its founder.

In 1887, the teaching powers were further increased by the establishment of a series of post graduate classes in connection with the Hospital.

The " Throat Hospital Pharmacopeia " has now become almost a text book. First edited by Mackenzie himself, and spoken of by the *British Medical Journal* in the following terms :—" Such a pharmacopeia has been long wanted and will prove most useful to practitioners," it has run through several editions, and has for long been a source of revenue to the Institution. The publication of this little work would in itself have justified the existence of the Hospital, had not the vast number of patients testified to this in another way.

The assistance always so cheerfully given by Sir Morell to members of the musical and dramatic professions has been well acknowledged by both the leaders and the rank and file of those professions. In the space of four years no less a sum than 1500*l.* was raised in a very remarkable and unprecedented manner. In 1878 Madame Christine Nillson gave a concert at St. James's Hall, when 900*l.* was realized, and in 1878 Madame Trebelli followed suit, clearing over 400*l.* Both these talented artistes were well supported by the profession, and patronized both by the Royal Family and the leading ladies of Society. In 1879 a still more remarkable performance was given in aid of the charity. Mr. Irving gave the use of the Lyceum Theatre for an afternoon performance, and appeared, with Miss Ellen Terry and other members of his company, in *Charles I.* Mr. Bancroft undertook the stage management, and, together with Mrs. Bancroft and the then Haymarket company, gave a selection from *Ours.* As a third piece Mr. Corney Grain, Mr. Arthur Cecil, and Mr. George Grossmith, gave the musical triumviretta " Cox and Box," Sir Arthur (then Mr.) Sullivan conducting his own music. This unique bill brought the Hospital between 250*l.* and 300*l.*

In the year 1881 the International Medical Congress met in London, and "the Hospital was selected as the most fitting place for the demonstration of exceptionally interesting cases, and of the various instruments and appliances used for the recognition and treatment of diseases of the throat." These demonstrations attracted a very large number of distinguished laryngologists from all parts of the world, and the Hospital received its due meed of recognition and appreciation.

The treatment of the Hospital by the two great collecting agencies, the Hospital Sunday and the Hospital Saturday Funds, is instructive, when the origin and aims of the two movements are considered. The Hospital Sunday Fund is practically an irresponsible body. It deals with other people's moneys, and cares little or nothing for the *principles* or usefulness of the respective Institutions. The Hospital Saturday Fund, on the other hand, is distinctly a responsible body. Its delegates are all elected from the contributing sources, it deals with its own moneys, and it *does* care for the principles and usefulness of the participating Institutions. This it shows by sending its own representatives to the governing bodies of the Hospitals, and in most cases they are given a hearty welcome ; and this Hospital, I may mention, not being ashamed of anything, has expressed itself quite willing to receive a delegate, and by pertinaciously insisting upon, and in many cases securing an evening attendance of medical officers.

And how have these two funds treated the Hospital for Diseases of the Throat? The Sunday Fund made a grant in 1873, in 1875, and in 1876 ; it was then dropped until 1887, in which year, and in 1888 and 1889, it made an award. In 1890 and 1891 it was again dropped. *The Hospital Saturday Fund made an award to the Hospital in the first year of its existence and has never missed its annual grant.* It soon occurred to Sir Morell, practically within the first two or three years of the foundation of the Hospital, that the provident principle was the only right one, and that while hospitals should be open free to the necessitous poor, those patients who could afford it should contribute something to the Institution from which they were deriving benefit. Accordingly, after the matter had been thoroughly examined and considered, a table of amounts

z 2

to be paid by patients, founded on wages earned, was drawn up and adopted, and in 1867—its fifth year—the sum of 289*l*. 9*s*. 6*d*. was received from this source. In 1868 it had increased to 337*l*. 3*s*., and it has gone on increasing ever since. It is this provident principle that, I understand, does not commend itself to the Hospital Sunday management, which systematically taxes those institutions adopting it, and which I am told is now given as the reason for not making a grant to the Hospital for Diseases of the Throat. The principle, however, commends itself to most thinking people, and is approved both by the public and by the patients, as is shown by the numbers who throng the Hospital. The system on which this Hospital acts was fully explained by Sir Morell in his evidence before the House of Lords during their recent Commission on Hospitals, and will be found in full in the *Blue Book* issued by that body.

Total number of out-patients, 132,729 ; in-patients, 5709. Total moneys received, nearly 100,000*l*. No record after the first few years has been kept of the attendances of medical practitioners, though, of course, all students are registered. But in the six years ending 1874 more than 2000 medical men and students availed themselves of the teaching.

With such results how can any one assert that the Hospital has not served a good purpose and filled a distinct want ?

APPENDIX E.

E.

THYROTOMY A DANGEROUS OPERATION.

THE German doctors maintained that the Emperor's case in the earlier stages was one specially favourable for the operation. See *British Medical Journal*, I. 1888, p. 1360. This view does not seem to have been entertained by Hahn, Krause, Billroth, and others, who maintained, with Mackenzie, that the operation is always dangerous. Mr. Prothero's remarks in the *Nineteenth Century*, November, 1888, may also here be read with advantage :—

" The False and the True Issue.

The *False* issue is this :—The German doctors suggest that in May, 1887, it was possible to extirpate the cancer by an operation which was comparatively simple, safe, and certain. To this operation, known as laryngotomy, the Crown Prince had consented—but—but Mackenzie's opinion that there was no evidence of the malignant nature of the growth, postponed its performance till too late. The reasoning by which von Bergmann minimizes the danger and exaggerates the efficacy of this external operation is misleading, if not disingenuous. It

was on the diagnosis of cancer that the operation was to be
performed. Cancer, and cancer only, was the plea for this
medical treatment. Either he trusted the diagnosis or he did
not. If he trusted it, the extirpation of the growth by the
excision of the whole or part of the larynx was his object. If
he did not trust it, his operation was unjustifiable. To see if a
disease is fatal, he offered to perform a life or death operation.
It is true the Crown Prince had consented to the treatment,
but its real nature was concealed from him. . . . There is no
external operation for laryngeal cancer known to surgery which
is not in the highest degree formidable, so hazardous in fact,
that many of the best throat specialists of the day consider it
to be under no possible circumstance justifiable.

"The True issue between the English specialist and the German
doctors was this :—In May, 1887, two German doctors, without
special skill in diseases of the throat, unsupported by any pathological evidence, trusting to the infallibility of their diagnosis,
and concealing from the patient and his family the nature of the
proposed medical treatment, advised an external operation, which
in 27·2 per cent. of the cases is immediate death, which in 54·54
of the cases hastens death, which nearly always destroys the voice
and which in only two cases (and in one of those Dr. Lennox
Browne doubts the existence of cancer) has effected a complete
cure. Against this proposal Sir M. Mackenzie took up a position from which he never swerved a hair's breadth. Without
asserting an opinion whether the growth was or was not malignant, he maintained that no external operation was justifiable without pathological evidence of the existence of cancer,
and that even if cancer were thus proved to exist, a palliative
treatment which prolonged life under normal conditions of
health for at least another year, was to be preferred to a radical
treatment. When the alternatives are so terrible the patient
himself must decide. In November, 1887, the Crown Prince
deliberately refused. His decision, in the opinion of every
important critic, concludes the controversy. The sole responsibility of re-opening the question rests with the German doctors,

and their charges against the English specialist compelled him to reply."—*Nineteenth Century*, October, 1888.

Mackenzie also says :—

"On May 5th, 1887, less than five months after a certain patient had submitted to thyrotomy, total extirpation had to be performed (three weeks before the date on which it was intended to operate on the Crown Prince). The patient survived this procedure only four weeks. Here we have an example of what would in all probability have been the fate of the Crown Prince, if von Bergmann had operated on him in May, 1887. His Imperial Highness would have suffered in May all the misery which he went through in the following February.

Name of Patient.		*Result.*
1. Scheidenreicht	...	Cured (?) but could not dispense with cannula. Recurrence. Death from suicide.
2. Hahn*	... ...	Cured. Recurrence five weeks after operation.
3. Richter	... ...	Death on the eleventh day through heart-failure. Operation only undertaken at urgent request of patient.

Instead of this, as the result of Virchow's report, the illustrious patient passed many

* The patient's name was the same as the operator's.

months of pleasant existence, during which he often told me that he felt as well as ever he had done in his life. If, when the time came for tracheotomy to be performed, the after-treatment of that operation had been carried out in an intelligent manner, not only would the illustrious patient have been spared much unnecessary suffering, but his life would, in all human probability, have been prolonged considerably beyond what actually was the case.

The average duration of life in cases of laryngeal cancer is two years, and there are well authenticated instances of patients undoubtedly suffering from the disease having lived for three and even four years. Taking the average period, however, the Emperor's "expectation of life" was till February, 1889. Thus several months of his existence were sacrificed through unskilful treatment, and the use of clumsy instruments.

Perhaps all the evil results ought not to be laid on the shoulders of Bergmann and Bramann, as the rapid development of the disease was, in part, probably caused by Gerhardt's extraordinary abuse of electric cautery. The slow progress of laryngeal cancer is universally recognized, the hard encasing cartilage resisting the progress of the disease. In this case, however, Gerhardt's reckless use of the red-hot wire no doubt set up the perichondritis which formed such a prominent feature in the case, and hastened the fatal result. (See also *British Medical Journal*, I., 1888, p. 1360.)

APPENDIX F.

F.

BISMARCKIAN POLICY AND THE EMPEROR FREDERICK'S DEATH.

IT is difficult to resist the impression that the Bismarck faction was extremely anxious to guide Providence into the right course of political action, by arranging for the translation of the Emperor Frederick to another world, if possible, before the death of his venerable father. Had Mackenzie declared him to be unfit to reign, Bismarck would have no doubt declared a regency; failing that, the passage of the Alps in mid-winter, which finished Mazzini, and has proved in more senses than one fatal to more heroes than one, seemed not inappropriate. When the Emperor at last arrived unexpectedly, fit and capable for the transaction of public business, there was nothing for it but to wait for his death with such patience and resignation as so fiery and unscrupulous a political faction could command, but upon the

whole situation the following extracts from the
Contemporary Review (Bismarck article) :—

" Sooner or later, then, it was certain, if the Emperor lived,
Prince Bismarck would have to go, and the probability was
that it would be sooner rather than later. Thus it came to
pass that, in the Chancellor's mind, there must have been constantly present, however much he repressed it, a haunting
temptation to wish that the Emperor might not recover; nay,
even that he might die before the inevitable crisis arrived. . . .

" The difficulty in his path was the danger that Sir Morell
Mackenzie would not certify the incapacity of his patient, and
also the probability, which deepened into a certainty after the
horrible accident of the cannula, that the Emperor would die
too soon to make it worth while to run the risk and to incur
the friction of the Regency. . . .

" Who could be surprised if he had wished that the cancer
would make haste ?

" That such evil thoughts may have brooded in the obscure
recesses of the great Prussian's mind is certain.

" When the old Kaiser died, there was for the moment a
period of painful suspense and indecision in the mind of the
Mayor of the Palace. What should be done ? How long would
the Emperor Frederick live ? Was there any need of there
being any Emperor Frederick at all ? From the point of view
of the Bismarck dynasty it certainly seemed desirable that
the succession should pass direct from the grandfather to the
grandson. For the young man was reared in the Bismarckian
tradition. He was a product of Blood and Iron. With him,
unless he is foully belied, the omnipotent Reichskauzler had
made sundry important and binding agreements, on the principle of *du ut des*. His father, on the other hand, was not a
Bismarckian. He moved in the midst of the Prussian Junkers,
like a cultured Athenian amidst the warlike Spartans. He
represented civilization, culture, peace. Above all, he represented the hateful principle of the right of woman to the
recognition of her faculties regardless of her sex, and he paid

to the genius of his wife the homage to which she was entitled as an intellectual force, without stinting the measure of his devotion because she was 'only a woman.' Of all the subjects of the old Kaiser the Crown Prince and Crown Princess probably regarded the coarse brutality of Count Herbert with most aversion. It is easy to imagine the pressure of the temptation suggested by the cancer which was eating into the throat of the invalid at San Remo.

" If the Crown Prince never came to the throne, Prince Bismarck's great danger would be averted, and if, at the same time that this peril disappeared, the Chancellor were to rivet his claims upon the young Emperor by placing him at once upon the throne without waiting for his father's decease, a double advantage would be secured. Opponents maddened by hatred accuse Prince Bismark of meditating the doing to death of the Emperor Frederick in order to gain his end.

" They assert that when the Imperial Chancellor brought Frederick III. from San Remo to Berlin, in the depth of winter, he calculated that the chapter of accidents might during the journey accelerate the progress of the disease. For what—it is asked by those who think the Chancellor capable of any crime which forwards his cause—what other conceivable motive could Prince Bismarck have had in declaring that he could not answer for the consequences if the unfortunate Emperor did not cross the Alps in the depths of a severe winter? Of two things, one—either the Emperor would have refused to risk the journey, in which case the Prince might have proclaimed a Regency, or he would, at any risk, proceed to Berlin, in which case he might die *en route.* Either alternative would have suited the Chancellor. As we know, neither alternative occurred. The Emperor stood the journey better than was expected, and Prince Bismarck, after seeing him, went so far as to declare that there never had been any necessity for the journey northwards. So easy is it for statesmen to persuade themselves after the event, when their schemes miscarry, that they have been entirely misunderstood."

A a

APPENDIX G.

A a 2

G.

THE NATURE OF THE ATTACK AND THE NATURE OF THE REPLY.

"*Die Krankheit Kaiser Friedrichs des Dritten*" is rather a popular appeal than a scientific treatise upon an obscure disease. Among its many unproved and unprovable assertions the only point which is clearly established is that the *spretæ injuria formæ* rankles as venomously in the breasts of the German professors as in the heart of a deserted woman. Their manifesto is a mere continuation of the Press Campaign inspired in every line by the Mackenzie-Hetz. Pride in their professional reputation, pride in the honour of German science alike dictated science. It is only vanity—personal or professional—which rushed open-mouthed into the streets to solicit sympathy. In the bitterness of their mortification the German doctors forget the honour of the profession, their personal pride, the dignity of German science, their own self-respect, and the teaching of experience.

" . . . The German doctors issue an elaborate manifesto to prove that if their advice had been followed the Emperor would now be alive and radically cured. Sir M. Mackenzie, under these circumstances, owed it to the Empress and her family to show that their unshaken confidence in him was not misplaced. He owed it to the German people, and, above all, to the memory of the late Emperor.—*Nineteenth Century*, November, 1888."

"The father's death had fought against the milder influences of the Liberal reign. The brief experiment ceased, almost before it had been well begun, and Prince Bismarck was left free to establish his dynasty in peace. Magnanimity is not a Bismarckian virtue. He had triumphed, but that was not enough to console him for the anxieties of the late reign. It was necessary to punish those who had in any way been associated with the sovereign who had dared to believe that Germany might continue to exist even if a Bismarck were no longer Reichskanzler. First and foremost came the unhappy lady who had shared for thirty years the sorrows and joys of the dead, and who had dared after all these years to remain English at heart. Half German by birth, naturalized German by marriage and residence, the wife of one German Emperor and the mother of another, she had never ceased to cherish with affectionate devotion the memories of the land where the sabre is not perpetually clanking in the street, and where there are other ideals of life than that of being a Prussian grenadier. With all her husband's aspirations she had keenly sympathized, and she had shared also in his antipathies. She had encouraged him to contemplate the emancipation of the Imperial throne from the ever-increasing shadow of the Bismarckian major-domo. Upon her, widowed and forlorn, fell the first vengeance of the offended Chancellor. To one who had for a twelvemonth nursed her husband at every step in the long stage that led to the grave nothing could be more tormenting than the accusation that, at some point or another in the treatment of the patient, mistakes had been made but for which his life might have been spared. Hardly had the obsequies ended when there was launched from the Prussian State Printing Press the pamphlet of the German doctors asserting, with brutal emphasis, that the Emperor had been subjected to a mistaken treatment, which had rendered his recovery impossible. All the blows aimed at Sir Morell

Mackenzie fell upon the widowed Empress, who had supported the authority of the English doctor, and who knew that her husband had trusted him and been grateful for his skill and attendance to the very last. Sir Morell Mackenzie replied. His pamphlet on 'Frederick the Noble' was promptly interdicted in Germany, while the accusations of his rivals were circulated everywhere."— *Contemporary Review.*

APPENDIX H.

H.

THE following fragments of Mr. Parkinson's interesting narrative I have with reluctance relegated to the Appendix, together with a characteristic letter by Mackenzie :—

In vain do I tax memory for the precise time and occasion of my first knowing Morell Mackenzie. It was certainly through the Edmund Yates's, and at one of their houses in town or country, where we were both frequent visitors, and with whom we were on terms of familiar and affectionate intimacy, but I cannot remember exactly where it was we met. We had been intimate so long that it seems like always. The very last time I saw Mackenzie was to consult him privately for Mrs. Yates as to his real opinion concerning her husband's health, who was then in the preliminary stages of the severe illness which lasted so long, but from which at this time of writing he has happily recovered. Mackenzie was then ill in bed, and expressed his keen regret he could not run down to Brighton to the Yates's, to relieve our dear friend's mind at once, and promising to do so " directly he was well enough—" a time which, alas! never arrived, for he never left his room again. An assuring telegram was, however, written by me that morning at Mackenzie's bedside, giving his views, which were emphatically that our friend Yates, however severe his attack might seem, was at that time in no danger, an opinion which gave infinite comfort and confidence when both were sorely needed.

In endeavouring to comply with the request that I should jot down some of my recollections of dear Mackenzie, I am met by the initial difficulty of not being able to explain the nature of the close and affectionate tie between us. Of different pursuits and habits, we had, it is true, many tastes and friendships in common ; but in looking back, neither this, nor anything else I can discover, is sufficient to account for our extraordinarily affectionate relations, which were more those of brothers than friends. I have only preserved one of his letters, the last I received from him, but it shows to some extent the sweet and gratefully sympathetic nature of the man. Here it is :

19, Harley Street,
Cavendish Square,
December 29th, 1891.

MY DEAR PARKINSON,—I have had a bad attack of influenza, and three distinct relapses, so that I find it very difficult to get well. Indeed I am afraid I shall have to go away in order to pull myself together. If anything, however, could do me good it would be such a kind letter as you have sent me. I think you must know that my feelings towards you are exactly similar to those which you entertain for me, and that there is no one with whom it is a

greater pleasure for me to associate than yourself. I do not feel equal to writing you a long
letter ; indeed I can scarcely express myself
properly, but I must assure you that your letter
has given me the greatest satisfaction. I have
very rarely received one which has so completely
touched me.

Hoping to see you soon, in the meantime,

Believe me,

Always your sincere friend,

MORELL MACKENZIE.

The above shows better than anything I can say the
sensitive high strung nature of the writer, who while credited
by the critics with being a born fighter, and who certainly
seemed to revel in the joys of a battle with his peers, had on
the other side of his nature, a heart as soft and tender as a
woman's, and one singularly open to the claims of friendship
and sympathy.

It was in the summer of 1878 during a Sunday afternoon's
ramble from the Temple, Goring, an exquisite river-side place
which the Edmund Yates's rented for several years, and at
which Mackenzie and myself were frequent visitors, that we
had a close talk, which made a lasting impression upon me,
for it was then Mackenzie first opened his heart to me, as
friend to friend, told me his secrets, lifted the veil from his
early struggles ; his difficulties in following the profession he
loved, and how and by whose agency they were removed ; his
distaste for the calling to which he was originally destined ;
his studies on the Continent ; his successes at home ; his
literary ambitions ; the appreciation he was gradually meeting
with abroad as well as in England ; his hopes and ambitions ;
his unremitting labours ; the opposition and jealousy he had

surmounted or was beset by (this was touched on very lightly, and in a humorous rather than complaining strain), and his well-grounded hopes for the future of his name and fame. We had been fairly intimate for some years before this, but I date from this conversation that community of feeling and close confidence which distinguished our later intercourse.

When Mackenzie resumed his London life our intimacy was maintained, and continued unbroken to the day of his death. We were members of the same clubs, and of other social institutions of which he was the ornament and pride, and we met frequently in private, always in fullest sympathy. I was never under him as a patient, never having the need for his professional services; but on all matters connected with the use and modulation of the voice, and on the cadences which gave oratorical force, and how far they can be strengthened by throat and chest management and the most skilful conservation of tone, were subjects we never wearied of discussing. But it was not by attainments or by knowledge or other possessions or endowments, material or intellectual, that Mackenzie's heart of hearts was reached. There was in his nature—little as his enemies or his critics suspected it—a vein of noble simplicity and unselfishness which impelled him to many a good deed in secret, which made him an absolutely devoted friend, to whom no sacrifice of time or energy was too great or too exacting, which lifted him above many a pretentious time-worn convention.

APPENDIX I.

I.

AMERICAN AND OTHER TRIBUTES.

I HAVE said in America Sir Morell was looked upon as an oracle. The following may serve as examples of the Transatlantic eulogies which followed him to his grave :—

Extract from the " Philadelphia Medical Times and Register,"
February 13th, 1892.

Sir Morell Mackenzie, the great English laryngologist, died February 3rd, of tuberculosis of the lungs. He was a great man, of consummate ability in his speciality, with enough pluck for seven men.

Extract from the " Daily Chronicle," February 16th, 1892.

The Baroness Burdett-Coutts in distributing the prizes to the Queen's Westminster Rifles " referred to the death of her; intimate friend, Sir Morell Mackenzie, who was the surgeon of the regiment."

Extract from the " Texas Sanitorian," February, 1892.

The Great Morell Mackenzie is dead ! He died in London on 3rd February inst., of bronchitis. Thus even the Goliath

B b

of throat and lung diseases may be filled by an infinitesimal microbe, perhaps.

Extract from " The Times and Register " of New York and Philadelphia, February 27th, 1892.

Dr. Cutter in a lecture delivered at New York, alluding to Sir Morell Mackenzie, said :—

" His words of good cheer and encouragement will long endure in my memory. Thus he brought me into society. Like the great-hearted Dr. Sims, he recognized co-workers in a very handsome way, and held out a helping hand to others."

.   .   .   .

" Thank God that Sir M. Mackenzie lived such a useful and brilliant life, and did so much good to others."

Extract from the " Journal of the American Medical Association," Chicago, March 26th, 1892.

The following beautiful tribute to one of the masters in our art is from the pen of Dr. Wm. Porter, and taken from the " Clinique."

SIR MORELL MACKENZIE.

" The master rests.   After the day of toil,
An urgent message came to him, and he,
Well used to sudden calls, in quiet haste,
With kind good-night went out and all was still.
And now his work is done ; to him no more
Will come the suffering ones and those who need
The helping hand and words of goodly cheer.
His last response completed all his work.
O strong and gentle heart, ours is the loss
Who knew thee well—and knowing loved thee more.
Ours is the loss and thine the great reward.
We crown thee victor, O thou kingly dead."

Extract from "Society," London, February 13th, 1892.

In Memoriam. Sir Morell Mackenzie.
Born 1837. Died February 3rd, 1892.

" Morell Mackenzie "—once it was a name
  To conjure with, wherever human skill
  Availed to baffle in any fleshy ill ;
And, far and wide, spread the great doctor's fame.

Yet death o'ercame him, who had wrestled long
  With that Arch-Conqueror, during his life,—
  Science avails but little in the strife
Which levels all, the weakly, wise, or strong.

Not as the surgeon honoured by a King,
  With prince and peer, as patrons, at his door,
  But as physician to the helpless poor,
His kindly sympathy for suffering
  Will cause him to be long-remembered here,
  And win a fadeless crown in brighter sphere.

To Sir M. M.

God gave thee to the world to lessen pain,
  And bring to many a stricken brother balm
In direst torments—surely not in vain
  For skill consummate thou dost not bear the palm !

Under no napkin hast thou dared to hide
  That talent given by thy Maker's hand,
But thou hast freely spent it far and wide
  To stem the tide of suffering in the land !

B b 2

Not only here, but in the Teuton's realm
   A truly noble martyr turned to thee !
In that last voyage he knew thee at the helm
   To smooth his course o'er death's tempestuous sea !

And though maligned by those who should have praised
   Thy leal devotion to their lord—we know
Our land's fair fame abroad thy skill has raised,
   And thy renown will through the ages grow !

                                        F. B. D.

APPENDIX J.

J.

A Letter from Mackenzie.

The following letter gives us a glimpse of Mackenzie at the *Schloss Friedrichskron,* and should no doubt have been included in the text of the book.

Schloss Friedrichskron,
June 10th, 1888.

My dear Anderson,—I am quite ashamed of not having written to you before, but I have been intending to write every day since I received your very kind invitation.

I am very sorry I cannot avail myself of your good nature, for if I leave here before August (and owing to certain symptoms which are threatening, I think it likely that I may not be here much longer, *but this is quite private*), I shall go away "far from the madding crowd."

Little did we think in those old days at

Vienna that my studies with the laryngoscope would end in my being der eŝste behandlender arzt des Kaisers.

I recollect seeing *your* copy of Czermak's first German pamphlet. You wrote the English translation of some of the difficult words in pencil in the margin ! ! You see what an impression your diligent application made on me at the time.

My time is completely taken up here, for when the Emperor is very ill, I am *obliged* to be constantly with him, and when he is better he won't let me out of his sight.

I hope you saw the scathing letters I wrote to the Berlin correspondent of the *Times*. The *Scotsman* stuck up for me well, and gave me a most eulogistic leader. The *Glasgow Herald* also came out well.

I hope you and all your family are well. I recollect Mrs Anderson so well as a very pretty, delicate and refined looking bride. How many years ago !

Yours always,

MORELL MACKENZIE.

June, 1893.

CATALOGUE OF RECENT WORKS

PUBLISHED BY

W. H. ALLEN & CO., Ltd.,

13, WATERLOO PLACE, S.W.

Publishers to the India Office.

Now Ready.

Super-Royal 4to, with 16 Chromo Plates, and 48 Plates in Photomezzotype.
£4 4s. *net.*

THE GREAT BARRIER REEF OF AUSTRALIA :

ITS PRODUCTS AND POTENTIALITIES.

Containing an Account, with Copious Coloured and Photographic Illustrations
(the latter here produced for the first time), of the
Corals and Coral Reefs, Pearl and Pearl-Shell, Bêche-de-Mer, other Fishing
Industries, and the Marine Fauna of the Australian Great Barrier Region.

By W. SAVILLE-KENT, F.L.S., F.Z.S., F.I.Inst., &c.

The Great Barrier Reef of Australia, represented by a vast rampart of coral origin, extending for no less a length than twelve hundred miles from Torres Straits to Lady Elliot Island on the Queensland coast, takes rank among the most notable of the existing wonders of the world. Built up by the direct and indirect agency of soft-fleshed polyps of multitudinous form and colour, it encloses betwixt its outer border and the adjacent mainland a tranquil ocean highway for vessels of the heaviest draught. To the naturalist, and more particularly to the marine biologist, the entire Barrier area is a perfect Eldorado, its prolific waters teeming with animal organisms of myriad form and hue representative of every marine zoological group.

The author's qualifications for the task he undertakes are emphasised through the circumstance of his having been occupied for the past eight years as Inspector and Commissioner of Fisheries to various of the Australian Colonies, the three later years having been devoted more exclusively to investigating and reporting to the Queensland Government upon the fishery products of the Great Barrier District.

A prominent feature in this work consists of photographic views of coral reefs of various constructions and from diverse selected localities, together with similar and also coloured illustrations and descriptions of the living corolla, coral-polyps, and other marine organisms commonly associated on the reefs. These photographic illustrations taken by the author are, from both a scientific and an artistic standpoint, of high intrinsic merit and also unique in character, representing, in point of fact, the first occasion on which the camera has been employed for the systematic delineation of these subjects.

London : 13, *Waterloo Place, Pall Mall, S.W.*

Crown 8vo.   Illustrated by W. W. RUSSELL, from Sketches by EDITH Œ. SOMERVILLE.   3s. 6d.

THROUGH CONNEMARA IN A GOVERNESS CART.

By E. Œ. SOMERVILLE AND MARTIN ROSS.

"A bright and breezy narrative of the adventures and experiences of two ladies in Connemara, who preferred independence and a mule to society and a mail-car. Is divertingly told. The narrative and its illustrations will provoke a frequent smile."—*Times.*

"Sketches of Irish life, the eccentricities of wandering Saxons, and descriptions of local scenery and events are worked up in a manner which makes the book a pleasant companion. Mr. Russell has, in his illustrations, ably supported the writers."—*Morning Post.*

"The freshness and vivacity of the holiday experiences comes like a savoury dish to a jaded palate, after all the dull bits of book-making in which so many globe-trotters find relief. They are related with a continual flow of conscious —and still more charming unconscious—Irish humour. The most prosaic details of travel are touched with so light a hand as to be invested with new interest."—*Bradford Observer.*

"To read such a joyous book as this makes us envy the happy faculty of the writers for seizing upon the incidents that make up the 'admirable drama of small things.'"—*Lady's Pictorial.*

"The authors have the knack of putting their readers in the situations in which they themselves were ; and so the book, light and smart as it is, is heartily enjoyable."—*Scotsman.*

Crown 8vo.   3s. 6d.

With Illustrations by F. H. TOWNSEND, from sketches by E. Œ. SOMERVILLE.

IN THE VINE COUNTRY.

By E. Œ. SOMERVILLE AND MARTIN ROSS, Authors of "Through Connemara," &c.

"A bright and artless narrative of travel."—*Times.*

"It is quite impossible in any sort of review to give a just idea of the vivacity and raciness of this delightful record of unimportant travel. . . We close the book with a feeling of regret—regret that we cannot forget it all, and so have the pleasure of reading it again quite freshly. But that pleasure we offer to others, with a last word of assurance that those who may be careless enough to forego it will miss one of the most joyous volumes of the season."—*Daily Chronicle.*

"There is not a dull page in the book. It is written in a vivacious style, and we can cordially recommend it to anyone who desires to be entertained during a few leisure hours."—*Manchester Examiner.*

"This lively and pleasant book is the story of an expedition to Bordeaux and its neighbourhood. . . Is agreeably told, and the book need only to be known to be popular."—*The Queen.*

"There is not a dull line in the volume from the first page to the last, and the authors have the rare gift of knowing when to stop."—*Lady's Pictorial.*

SIR W. W. HUNTER'S "INDIAN EMPIRE."

Demy 8vo, 852 pages, with Map, 28s.

Published under authority of the Secretary of State for India.

THE INDIAN EMPIRE:

ITS PEOPLE, HISTORY, AND PRODUCTS.

By Sir W. W. HUNTER, K.C.S.I., C.I.E., LL.D.

"It should be mentioned that this new edition is not a mere reprint, but has carefully been brought up to date. How thoroughly this has been done may be seen from the references to the events which have happened in the present year. More than this, the volume actually anticipates the official report of the Indian Census of 1891. The mere mention of such facts is better than the best recommendation."—*Glasgow Herald*.

"The book is a most valuable library of information, embracing almost every subject which can interest and instruct people who wish to know what India has been and is. . . It may be safely said that all who desire to know what India was, and is, and may be in the future, will find in Sir W. W. Hunter the ablest and most attractive guide."—*Overland Mail*.

"A solid and substantial volume, it will well repay careful study, and will be a valuable addition to any library."—*Manchester Examiner*.

"The most lucid, comprehensive, and able summary of facts and forces which are indissolubly bound up with the honour as well as the welfare of England. . . History, ethnology, geography, science, religion, education, and commerce are all represented in their just proportions and with amplitude of detail in this authoritative work of reference; and scrupulous care has been taken to bring the wide array of facts and figures abreast of the times."—*Standard*.

"This work is absolutely indispensable to anyone who aspires to an accurate knowledge of our great Indian Empire. . . Numerous appendices and a full and excellent index add greatly to the value of this important work."—*United Service Gazette*.

"It is a vast monument of skill, labour, and patience."—*National Observer*.

BY THE SAME AUTHOR.

Demy 8vo, 10s. 6d.

THE INDIAN MUSALMANS.

London : 13, *Waterloo Place, Pall Mall, S.W.*

Royal 8vo, with Maps and Plates, 21s.

NAVAL WARFARE:

Its Ruling Principles and Practice Historically Considered.

BY

VICE-ADMIRAL P. H. COLOMB,

Gold Medallist Royal United Service Institution, and Lecturer on Naval Strategy and Tactics in the Royal Naval College at Greenwich.

"The book is almost a pioneer of its class, for, strange to say, the literature of the greatest naval power in history has no authoritative treatise on the principles of Naval Warfare. . . . Ought to have an absorbing interest to every Englishman who loves his country and cares for its history."— *The Times.*

"A serious and important contribution to a vastly interesting study."—*Daily Telegraph.*

"There are other roads to fame than the path which leads to victory, and there are services which a man may render to his country perhaps greater than to die. Englishmen have reason to be proud of the wisdom, the public spirit, the wide knowledge, and the singleness of purpose displayed in every page of Admiral Colomb's great work. . . . Into the technical details we have no space to enter, but we can only hope that so great a master of naval tactics will give the world the further benefit of his researches and experience in some future volume."—*Murray's Magazine.*

"Such a work ought to find its way into every reference library, as well as into the hands of all who are preparing for the service."—*The Standard.*

"This able work should be highly appreciated."—*Morning Post.*

"The gallant author, who is a most prolific writer on professional subjects, deals with every phase of the question of Naval Warfare. . . . There are numberless illustrations, plans, diagrams, maps, &c., to assist the reader, and the bulky volume should, upon its merits, generally find many readers."—*Hants Telegraph.*

Crown 8vo, with Plans, 6s.

ESSAYS ON NAVAL DEFENCE.

By VICE-ADMIRAL P. H. COLOMB, Author of "Naval Warfare."

"Admiral Colomb has done the country a service in keeping it well in mind of its perils. Highly technical as much of his work is, we hope it will receive from the general reader the attention it deserves."—*Yorkshire Post.*

"The papers may be regarded as the latest voice of science on the great and complex problem of naval defence."—*Scotsman.*

"An admirable manual for the naval student."—*Daily Telegraph.*

"Is both well-timed and welcome. . . This present handy volume ough to find favour with all who feel that the prosperity—nay, the very existence—of this country depends on the efficiency of its sea forces. Every thoughtful executive naval officer should possess a copy of this book, and there are many civilians capable of reading it with much interest and profit."—*World.*

"Throughout the entire work Admiral Colomb shows himself to be thoroughly master of the subjects with which he deals ; and while some of the principles of Imperial defence he sets forth may be and are contested, and some of the facts behind them are denied, the Admiral's views, as given in this excellent series of essays, are entitled to the most serious and careful consideration. The volume is beautifully printed in clear, readable type, and handsomely bound, and forms a most valuable contribution on a highly important subject. There are nine plates of diagrams throughout the book."—*Steamship.*

"On the problems of Imperial defence the opinions of Admiral Colomb are always worth studying, and the republication of these essays is an inducement to re-read and re-study them."—*Athenæum.*

"Through the whole work Admiral Colomb shows a thorough familiarity with his subjects, and although he deals with some questions on which other authorities differ from him, he is everywhere worthy of careful attention."— *Glasgow Herald.*

London : 13, Waterloo Place, Pall Mall, S.W.

Medium 8vo, 12s. 6d.

DEDICATED BY PERMISSION TO

ADMIRAL H.R.H. THE DUKE OF EDINBURGH, K.G.

THE STEAM NAVY OF ENGLAND:

PAST, PRESENT, AND FUTURE.

BY

HARRY WILLIAMS, R.N.,

Chief Inspector of Machinery.

OPINIONS OF THE PRESS.

" It is a series of essays, clearly written and often highly suggestive, on the still unsolved, or only partially and tentatively solved, problems connected with the manning and organisation, and propulsion of our modern war-ships, . . . being laudably free from technicalities, and written in a not unattractive style, they will recommend themselves to that small, but happily increasing, section of the general public which concerns itself seriously and intelligently with naval affairs."—*Times.*

" We strongly advise all who are interested in naval matters to procure a copy, seeing that they will find in it information which they cannot obtain in so well-arranged a form in any other work hitherto published."—*Hampshire Telegraph.*

" Its manifest object is to promote the efficiency of our steam navy in times to come, keeping which aim steadfastly in view, Mr. Williams has brought great knowledge and ability to bear upon the endeavour to forecast what provision it would be well to make in order to meet the full requirements of the British nation. A highly instructive work."—*Daily Telegraph.*

" His opinion on naval matters is the result of deep thought, of wide experience, and of a single-minded desire for efficiency with economy. A work of the very first importance, not only to the navy, but to the safety of the Empire in time of trial."—*Daily Chronicle,* December 23rd, 1892.

" Mr. Harry Williams, a naval engineer of long experience and high rank, discusses the future requirements of the fleet. He is naturally most at home when dealing with points which specially affect his own branch of the service, but the whole book is well worth study."—*Manchester Guardian.*

Crown 8vo, 6s.

THE STORY OF A DACOITY.

NAGOJI THE BEDER NAIK, AND THE LOLAPUR WEEK.

By G. K. BETHAM, Indian Forest Department.

"Graphic sketches of Indian life, narrated with a good deal of spirit and picturesque force. . . The author has the knack of enlisting the attention of his readers."—*Daily Telegraph.*

"The author gives a spirited narrative of the adventures and ultimate capture of one Nagoji Naik. . . Mr. Betham's intimate knowledge of the natives and their ways has enabled him to render the scenes and incidents of this tale with truthful vigour."—*Morning Post.*

"Will be found to convey a life-like impression of scenes in which natives and Europeans, sepoys, police officers, and dacoits, tell their own tale, and throw unwonted lights on India as it is now. There is much to be learned from this book, and many of its passages are marked by great graphic power."—*Globe.*

New Edition, Crown 8vo, 6s.

THE CHRONICLES OF BUDGEPORE;

Or, Sketches of Life in Upper India.

By ILTUDUS PRICHARD.

"This is an interesting book, and one of the most depressing ever written. . A very interesting production."—*Pall Mall Gazette.*

"With many incidents, grave as well as gay. Mr. Prichard illustrates the many phases of the society to be found in Modern India, and, amongst the minor parts, old Indians will appreciate with a smile the well-known names with which he vests his official characters. . . English readers, whether they have passed any part of their lives in India or not, will find it quite worth their while to read these sketches."—*Colonies & India.*

London : 13, *Waterloo Place, Pall Mall, S.W.*

Demy 8vo, 680 pages.   18s

THE LIFE AND TEACHINGS OF MOHAMMED

Or, The Spirit of Islam

By Syed Ameer Ali, M.A., C.I.E., Barrister-at-Law,
a Judge of the High Court of Judicature in Bengal,
Author of " The Personal Law of the Mahommedans," &c.

" It has been reserved for Mr. Justice Ameer Ali, well known as one of the most prominent and enlightened followers of Islam in India, to defend and recommend his faith in an English work intended chiefly for circulation among Christians—a work equipped with all the resources of western thought and learning.   Mr. Ameer Ali writes with enthusiasm, but with no trace of fanaticism."—*Times.*

" This volume can be cordially recommended to the consideration of the English reader.   There may have been more detailed lives of the Prophet of Islam written by European as well as Oriental pens, but we may venture to assert that none of them reveal more boldness or greater breadth of vision."—*Daily Graphic.*

" A clear-sighted, clearly-stated, and forcible exposition of Mohammedanism as a moral force, and has an advantage over the few good books on the subject that an English reader can obtain."—*Scotsman.*

" The historical value of the book is very considerable. . . . Those who care nothing for the polemics of the matter may still find profit and pleasure from the narrative portion, while to others it may suggest a new and important view of the development of the human mind."—*Academy.*

Crown 8vo, 3s. 6d.

WORDS ON EXISTING RELIGIONS.

By the Hon. A. S. G. Canning, Author of "Thoughts on Shakespeare's Historical Plays," " Revolted Ireland," &c., &c.

" The attention which has been latterly devoted to the comparative study of religion is one of the most remarkable features of the thought of the century, and those who are curious to know what the results of that study of them will find them admirably summarized in Mr. Canning's book."—*Scotsman.*

" An interesting and instructive volume, mainly historical, have the merit of originality of thought, and is carefully written. . . . The work is characterised by profound thought and great research, and, to be duly appreciated, must be carefully studied."—*Belfast News Letter.*

" Mr. Canning has produced an interesting volume."—*Publishers' Circular.*

" ' Words on Existing Religions ' is the outcome of Mr. Canning's wide reading of the many standard religious works of the day, which he has evidently read and digested to no mean advantage.   No statement is made in its pages without an authority, which places it almost beyond the range of general criticism, and from its pages a good deal of really useful knowledge may be gleaned relating to the various forms of religion now existent in the world."—*Public Opinion.*

" Is readable, and gives a very just and sympathetic survey of the world's religions."—*Daily Chronicle.*

𝕭ooks on 𝕾port.

By PARKER GILLMORE ("Ubique").

New Edition, Crown 8vo, 6s.

GUN, ROD, AND SADDLE.

"Teem with valuable information and pleasant narrative."—*Daily Telegraph.*

"The author has shot and fished in almost every part of the world, and has had his full share of adventures. He shows a considerable knowledge of natural history, and is evidently a keen observer, so that the sportsman will read his pages with profit and interest."—*Scotsman.*

"Deserves cordial acknowledgment. It is a record of personal experience and of advice, the outcome of such experience from the pen of one who has travelled, and kept his eyes open, everywhere. Here he discourses of subjects so various as wolf-coursing and dog-breaking, the Cape buffalo and Japanese salmon, shooting in Morocco and shooting in America, catching sharks and catching grey mullet, the breeding of oysters, and the training of the race-horse. No reader who has a taste for sport will find this volume devoid of interest."—*Yorkshire Post.*

"The personal experiences recorded in this volume have been gathered in all parts of the world . . . they convey an immense amount of out-of-the-way and valuable information. . . His book is as instructive as it is interesting, and will afford pleasant reading to a good many outside the circle of the 'sportsmen naturalists.'"—*Glasgow Herald.*

"A highly readable and entertaining volume."—*Bookseller.*

"The book is full of interesting reminiscences and anecdotes."—*Publishers' Circular.*

Crown 8vo, with Portrait, 6s.

LEAVES FROM A SPORTSMAN'S DIARY.

London: 13, *Waterloo Place, Pall Mall, S.W.*

Books on Sport, by PARKER GILLMORE ("Ubique"),
continued.

Third Edition, Crown 8vo, Illustrated, 3s. 6d.

ENCOUNTERS WITH WILD BEASTS.

"Mr. Gillmore has well earned his *nom de plume* of 'Ubique.' . . Contains twenty-one chapters on the varieties of game to be found in the northern states of America, and they form a useful and interesting guide to intending visitors."—*Land and Water.*

"Has additional interest because, with but few exceptions, all the adventures related befell the author himself in South Africa and America. Mr. Gillmore tells the stories well without any of the self-glorification and evident exaggeration that sportsmen are usually guilty of in recounting their own adventures. The book should be a popular one with boys, and all into whose hands it may happen to fall. Not the least interesting parts of it are those which deal with the manners and customs of the tribes that Mr. Gillmore fell in with in his search for big game."—*Notts Daily Guardian.*

"Are full of thrilling stories, and are freely illustrated."—*Yorkshire Post.*

Second Edition, Crown 8vo, Illustrated, 3s. 6d.

PRAIRIE AND FOREST:

A GUIDE TO THE FIELD SPORTS OF NORTH AMERICA.

"We are glad to welcome a second edition of 'Prairie and Forest,' in which 'Ubique' so graphically describes the field sports of North America. . . 'Ubique's' descriptions are the more valuable because they are written by a sportsman and not a mere tourist picking up information second hand."—*Daily Telegraph.*

"This admirable guide to the field sports of North America has already attained well-deserved popularity. It is a book which 'the new hand' may read with profit and an enthusiastic desire to learn how to attack his quarry, whether in the air or on the earth, or in the water; whilst 'the old hand' will certainly peruse it with pleasure."—*Home News.*

"The author is such an authority on field sports in general that everything he signs is sure of a standing welcome."—*Bradford Observer.*

"The book is a valuable addition to the Science of Natural History, told in a popular form, and made interesting from the fact that the author has had a very practical acquaintance with the animals he is describing."—*Notts Daily Guardian.*

New Novels.

With Numerous Illustrations by the Author.   Crown 8vo, 6s.

ABSOLUTELY TRUE.

By IRVING MONTAGU, late Special War Correspondent " Illustrated London News."

" The plot of this romance is cleverly and ingeniously worked out, and the reader is certain not to close the book until he has devoured the last page."— *Academy.*

" All the characters are well drawn, some of them are exceedingly so. . . The interest which is awakened in the very first chapter is maintained throughout."— *Pall Mall Gazette.*

" A story of much power, told in fervid and stirring language. The incidents are neatly arranged, and the interest never flags, while the humour is consistent, and not over-strained."—*Daily Telegraph.*

" We accept Mr. Montagu's declaration that the incidents in his delightful story are *absolutely true;* and as one lays down the volume one exclaims that, in all truth, fact is stranger than fiction. The book is not only charming as a tale, but it is written in excellent taste and with conspicuous literary power. . . It should be added that the book is beautifully illustrated from sketches from Mr. Montagu's powerful pencil, and that these add immensely to the attractiveness of an altogether delightful work."—*Scotsman.*

" There is a good deal of ingenuity in the plot of this book, and only the very accomplished novel reader will be able to unravel the plot without reading on to the end."—*Daily Chronicle.*

---

2 Vols., Crown 8vo, 21s.

AN AMERICAN MONTE CRISTO.

A Romance.

By JULIAN HAWTHORNE.

" There is a touch of supernatural in the story wisely left unexplained, and for the rest, though wildly romantic, it is not a book to begin and lay aside."— *Daily Graphic.*

" Mr. Julian Hawthorne bears an honoured name in American literature, and a new work from his pen cannot fail to be of interest. ' An American Monte Cristo ' possesses a great deal that is fine . . . it is of the sensational order, certainly very exciting, and filled with startling incidents enough."—*Saturday Review.*

" Full of interest, excitement, and general ' go.' Mr. Hawthorne rises to the height of his great opportunity, very good indeed."—*Daily Chronicle.*

" Its author has written stories more coherent, but none in which the mingled charm of mystery and romance are secured with better effect."—*Scotsman.*

" The scheme of the story is extremely ingenious, and enchains the reader rom first to last. . . A very moving drama."—*Bradford Observer.*

" Will be thoroughly enjoyed by the reader. . . The interest is kept up to the very end of the story."—*Publishers' Circular.*

" The reader is not likely to lay down the book until he has reached the last page."—*Daily News.*

" The plot of this romance is cleverly and ingeniously worked out. It contains all the exciting ingredients of love, jealousy, hypnotism, and crime ; and the reader is certain not to close the book until he has devoured the last page."— *Academy.*

London : 13, *Waterloo Place, Pall Mall, S.W.*

Mew Movels Just published.

3 vols. Crown 8vo, 31s. 6d.

THE HARLEQUIN OPAL.

A ROMANCE.

By FERGUS HUME,

Author of "The Island of Fantasy," &c.

" Something exciting is always either happening or about to happen, and the book is always refreshing and entertaining."—*Scotsman.*

" The thrilling and mysterious in Mr. Fergus Hume's story is pleasantly relieved with scenes and incidents which are comparatively ordinary, though they all belong to South America.   He every now and then gives us a rest from the harrowing and exciting, by introducing bits brightened up with wit and humour, and if we have strange heathen priests and Napoleonic adventures, and secret passages, and human sacrifices, and impenetrable forests, and blind-folding, and hideous yells, we have also a delightful Irishman, a prim aunt, and plenty of pretty love-making and friendly chaff."—*Glasgow Herald.*

" It is certainly an interesting story, and shows a vivid imagination and much dramatic ingenuity."—*Birmingham Gazette.*

---

2 vols., Crown 8vo, 21s.

THE PRIVATE LIFE OF AN EMINENT POLITICIAN.

By EDOUARD ROD.

(Rendered into English from La Vie Privée de Michel Teissier.)

" The cleverness of the book is remarkable, its skill in developing emotional situations unquestionable, its boldness refreshing, and its modernity quite new."—*Scotsman.*

" The book is a very remarkable and superior one."—*Glasgow Herald.*

" The story is profoundly interesting and deeply pathetic. The psychology is exceeding subtle, and many of the situations intensely dramatic."—*Daily Chronicle.*

A tale of French political and domestic life. It is, however, true not only to nationality, but to human nature, and is therefore as interesting to the English as to the foreign reader."—*Globe.*

" The main business of the novel writer is to catch and hold your attention, and this M. Edouard Rod is able to do in all the works of his I have hitherto read.   The book which is before me, translated with real excellence, is, as a story, one of the best constructed I have read for a long time.   You are brought into contract with the catastrophe almost in the first page.   There is scarcely a pause in the narrative until you reach the final and inevitable end."—*Weekly Sun.*

London : 13, *Waterloo Place, Pall Mall, S.W.*

New Novels.

Crown 8vo, 6s.

THE BOW OF FATE.

A Story of Indian Life.

By SURGEON-MAJOR H. M. GREENHOW.

"His pictures of Anglo-Indian life are very graphic in their simplicity, while the period of the story—that of the great Mutiny—gives ample opportunity for the introduction of much dramatic incident, which lends the book more than ordinary interest."—*Morning Post.*

"The author has thought out an interesting plot, yet the attraction of the book lies rather in the events than in the characters . . . the *times* in which their creator has placed them were real enough, and we follow with fresh excitement this recital of the surprises and terrors of 1857."—*Glasgow Herald.*

"It is a well-written story, interesting in its subject, and containing powerfu scenes —*Manchester Examiner.*

Crown 8vo, 6s.

CAVERTON MANOR, or FORESHADOWED.

By MAY BROTHERHOOD.

"Many of the incidents narrated will be found to be more than usually fascinating by the majority of the readers."—*Evening News and Post.*

"The author deals with nature and animal life in a way that is fresh and exciting."—*Daily Telegraph.*

"A pleasantly-told tale of life in a hunting country, and will interest."—*Glasgow Herald.*

"There are traces of originality and power about this story of love and jealousy."—*Bookseller.*

2 Vols., Crown 8vo, 21s.

CAPTAIN ENDERIS, 1st WEST AFRICAN REGIMENT.

By ARCHER P. CROUCH, Author of "On a Surf-bound Coast," "Glimpses of Feverland," &c., &c.

3 Vols., Crown 8vo.

WHAT AILS THE HOUSE?

By A. L. HADDON.

New Edition, Crown 8vo, 3s. 6d.

SIGNOR MONALDINI'S NIECE.

A Novel of Italian Life.

Crown 8vo, 3/6.

ORNITHOLOGY

In Relation to Agriculture and Horticulture.

Edited by JOHN WATSON, F.L.S., &c.

List of Contributors.—Miss Eleanor A. Ormerod, late Consulting Entomologist to the Royal Agricultural Society of England; O. V. Aplin, F.L.S., Member of the British Ornithologists' Union; Charles Whitehead, F.L.S., F.G.S., &c., Author of " Fifty Years of Fruit Farming"; John Watson, F.L.S., Author of "A Handbook for Farmers and Small Holders"; The Rev. F. O. Morris, M.A., Author of "A History of British Birds "; G. W. Murdock, late Editor of *The Farmer*; Riley Fortune, F.Z.S.; T. H. Nelson, Member of the British Ornithologists' Union; T. Southwell, F.Z.S.; Rev. Theo. Wood, B.A., F.I.S.; J. H. Gurney, Jun., M.P.; Harrison Weir, F.R.H.S.; W. H. Tuck.

"In these days of agricultural depression it behoves the farmer to study, among other subjects, ornithology. That he and the gamekeepers often bring down plagues upon the land when they fancy they are ridding it of a pest is exceedingly well illustrated in the series of papers."—*Scotsman.*

" Will form a text book of a reliable kind in guiding agriculturists at large in their dealings with their feathered friends and foes alike."—*Glasgow Herald.*

"This is a valuable book and should go far to fulfil its excellent purpose. . . . A good book that every agriculturist should possess if he wishes to know friends from foes among the birds."—*Land and Water.*

" This many-authored book is full of interesting and instructive matter.' — *Saturday Review.*

"This volume may be confidently recommended to farmers, gardeners, and lovers of birds."—*Academy.*

" It is well to know what birds do mischief and what birds are helpful. This book is the very manual to clear up all such doubts."— *Yorkshire Post.·*

"If landowners were to make a present of the book to their gamekeepers, much useful knowledge would be disseminated among a class that is sorely in need of enlightenment. We can cordially recommend the volume to all who are interested in British birds."—*Manchester Examiner.*

Crown 8vo, 2s. 6d.

THE FUTURE OF BRITISH AGRICULTURE;

How Farmers may best be Benefited.

By PROFESSOR SHELDON.

London : 13, *Waterloo Place, Pall Mall, S.W.*

Second Edition, Crown 8vo, 7s. 6d.

THE CHURCH UNDER QUEEN ELIZABETH.

An Historical Sketch.

By Rev. F. G. LEE, D.D., Vicar of All Saints', Lambeth.

"This is in many ways a remarkably fine book. That it is powerfully written no one acquainted with Dr. Lee's vigorous and even slashing style would for a moment dispute.—*Morning Post.*

"His valuable contribution to English history ought to be greatly appreciated. Dr. Lee is an able and painstaking scholar, and the fruits of his undoubted labour deserve to be widely read."—*Public Opinion.*

"His vigorous style must command the admiration even of those who most strongly dissent from the views he puts forward. Politics, intrigue, patriotism, religion, fanaticism, and superstition, were wonderfully blended in Queen Elizabeth's reign, and the condition of the society thus produced is well adapted to give full scope to Dr. Lee's controversial and critical powers. No reader is likely to complain that the 'historical sketch' is dull, or that it is lacking in argumentative power."—*Liverpool Mercury.*

"The author's learning is great, his pen is a fearless one, and his work will do much to take from Queen Elizabeth claims to honour attributed to her by many an earlier historian. The statements by the author are fortified by foot-notes on almost every page."—*Public Opinion* (Washington).

Second Edition, Crown 8vo, 5s.

ADDRESSES FOR A RETREAT OF FOUR OR SIX DAYS.

By The Very Rev. R. W. RANDALL, Dean of Chichester.

Part I.—Union with God; Part II.—From Life to Life.

"This excellent volume will be found not only suggestive for conductors of retreats, but will also be of the greatest use to any of the clergy who hold solitary retreats for themselves at home. We hope we may anticipate for this book the circulation it deserves."—*John Bull.*

"Dealing as it does with the great problems of faith, patience, and the life to come, we can confidently recommend it to that larger circle which is sometimes known as 'The Religious World.' It is full of deep thought, wide reading, and a profound insight into the spiritual life; and from its great catholicity should be of use far beyond the bounds of the class and church to which it is dedicated."—*Academy.*

"The main object of these meditations is to bring clearly before the soul that life is given that we may live for the glory and honour of God; to awaken the soul to the misery of missing this great end of life; to guard it from what threatens to lead it astray; to point to the example and love of Christ, and the joy of being true to God. . . The subjects dealt with are serious, solemn, as benefited the occasions on which the addresses were delivered. The meditations are short, pithy, and instructive, and are characterised by deep spirituality and intense earnestness."—*Manchester Examiner.*

Crown 8vo, 5s.

SCRIPTURE PORTRAITS

And other Miscellanies collected from his Published Writings.

By ARTHUR PENRHYN STANLEY, D.D.,

Dean of Westminster.

Many of our readers will be pleased to see this volume. It is a selection from the author's works generally, and contains much beautiful writing in the way of biography, travel, history, and exposition."—*Liverpool Mercury.*

"The reader will find here many most striking passages; his writings are a valuable contribution to the proper understanding of Jewish history. His style is beautifully chaste and poetical, and fascinates the reader at once."—*Bradford Observer.*

Uniform with the above.

Crown 8vo, 5s.

WORDS OF TRUTH AND WISDOM.

By Very Rev. FREDERICK W. FARRAR, D.D., F.R.S.,

Archdeacon of Westminster.

"A selection of serene and beautiful extracts characterised by elevation and clearness."—*Liverpool Mercury.*

"Are widely known and deservedly popular, but these selections from them will be useful to those who cannot afford to possess them in a complete form. The choice of passages have been made with careful and discriminating judgment, and the reader will have no difficulty in finding many of great eloquence and power. Such 'Words of Truth and Wisdom' cannot fail to do good."—*Bradford Observer.*

Uniform with the above.

Crown 8vo, 5s.

HEROES OF HEBREW HISTORY.

By SAMUEL WILBERFORCE, D.D.,

Bishop of Winchester.

"With graphic eloquence the bishop sets forth before his readers a living portrait, bringing into their proper proportion sentences of the sacred text which might be passed over by the superficial, and yet one of great importance to the right understanding of the subject. Anything from the pen or the lips of the great Bishop of Winchester is of great value, and much may be learned from this very cheap and most interesting volume, one especially valuable for the Sunday School teacher."—*Liverpool Mercury.*

"Will be found a rich mine of golden ore to the busy preacher of to-day."—*Perthshire Advertiser.*

Crown 8vo, 3s. 6d.

ANGLO-INDIAN AND ORIENTAL COOKERY.

By MRS. GRACE JOHNSON.

"Overflows with all sorts of delicious and economical recipes."—*Pall Mall Budget.*

"Housewives and professors of the gentle art of cookery who deplore the dearth of dainty dishes will find a veritable gold mine in Mrs. Johnson's book."—*Pall Mall Gazette.*

"She has thoroughly and completely investigated native and Anglo-Indian cuisines, and brought away the very best specimens of their art. Her pillau and kedgeree are perfect; curries are scientifically classed and explained, and some of the daintiest recipes we have ever seen are given, but the puddings particularly struck our fancy. Puddings as a rule are *so* nasty. The pudding that is nourishing is hideously insipid, and of the smart pudding it may be truly said that its warp is dyspepsia and its woof indigestion. Mrs. Johnson's puddings are both good to taste and pretty to look at, and the names of some of her native dishes will brighten any menu."—*Daily Chronicle.*

Fifth Thousand. Cloth. One Shilling.

PUDDINGS AND SWEETS:

Being Three Hundred and Sixty - five Receipts, approved by Experience.

By LUCY JONES.

"Those whom the matter concerns will find a faithful and fertile source of information."—*Saturday Review.*

"Contains a fresh recipe for every day of the year, is clearly printed, and of a handy size. The recipes are clearly set forth, and likely to be of practical assistance to cooks and housewives, since they have all been approved by experience."—*The Caterer.*

"A useful little cooking book."—*Home News.*

"Miss Lucy Jones' 365 receipts are admirable for their terseness and for the ease with which they can be understood. This handy book is a veritable treasure to young housekeepers."—*Public Opinion.*

"The collection as a whole in this handy and useful volume will be highly prized."—*British Weekly.*

"We could not recommend a better work."—*Army and Navy Magazine.*

"A considerable number of the recipes are out of the ordinary run, and those which we have examined in detail appear to be constructed on sound principles."—*Manchester Guardian.*

"Will be found extremely serviceable."—*Metropolitan.*

London : 13, *Waterloo Place, Pall Mall, S.W.*

Second Edition, Crown 8vo, Illustrated, 6s.

WANDERINGS OF A WAR ARTIST.

By IRVING MONTAGU, late Special War Artist "Illustrated London News."

"Mr. Montagu is to be congratulated on an eminently readable book, which, both in style and matter, is above the average of productions in this kind."—*Morning Post.*

"The adventures of Mr. Montagu are narrated with humour, and are seldom dull reading."—*Glasgow Herald.*

"It is seldom that a more exciting and readable book than the 'Wanderings of a War Artist' comes into our hands, and we congratulate Mr. Irving Montagu on his excellent production. Here we have racy anecdotes, full of life and humour, illustrated so well that we see the whole scenes rise vividly before us again. . . . The spirit of enterprise and daring breathes in his every page, and old and young alike will derive healthful amusement, together with information and instruction by following the author through his many vicissitudes and experiences in his capacity as a war artist."—*Admiralty and Horse Guards' Gazette.*

BY THE SAME AUTHOR.

Second Edition, Crown 8vo, Illustrated, 6s.

CAMP AND STUDIO.

By THE SAME AUTHOR.

"Is a bright, chatty record of war scenes and adventures in various parts of the world."—*Echo.*

"His animated pages and sketches, however, have a more than ephemeral interest, and present a moving picture of the romance and the misery of countries and populations ravaged by great opposing armies, and many a picturesque episode of personal experiences; he is pleasant and amusing enough."—*Daily News.*

"Will turn with pleasant anticipation to this recital of adventurous experiences, and will assuredly not be disappointed. Mr. Montagu has plenty to tell, and an easy way of telling it which is delightful. His vivacity is not spoilt by laborious effort, his pathos is not vitiated by sentimentality, and he possesses the rare gift of exciting interest in his own doings without so much as a saint of egotism."—*Broad Arrow.*

"Brightly written and cleverly and interestingly illustrated the book ought to become exceedingly popular. From first to last the author has avoided dry etail, and while consecutiveness is not lost sight of, there is scarcely one out of the 400 pages into which the matter is compressed that is not sufficiently interesting in itself to claim the reader's attention."—*Evening News.*

Crown 8vo, with Maps specially drawn for the work, and numerous
Illustrations, 7s. 6d. Second Edition.

MOROCCO AS IT IS.

WITH AN ACCOUNT OF THE RECENT MISSION OF

SIR CHARLES EUAN SMITH.

By STEPHEN BONSAL, Jun., Special Correspondent "Central News."

"There are several new and interesting features in the work, which gives
much valuable information."—*Daily Telegraph.*

"Will be read with interest by all who are anxious about the present prospect
of affairs in Morocco."—*Scotsman.*

"Deserves to be widely read. . . . Any who desire a full and picturesque
account of this mission this book will be of special interest."—*Manchester
Examiner.*

"A vivid account of Sir Charles Euan Smith's abortive mission to Fez forms
a prominent part of this volume, and Mr. Bonsal gives an independent version of
what really happened."—*Daily Graphic.*

New Edition, Demy 8vo, 1,200 pages, £1 11s. 6d.

Dedicated by special permission to the Right Hon. W. E. GLADSTONE.

THE BOOK OF DIGNITIES,

CONTAINING

LISTS OF THE OFFICIAL PERSONAGES OF THE BRITISH EMPIRE,
CIVIL, DIPLOMATIC, HERALDIC, JUDICIAL, ECCLESIASTICAL,
MUNICIPAL, NAVAL, AND MILITARY.

From the Earliest Periods to the Present Time, together with the Sovereigns and
Rulers of the World from the Foundation of their respective States; the
Orders of Knighthood of the United Kingdom and India, and
numerous other lists.

*Founded on Beatson's " Political Index " (1806). Remodelled and brought down
to 1851 by the late JOSEPH HAYDN. Continued to the Present Time, with
numerous Additional Lists, and an Index to the entire work.*

BY HORACE OCKERBY,

Solicitor of the Supreme Court.

"It is probably the most complete official directory in existence, containing
about 1,300 different lists."—*Times.*

"The value of such a book as this purports to be can hardly be overrated."—
Saturday Review.

London : 13, Waterloo Place, Pall Mall, S.W.

Imperial 8vo, 1,539 pages, £3 3s. net.

A COMPREHENSIVE PERSIAN-ENGLISH DICTIONARY:

Comprising such Arabic Words and Phrases as are to be met with in Persian Literature; being JOHNSON & RICHARDSON's Persian, Arabic, and English Dictionary, Minutely Revised, Enlarged from Fresh and Latest Sources, and entirely Reconstructed on original Lines.

By F. STEINGASS, Ph.D., Author of both the Student's Arabic-English and English-Arabic Dictionaries.

" The author has spared no pains to make his work as complete and useful as possible."—*Times of India.*

" Messrs. W. H. Allen & Co. have added another to the long list of useful books with which Oriental students associate their name. Dr. F. Steingass has been responsible for the preparation of this volume, which comprises all such Arabic words as are to be met with in Persian literature. The excellence of the work is attested by the fact that it has been brought out under the approval of the Secretary of State for India."—*Daily Telegraph.*

" Dr. F. Steingass' *Persian-English Dictionary* has been delayed some time, but no one will regret this who considers the thoroughness with which the work has been executed, and the enormous labour necessary for its completion. It is by far the most complete and most generally satisfactory book of the kind yet offered to English students. The title-page modestly describes the volume as 'Johnson and Richardson's Persian, Arabic, and English Dictionary, revised, enlarged, and entirely reconstructed.' But the truth is, it is practically a new lexicon. Dr. Steingass has, indeed, had the advantage of the labours of some predecessors distinguished in lexicography, just as Johnson had the advantage of Richardson's in producing the dictionary known under their joint names. But so much, both in substance and in the arrangement of the work, is due to Dr. Steingass' own labour, and to the newer elements that the mere lapse of time has made available, that the lexicon is not properly regarded as only an enlargement. It has in it all—so far as Persian is concerned—that is in Johnson and Richardson, and the kernel of the recent French lexicons, and of Vuller's Persian-Latin Dictionary ; while Dr. Steingass has very fully supplemented this rich matter by his own wide reading, which ranges from the acknowledged and historical classics to the Shah's diaries. The difficulty in a work of this kind is always that of the importance to be assigned to Arabic. Dr. Steingass has overcome this in such a way as to make his lexicon satisfactory both to those who wish to be scholars in Arabic and to those who care nothing about that speech except in so far as it has been adopted by Persian writers. The work, on the whole, is a conspicuous monument of labour and learning in Oriental philology, and will without any doubt at once take its place as the standard dictionary for English students of the speech of Sadi."—*Scotsman.*

" This is a minute revision of Johnson and Richardson's Persian, Arabic, and English Dictionary, with enlargements from the latest sources, and the whole work has been reconstructed on fresh principles. The Arabic element has been reduced and recast, but the dictionary still comprises all such Arabic words and phrases as are to be met with in Persian literature. The volume bears marks of assiduous care and indefatigable research, and will find an honoured place on the shelves of all serious students of Oriental literature."—*Daily Chronicle.*

" This volume, comprising over 1,500 imperial 8vo pages, seems to have been prepared regardless of cost or labour. It is a minute revision of Johnson and Richardson's Persian, Arabic, and English Dictionary, and all Arabic words and phrases to be met with in Persian literature are included in it. It was at first intended to reduce the Arabic and increase the Persian in the original dictionary, but the additions which were found necessary have carried the work beyond the dimensions contemplated. Dr. Steingass appears to have at last placed at the disposal of English students of Persian life and Persian literature a first-class dictionary."—*Home News.*

" Dr. Steingass has brought a most laborious work to a successful termination, and deserves the profound gratitude of all students of Persian for the conscientious manner in which the book has been compiled."—*Saturday Review.*

Royal 4to.

Cloth, with 51 Illustrations, £3 3s. net.

MAHÂBODHI; OR, THE GREAT BUDDHIST TEMPLE UNDER THE BODHI TREE AT BUDDHA-GAYÂ.

BY

MAJOR - GENERAL SIR ALEXANDER CUNNINGHAM

R.E., K.C.I.E., C.S.I.

"'The author gives an elaborate account, illustrated with numerous photographs, of the results of the excavations and restorations recently undertaken at the Great Buddhist Temple of Buddha-Gayâ. The importance, as he says, 'of the Temple for the history of art is quite unique, as it gives us the oldest existing remains of both sculpture and architecture. The sculptures of the Bharut Stûpa date from the flourishing period of the Sunga dynasty, about B.C. 150, whereas the Mahâbodhi remains belong to the period of Asoka, just one century earlier.' All Oriental archæologists will recognise the importance of these remains and the value of Sir A. Cunningham's monograph upon them."—*The Times.*

" A handsome volume which will be warmly welcomed both by archæologists and the wider circle who interest themselves in Indian Art. Mahâbodhi is a monument of careful and patient investigation, and bears on every leaf the stamp of its author's ripe acquaintance with a branch of learning, which in India has been peculiarly prolific in practical results. . . . It is elaborately illustrated with a series of over thirty plates, which reveal some of the finest masterpieces of Indian sculpture and architecture extant."—*Pioneer* (Allahabad).

Sir A. Cunningham is the greatest authority on the ancient monuments of India, and his volume, historical, descriptive, and illustrative of the *Mahâbodhi* is a work of unusual interest and value. . . . The work is illustrated by a series of beautifully executed plates, and these, together with the letterpress, give us a very clear and complete idea of this famous temple."—*Scotsman.*

"This handsome volume will increase the deservedly high reputation of its author."—*Manchester Guardian.*

" Sir A. Cunningham's work is one of great value, and abounds with matter of a highly suggestive character."—*Indian Magazine.*

London : 13, *Waterloo Place, Pall Mall, S.W.*

In 2 vols. Demy 8vo. 30s.

With 18 Maps of Collectorates.

THE LAND REVENUE OF BOMBAY :

A History of Its Administration, Rise, and Progress.

By Alexander Rogers, Bombay Civil Service (retired).

"Mr. Rogers has produced a continuous and an authoritative record of the land changes and of the fortunes of the cultivating classes for a full half-century, together with valuable *data* regarding the condition and burdens of those classes at various periods before the present system of settlement was introduced. He commences with the northern division of Bombay, in which his service was chiefly spent, and works southward, giving a detailed account of each district within the Presidency, exclusive of Bombay Island and Sind. His work thus supplements the valuable selections of records which have from time to time been published by the Bombay Government. These selections deal chiefly, although not exclusively, with periods of special interest or with measures of particular importance. Mr. Rogers now presents a comprehensive view of the land administration of Bombay as a whole, the history of its rise and progress, and a clear statement of the results which it has attained. The narrative is by no means one of unchecked prosperity. But in spite of famine, droughts, floods, and the other recurring calamities of nature in a country dependent on the tropical rainfall ; in spite, also, of the occasional blundering officials, it is a narrative of which all patriotic Englishmen may feel proud. The old burdens of native rule have been lightened, the old injustices mitigated, the old fiscal cruelties and exactions abolished. Underlying the story of each district we see a perennial struggle going on between the increase of the population and the available means of subsistence derived from the soil. That increase of the population is the direct result of the peace of the country under British rule. But it tends to press more and more severely on the possible limits of local cultivation, and it can only he provided for by the extension of the modern appliances of production and distribution. Mr. Rogers very properly confines himself to his own subject. But there is ample evidence that the extension of roads, railways, steam factories, and other industrial enterprises, have played an important part in the solution of the problem, and that during recent years such enterprises have been powerfully aided by an abundant currency."—*The Times.*

London : 13, *Waterloo Place, Pall Mall, S.W.*

Tenth Year, 1893.   Price 2s.

THREE HUNDRED ILLUSTRATIONS.

ACADEMY SKETCHES.

A VOLUME OF SKETCHES OF PAINTINGS, WATER COLOURS, &C.,

IN THE

ROYAL ACADEMY, THE NEW GALLERY, THE WATER-COLOUR

SOCIETIES, AND OTHER EXHIBITIONS.

Edited by

HENRY BLACKBURN.

"A capital selection of illustrations of paintings and sculpture in the eight principal art exhibitions of the year."—*Saturday Review.*

"It is not only valuable as a companion to the various picture Exhibitions, but as a memento of them, and as giving some idea of the majority of the pictures to residents abroad, or persons who are prevented by circumstances from seeing the originals. It is particularly well got up, and, as many of the plates are reproduced by the Meisenbach and kindred processes, they will bear looking into, even with a magnifying-glass."—*Lady.*

"The most complete representation of the works of art shown in the various London exhibitions. It is an admirable *souvenir* of the art work of the year."—*Scotsman.*

"Sketches from all the leading exhibitions, and will serve to indicate and to recall some of the best pictures of the season."—*Life.*

London : 13, *Waterloo Place, Pall Mall, S.W.*

Crown 8vo, Cloth, 1s.

Twelfth Year of Issue, Revised and Enlarged.

LONDON IN 1893.

ILLUSTRATED BY

Twenty Bird's-Eye Views of the Principal Streets,

ALSO BY

A LARGE GENERAL MAP OF LONDON.

Originally Compiled by HERBERT FRY,

Editor of the "Royal Guide to the London Charities," "Handbook to Normandy," " The Road to Paris," &c.

THE great object of this Book is to provide the stranger in London with *information at a glance* respecting each of the main thoroughfares ; and with this design both the plan and the style of its unique illustrations have been projected. Moreover, instead of the usual arrangement of Guide-Books, where the traveller is set down before a very maze of streets, with a list of places and institutions alphabetically strung together, street-by-street particulars, such as are of the most general interest, are given, and an Index supplies an alphabetical means of reference.

This manual not only serves as **the Easiest and Clearest Guide about the Great Metropolis,** but both for the accuracy with which its novel illustrations depict the main thoroughfares and their principal buildings, and for the descriptions corresponding therewith, the book is esteemed an interesting *souvenir* which visitors carry home with them, and also *purchase as an appropriate present for their far-off friends.*

The first annual edition of this book contained only Thirteen Illustrations. **"London in 1893"** has **Twenty Double-page Street Views,** and is carefully revised to present date, so as to exhibit the latest alterations and changes in this ever-improving and enlarging metropolis.

OPINIONS OF THE PRESS.

" The bird's-eye views of the chief thoroughfares are a new feature I streetography, and far more useful than maps. Altogether it is a most valuable handbook to the metropolis."—*Graphic.*

" Very extensive in its information and interesting in its details—as a text-book for explanation and as a historical book of reference it will be found most useful and entertaining."—*Daily News.*

" An admirable guide, full of information. The bird's-eye views are very interesting. They often give even those who are familiar with London a new idea of the relation of localities."—*Illustrated Sporting and Dramatic News.*

" In addition to an admirably-arranged and vivaciously-written description of all the places and sites of interest in London, interspersed with numerous historical notes and details, the guide contains a feature which is absolutely unique in a series of eighteen bird's-eye views of the principal thoroughfares and the buildings of importance which abut upon them. It is unquestionably one of the most serviceable of the works issued for the behoof of visitors to the metropolis."—*Scotsman.*

" The usefulness of this work, both to residents and visitors, is now pretty well known."—*Christian World.*

" This handbook is not only of great practical value, but abounds anecdotes and curious incidents."—*Army and Navy Gazette.*

" It would be difficult to find a book which better fulfils its avowed purpose than this most excellent compilation."—*Knowledge.*

" Emphatically the best London guide."—*Broad Arrow.*

" By far the most comprehensive guide."—*Whitehall Review.*

" May be described as an established fact. Good to begin with, the guide to the metropolis has got better every year, until it is now more serviceable than ever."—*Derby Mercury.*

London : 13, *Waterloo Place, Pall Mall, S.W.*

www.ingramcontent.com/pod-product-compliance
Lightning Source LLC
Chambersburg PA
CBHW020238110726

47898CB00004B/1306